1-10pm Sept

To Karen
gine.

Good on you, Karen

Jonathan Goteley.

CW01494501

PERCY LONGPRONG

JONATHAN GOTELEY

JONATHAN GOTELEY
68 Marmion Road, Hove, Sussex, BN3 5FT, England.

First published in Great Britain 1998 by
JONATHAN GOTELEY
68 Marmion Road, Hove, Sussex, BN3 5FT, England.

British Library Cataloguing-in-Publication Data.
A catalogue record for this book is available
from the British Library.

ISBN: 0-9533804-0-8

© Jonathan Goteley, 1998

All rights reserved.

Jonathan Goteley asserts his moral right to be identified as the author of
this work in accordance with the Copyright, Designs and Patents Act, 1988.

This book may not be reproduced, in whole or in part, in any form (except
by reviewers for the public press), without prior permission in writing from
the publisher.

Printed by *Manuscript ReSearch Printing*
P.O. Box 33, Bicester, Oxon, OX6 7PP, England.
Tel: 01869 323447   Fax: 01869 324096

ACKNOWLEDGEMENT

My thanks to *Valérie,*
without whose encouragement and support
the publication of this novel would not have happened.

ONE
'Ow This 'Alf Lives

Percival Albert Longpre was born in the early twenties. His father, named Horace, was an alcoholic, and Lucy, his mother, had very little to apply emancipation to, in the circumstances, even had she fully understood its meaning.

Amongst his early memories was that of his mother breast feeding him, and tasting his own tears as they slid along his cheek to her teat. Being able to remember such a thing he assumed, correctly, that he had been way past the time of being nourished from this source, but evidently there was nothing else. Other memories included nearly drowning at the age of about three when he had sand thrown in his eyes on the seashore, and stumbled blindly into one of the deep pools that remain at the ends of some of the groynes when the tide goes out; his head being trapped in some railing; a milk cart falling on him, and his father calling a policeman to him in the street at the age of six, for smoking.

With his parents and a sister named Sylvia, three years his senior, an existence of impoverishment was carried on in a damp, gloomy and haunted basement in a road leading directly on to the coast highway near the border of Brighton and Hove. As far as furniture went he could not recall ever sitting at a table for a meal but remembered only lying on a string-supported bed watching, unafraid, the dismal spectres coming and going through the wall while his sister slept peacefully beside him.

His father, already sightless in one eye from shrapnel in the Great War, became totally blind when a cat he had tormented leapt upon his head from the stairs leading to the ground floor, and rendered the other one useless. Percy called out to his father to kneel down and so place the cat within his reach, but instead the bewildered man struggled to the yard where he proceeded to charge at the wall head first until the enraged creature gripping him was practically pulp. Nevertheless the cat managed to drag itself to a corner where it lay, still feared, until maggots came from its mouth.

The incident put an end to the rare visits to the picture house where Percy would be taken, on the spur of the moment, to marvel at Charlie Chaplin and Mickey Mouse. He became his father's guide to the local pubs in the evenings and had to bear the brunt of the disparaged man's unstable temperament. Two or three bars would be visited according to the availability of sympathisers to supply the drinks. If things were quiet in the Western Road vicinity a few coppers would be invested in bus fares to Portslade. "Keep a watch out for Billy Coats and Alby Fisher, boy," he'd say as the bus rattled along.

These were two particular mates of his who would not only keep forking out the money for his drinks but supplied Percy with lemonade and crisps as well, then paid their bus fare home. Percy liked these excursions for he could watch the trains go over the crossing while he was waiting for his father to get tranquilised.

There were others though who were totally unsympathetic towards the pair and Percy was constantly warned to spot Barney Watts and Jock Moses before they spotted them. Not that Percy needed any warning after the feared pair had caught him and his father on one of the many occasions they were forced to walk home through the lack of benefactors to give them their fare. While one held Percy and systematically boxed each of his ears in turn, the other ducked under the swipes of the short, lead-loaded cane wielded by his father and picked his punches at will. "That'll di yer nae guid at all now, Horry," the man scoffed as each of his determined blows brought renewed gasps from his victim. All the time Percy was trying to free himself in order to push the assailant into his father's grasp an he had been instructed to do if such an occasion arose, but the grip on him was only relaxed when he was slung to the ground beside his groaning and bloody parent. He never asked the whys and wherefores of the beatings but just accepted it as being the way of the world, and that someone might wish to destroy him for no apparent reason,

In a sober rage his father would strike him one minute and caress him repentantly the next and soak his face with tears from his dead eyes. While in the realm of intoxication Horace would re-live to the amazed lad the glorious clashes of his regiment the Royal Horse Artillery, in the greatest struggle man had yet seen. "Teams of beautiful horses boy, and wonderful mates, blown to smithereens." He would go silent and sob, then angrily exclaim that there was no honour in the country and that it all died in France. "Those Prussians will be back, lad, you mark my words. They're just restin'. We know 'em, them of us that's left." Like thousands of others his concern came from a fixation of the hardships endured for an inconclusive armistice, so became a personal challenge on the side for all involved to pass on to their offspring.

Even at the age of eight Percy was already resigned to the idea that fighting Germans was a duty passed on from father to son, and the future would see him retracing his father's steps. When he thought about it he was always a small boy carrying a big gun and having to combat grown men for he could not imagine himself being any bigger than he was then. But he did not dwell on things so far in the future even though he was constantly reminded of the war by his father playing old soldiers' tunes on a mouth organ, as well as the chatter about their escapades amongst the fraternity of ex-servicemen that was still as commonplace as the Woodbines they smoked.

"Are the Germans worse than the two who beat us?" Percy once asked.

"Lord no, boy," his father replied indignantly. "They were gentlemen, the same as us." Then hesitantly, 'Well, most of 'em."

"Wouldn't they beat you when you were caught then?" inquired Percy.

"Beat you, boy, good gracious no," said his father. "Shoot you maybe, but nothing else, not soldier to soldier."

"I'd ask them to beat me instead," said Percy.

"No honour in that though, lad," replied his father.

"No sense in being dead either," argued Percy. "Not for anything."

There was a time when the young lad limped about like a wounded warrior, but not on account of a direct human encounter. Horace had been asked to leave a saloon bar because his trousers were in such a ragged state. It fell to Percy, or so he felt obliged, to forage for another pair. Through the hole in the fence of a garden that Percy passed on his way to and from school, he had observed the preparations for a bonfire night.

The guy, in Percy's opinion, was wearing a suit that was far too good to go up in flames. If he had not stood so long looking at the remains and thinking how unlike a human it now looked after he had deprived it of the suit, he would have beern out of the gate and away.

But his thoughts of how horrible it was to even burn a man's effigy, which sentiment stayed with him for life, were broken first by the growls of a bull terrier, that had been turned loose from the back door of the house, then by its bite as it sunk its teeth in Percy's leg just above the knee. As he screamed with pain and fear, a man named Mr. Potter called the dog off and grabbed the terrified lad by the hair. "You thieving little tyke, I should have let him bite your hands off, that would teach you a lesson." He seemed to spit the words, for Percy felt the man's saliva on his tear-soaked face, and was sure he was in for a hiding that would surpass anything he had yet experienced.

He closed his eyes expecting the man's free hand to come smashing into his face, but instead he was thrown to the ground.

"You two had better deal with him," the man remarked to his two sons, Denis, eleven, and Arthur, twelve, who had arrived on the scene. "Teach him the error of his ways," their father urged, and Percy knew he could expect far less mercy from them than from the man, for the pair had punched him and his sister before, quite often. One pulled him up off the ground by his collar and held him while the other pinched him viciously on his bottom and legs. Then he was punched in the face, chest and back, and his toes stamped on, while the dog growled and barked about him, waiting for a command from its master to tear the hapless child to pieces.

Just as Percy was expecting to be beaten to death the man called upon his sons to stop, which they did reluctantly, but not before one knelt behind him and the other pushed him over. All this time, feeling guilty, he had said nothing, but just cried bitterly.

"Come on, son, dry your eyes, it's all over," said the man as he wiped Percy's face with a piece of sponge he used for washing his Morris Cowley car down with. But the sobbing lad never saw the wink the man gave to his grinning young cowards who stood eagerly waiting to participate in the next round of torment.

"Shall we let him feed the chickens, boys?" said Mr. Potter with sarcastic tenderness as the boys chuckled and nudged each other.

Taking no notice of Percy voicing through his sobs that he wanted to go home, they took him behind a large hedge to where a chicken run lay at the end of a vegetable patch.

"There you are, look at those lovely hens all waiting for you to feed them," coaxed the man as he took the lid off a tin and tipped corn into Percy's cupped little hands, while Denis and Arthur opened the entrance to the run.

Quite unsuspectingly he entered the enclosure but wondered why the boys seemed to be standing guard at the wire mesh gate they had quickly snapped shut behind them.

"Throw some feed down to them then," advised the man, which Percy began doing, and was amused to see how the birds came flocking around his feet. He wiped the tears from his eyes with the sleeve of his shabby little jacket and set to seriously seeing that each one was going to get a share of the corn.

"Here, boy, come on boy," he said cheerfully. The boys

laughed and remarked to their father that he didn't know the difference between hens and cockerels. Percy glanced at them and smiled, thinking they were now good naturedly well disposed towards him.

"He'll know the difference any second now," declared the man as he pulled a cord that lifted a trap and let loose a squawking cockerel to shatter the tranquillity of the pen. Percy screamed with fright as the creature fluttered up in an attempt to peck his face.

He could not have been more terrified if it had been an eagle attacking him.

"Here you are, boy, " he called out as he tried to bargain with it by dropping all the corn he had left. The bird's attack was unrelenting and Percy's cries of, "Don't, please don't, oh, get it off me!" were pitiful, heartbreaking, and unheeded by the boys, now in fits of laughter, and their father grinning with satisfaction.

"Now you've got it right," called Arthur. "That's the *boy*, chicken."

Percy made his way to the exit but it was barred against him. He pleaded to be let out, and pressed his tear-stained face against the wire as the cockerel viciously pecked his legs. But, as if in the grip of sadism, those keeping him in just jeered and laughed and taunted the frantic youngster. Denis went even further and struck at Percy's fingers, protruding through the wire, with a stick, telling him to get back as if he were shouting at a disobedient animal.

At such times when humanity, in the form of individuals, is confronted with such a varied array of traumas, a reaction in some form usually occurs. Percy felt that one way or another his life was being jeopardised, and if not he would at least be maimed in some way by these three who had lost all restraint.

Even at his tender age he considered the punishment he'd had and was receiving far outweighed his crime. So out of sheer anger and a will to survive, still crying bitterly, he hurled himself at the wire fencing again and again until he broke down the supports and tumbled free of the enclosure.

"Look what he's done," yelled Arthur indignantly, as if Percy had no right to save himself at all, let alone in the manner he had.

"I can see what he's done, you stupid oaf," said his father angrily, "Lift it up quickly before the chicken get out." He made a grab at Pery who was just picking himself up.

"Oh no, you don't, you little swine, you're responsible for this," he spat viciously, but Percy ducked under his hand and made for the garden exit.

"Get him, Rex," snapped the man to his dog, which at that moment was hurled into the chicken run by the action of the two boys pulling the fence back up just as the animal was crossing it to get at the cockerel, and with the carte blanche of his master's approval the beast ploughed through the hens, knocking them this way and that in its frenzy to fulfil its previously frustrated desire to tear the cockerel to pieces. The hen-house, in which the cockerel, knowing as animals do how the dog felt about him, was hiding, splintered like matchwood under the force with which Rex hit it.

Amidst the growls, whines and whimpers of the dog in its element were the screeches of the terrified bird and the shouts of the man for the boys to lower the fence again to give him access to the creature that, to him, had gone mad. The boys argued that if they lowered the fence the chicken would escape.

But their father wrenched it from their grasp and tore it down, but tripped over it in his haste to rescue the cockerel. Then with his mouth imitating a scoop, his face slid amongst the droppings in the pen.

When the two minute pandemonium subsided and the near-dead bird was retrieved from the dog's mouth by way of a slap on his testicles, only two of the fifteen hens remained in the garden.

Randolph, which was what they had named the cockerel, fluttered from the man's hands only to land lopsided on the ground, on account of a damaged wing.

As it attempted to walk it could do no more than push itself round in a circle like a man rowing a boat on only one side.

Denis broke the silence as they watched the struggling creature by asking if it was finished. The man looked at his son in surprise for some seconds before answering with the question of, "What the damn hell do you think?" then adding, "It's got a broken leg one side and a half chewed off wing the other."

"Won't that balance him up?" said Arthur, "especially if you put a splint onthe leg." His father shook his head in silent exasperation, then walked off to the shed and returned with a chopper.

"You're going to make a splint for it then ?" inquired Arthur, with an air of certainty. But his father, ignoring the remark, picked up Randolph and resting the bird's neck on the base of the hen-house, lopped its head off.

The boys burst out laughing as the headless bird fluttered vigorously round the pen and was pounced upon once more by Rex. He had ventured out from his place of refuge under the garden shed to join in the excitement, but was driven off whimpering by a boot in the bottom from his master.

"Why can't he have it now?" asked Denis with surprise.

"Because he'll start on the hens if he gets a taste for it," was the reply.

"No he woudn't," said Arthur. "He was only annoyed at Randolph."

"Don't be stupid," said the man.

"Why did he bash straight through the hens to get at him then?" challenged Arthur. "He didn't bother to get one of them, did he? And he could have, easy."

"All right, then, why didn't he?" inquired the man.

The two boys looked sheepishly at each other and grinned.

"Well, come on," said their father impatiently. "Tell me."

But the lads just giggled.

The man became angry and grabbed Arthur by an ear. "Now listen, if you know something I don't, then you'd best tell me and be quick about it," he said.

"You know, you know yourself what the dog's like," squealed Arthur.

"What do you mean, I know?" went on his father.

"You told the coalman what a dirty, randy swine it is, and that it would 'thingy' a frog if it would stop hopping."

"Thingy a frog?' said his father curiously. "What's that?"

"Well, fix it then, that's what you said," whined Arthur, now rubbing his ear after his father had let go.

What's that got to do with his dislike for Randolph?" demanded the man angrily.

"He didn't like Randolph being with the hens so much," said Denis quietly. A look of utter disbelief came upon their father's face. What utter drivel," he said sharply. "Jealous of a cockerel going with hens?" He tutted in amazement.

"It's true," shouted Arthur. "We've watched him, haven't we, Denis ?" His brother agreed.

"Watched him at what ?" asked their father angrily.

"When he's been going round the hens dipping his dangler," giggled Denis.

"What, Rex going with hens?" shrieked the man.

"No, watching Randolph," explained Arthur. " We've seen him, haven't we, Denis?" and again his brother bore him out, adding that Rex crept round the pen growling.

"Well, you said he'd fix a frog, didn't you?" reasoned Arthur.

Feeling that any further discussion on the subject would be useless the man ordered his sons back into the house, but on passing what once was the guy, all three stopped and looked around. Denis voiced the question they all were about to ask. "Where's the suit?" And the man just stared at the gate and whispered, "Little bastard!"

Percy arrived home, scarred and trembling, with the suit under one arm and a half-dead hen under the other. His hazardous endeavour to supply his father with presentable clothing, plus a luxury meal for the family as a bonus, resulted in little or nothing of benefit.

The sight of Horace in the suit brought tears of joy to Lucy's eyes, and excited praise from Sylvia, while Percy stood at his father's side feeling very proud of himself. Nevertheless the sentimentality of Horace was limited strictly to those who were reminiscent of shell-holes and machine-gun chatter, and anyone or anything unconnected with these things was superfluous.

That evening both the hen and the suit were sold to a man in a back street pub, who paid only half the agreed amount, along with a promise to settle the remainder the following night. Horace left the pub drunker than he'd been for many a day. Not a penny was left from the transaction through the crowd of friends who gathered to drink his health. Not least among them was the man who bought the goods. He drank back almost half the money he had paid Horace, who he said had left him momentarily embarrassed financially because of the deal.

Getting his father home that night was a greater difficulty than Percy ever remembered—worse even than the time they were beaten by his father's enemies.

Even had there been the few pennies left for the tuppenny and a pennorth promised to Percy in place of a chicken dinner there would have been no opportunity to get them. For if he left his father on the ground, he knew he would never have got him up again.

Arriving home Percy was on the point of collapse, and had to call his mother out as he dared not attempt to manoeuvre his father down the basement steps on his own.

And so, with a last chorus of "One Night of Love," which he had been attempting to sing all the way from the pub, Horace was guided perilously down the steps and put to bed only minutes before Percy dropped fast asleep from what had proved to be for him, a very exhausting day.

Soon after he awoke the following day he remembered that the footsteps he and his father had taken the previous evening must be retraced to collect the money outstanding for the suit and the hen. All through the day he felt doleful at the thought of the ordeal that was to be repeated. Percy considered the locality of the pub to be boring. There were no trains or buses going by, nor were there any other kids outside to keep him company while their fathers too boozed away the food and rent money. But getting the almost dead weight of his drunken father home was the task that put Percy's limited energy to the test.

And he knew he could not stand too many nights like the one before, not one after the other anyway.

As there was no contact that evening with the man who owed the debt, Horace had to be satisfied with a free pint from the landlord, out of sympathy. Also keeping out of his way were the spongers, who had so readily kept him company when he had a few shillings. They all remained quiet in a corner so as not to attract his attention in case it cost them a drink or two. No penny biscuits or lemonade came Percy's way that evening, but only an enraged Horace, escorted off the premises by the landlord. All the way home Percy took the fury of his father's disappointment. The hand on his shoulder would grip viciously and only relax to cuff his ear when he cried out in pain. Falling asleep that night to the sound of his mother crying as a result of his father's abuse further proved to the unhappy lad what a waste all his efforts had been. He still loved his father, for the thought that the love was never being returned to him or his mother and sister never entered his head.

Far from being the bulwark of his family's survival, Horace was its parasite. He guzzled away the pittance earned by Lucy from her charring, as he had the few stocks and shares left her by her father. She was from a middle class family, hence her upbringing fell short of being equipped to remonstrate with such conditions as Horace brought about. Indeed, the scheming of alcoholics has proved to be the destruction of many a woman from even a hardier and more robust background, and no doubt it was the sense of devotion and duty which were the watchwords instilled in young women of her class in that day, that guarded Lucy's sanity.

Amidst all the gloom and disparagement that seemed an eternal monotony to her, there came a happening that, although born out of the unbearable despair of another, eased some of the ache in her heart and mind. Through grief over the death of his wife, the landlord took poison and the building went up for sale. Consequently the Longpres were allocated a council house on a brand new estate at the North-west outskirts of the town. Adding to the family's happiness on the day of moving, the weather was beautiful. Percy sat next to the driver of the cart and was allowed to hold the reins. He waved excitedly to his mother and sister, who through there being no room on the small cart, were forced to walk to their new home.

Horace was propped up just inside the tailboard and did nothing but insult the performance of the man's horse for the whole of the journey.

"Call that a horse?" he would say with a "Tut!" "We'd 'ave 'ad 'im on toast and greased the axles with the drippin' over there, mate."

Percy looked with embarrassment at the removal man, and was pleased with the smile along with a wink and a friendly understanding nudge that the man gave him.

"We'd 'ave needed fifty like 'im to pull the gun," went on Horace. "'Allo, sounds like all 'is legs aint the same lengf eiver," he continued. "Got splints on it, ave yer mate? We 'ad 'em pullin' better wiv free legs. 'Ere, that is an 'orse aint it? Or is it a goat? 'Cause it aint bad for a goat."

Arriving at the house made Horace think the horse had dropped dead, and he asked if it had.

The man from the council was there to hand over the keys. He also explained to Lucy the working of the cast iron cooking range situated in the parlour. He demonstrated how the oven could be opened by pushing his foot on a treadle that operated the door, which she thought was very up to date. All the shabby sticks and bits of furniture went into the house easily enough. The mahogany table given to Lucy by her father, however, had to have some three inches cut from each leg before it would pass through the doorway.

Horace had on different occasions brought antique dealers home to buy the heirloom, but on seeing how upset Lucy was, none of them would bid for it.

The immediate neighbours of the new dwelling seemed to sum up Lucy's unenviable position right away, and were ready to give assistance, in as much as anyone in the same hard-up and happy state could, that is.

Not that Lucy could, so far, be associated with happiness. She did, however, feel she was standing on a clean new threshold of life, even though the family was reduced to the soup kitchen existence. Percy and Sylvia romped as gleefully around the hard undug ground at the back of the house as if it were the garden of a country estate, and their steps echoed as they ran upstairs and downstairs and from room to room on the bare floorboards that first day. Indeed, the boards were destined to remain so for quite a time before they were covered with scraps of oilcloth cast out by a removal firm.

Even Horace remarked how cool and sweet the air of the Downs felt and smelt. Lucy and the children were hopeful that he would find an existence that was not dominated so much by the pub opening times.

Percy was allowed to join the Cubs. They met in a large hut at the top of the road. His uniform, consisting of cap, neckerchief, toggle and garters, cost half a crown but a dispensation was made for him to pay it off at threepence a week. It was all very exciting to him, and he looked forward immensely to the meetings. Even more, he thrilled at the thought of the country rambles and later, camping, when he became old enough to join the Scouts, who also used the hut on other evenings. Also, the premises were used for a Sunday school by the Salvation Army at which Percy attended on account of the fruit-drops that were doled out to those present. They all sang children's hymns to the accompaniment of a heavily moustached old gentleman's talent with a little concertina that would have been similarly ideal for sea shanties on a windjammer.

Percy's life took on a more natural existence for a boy than he had experienced so far in his few years of limited understanding. His father reluctantly made do with a couple of nights a week at the pub, and a pint of beer at other times, fetched by Percy from the bottle and jug department.

It was on his way home from one such errand that he had the misfortune to be caught by Denis and Arthur. While they pummelled him on the ground he watched his father's precious beverage escaping from the broken bottle at his side. He then felt the liquid as it soaked into the sleeve of his jacket. Suddenly in the midst of Percy's misery, the two bullies, who had been kneeling one on each of his arms as they beat him, were dragged off by a youth whose grip on their hair made them shriek with pain. Percy sat spellbound in the puddle of beer as his rescuer thrashed the brothers, and they were well into a deserved state of bloody noses and blushing ears before they were set free. The boy had not uttered a sound all through the fracas, and the anger only left his face when he looked at Percy and smiled before walking away.

Arriving home with only an egg cup full of beer in the broken bottle brought further violence to the unhappy lad from his enraged father. Even had he been able to see the bumps and bruises of Percy's earlier encounter it is doubtful whether any pity would have found its way into the man's heart when it came to being deprived of alcohol. The tranquillity of the past weeks had already been under great strain through the restriction of Horace's pub attendances, and he lashed out mercilessly, first at his son and then at Lucy as she stepped in to protect the lad. With exhaustion and heartbreak in her voice she bade Percy to go and attend the Cubs as she struggled with her seemingly demented husband. For a while the young boy stood sobbing as he stared at his father as if seeing him as he really was for the first time. As he looked like going against all his previous sense of propriety and about to start an attack on his father, his mother shouted at him to leave the house, with an urgency in her voice that bordered on hysteria. Still sobbing he arrived at the Cub meeting minus his uniform and his penny for subscription. He burst into tears as he asked Akela if he would be allowed to stay without them, and was comforted by the young woman saying it was all right. He was further consoled by being told that he did not have to worry any more about the payment for his uniform. Soon he was joining in the games and laughing with the other boys as if his life were as trouble-free as theirs seemed to be.

Turning to see what was causing the commotion in the doorway, made the happiness vanish like a mask from his face.

23

His father was on the floor after barging in and falling over a Cub who was kneeling down in a game. Bad language and abuse flowed from Horace's mouth as Akela helped him to his feet. He demanded that Percy should be handed over to him, as an important errand was required of the lad. In spite of strong remonstrations from the Cub master against upsetting Percy any more than it was obvious he had been, the lad was forced to go with his father. But not before a warning was given to Horace concerning the bruises around the youngster's face and arms, that the authorities would be notified should the child be seen in that state again. Even though the marks of a beating were mostly from the Potter boys the warning was well directed, for had many of Horace's lunges landed on Percy the results would have been far worse.

That evening saw Percy more or less back on the old familiar route of the pub crawls. The only difference being that the dwelling he so laboriously brought his father back to was without the risk of them both falling down basement steps. Horace did however have to be propped up until the door was opened and then quickly grabbed by Lucy before he fell back on top of Percy and then into the privet hedge.

Since Percy had become his father's guide on the evening pub excursions he had the sympathy of all the bar staffs on the round. Some thought that Horace should be reported for leaving a child outside in all weathers. But the fact that the bulk of their patronage still consisted of ex-servicemen deterred any action that could be construed as victimising so obvious a patriot as Horace was considered to be.

Many a time Percy was dragged in from the bitter cold by a kindly landlord. He would sit beside the fireplace observing the phlegm coughed up by some of the patrons, sizzling and bubbling on the hot coal and metal. He had witnessed the same at home from his father, who was in quite an advanced state of consumption, but ignorant of the fact. Due to his total blindness, however, Horace was more off target than on, and so had to eject the slime into an old cocoa tin. This had to be emptied into a back drain by Percy, who vomited violently on every occasion.

It was when he was allowed on the licensed premises that he unwillingly observed the embarrassing antics of his father. Horace would grope along the bar and clutch at a glass that had far more in it than the one he had put down. Likewise he would feel his way along the chairs and stumble as he came across a female form, with the result that somehow one of his hands would either find its way momentarily between her legs or on her breast.

According to the amount of commotion this sparked off, husbands were more understanding than were fiances, some of these being about to manhandle Horace until restrained by their affronted female, out of pity. Ironically the incident was usually resolved with a pat on the back or a handshake from the man and, what was far more important to Horace, a few drinks thrown in to boot.

On the whole, he used his blindness to the hilt, for he and Percy complemented each other in the pitiful sight they represented. However, there were limits to which sympathy was spontaneous, and as Horace found out to his final downfall, stealing was one of them. On school holidays Percy was required to take his father to some of the morning drinking sessions, providing, that is, that the previous night's intake had not left the man incapable of leaving his bed. But this was not the case, unfortunately for Horace, as he attended his last drinking bout in this world at the "Horn and Slipper".

Outside, Percy's interest was taken by the draymen sliding the barrels down through the pavement flap into the cellar beneath the public house. After a while he turned his attention to the magnificent creatures in harness at the kerbside. He had of course seen many different horses and trailers before, but the opportunity to pat and fondle the animals had not been possible when they were trotting along. As he stretched up timidly to pat their soft noses in turn, he likened them to the poor beasts that were blown to bits in the war, as described many times by his father. " 'Ow could they do that to you?" he whispered sadly to the huge animals towering above him. "Yoi'd never 'urt anyone would you?"

"Luvly aint they, boy?" exclaimed the man as he slid another barrel off the dray.

Percy readily agreed, adding that his father rode one just like them in the war. To this the man answered that he was lucky and he supposed the lad wanted to do the same thing. But Percy lowered his head and said it was cruel.

At that moment Horace came stumbling out of the pub door and moved too quickly for a blind man towards the spot where Percy usually waited. Alas, in between lay the open flap guarded solely by a low chain which only the sighted could observe. Close on his heels as he left the pub door had been a woman and two men who now stood at the edge exclaiming "Christ!" and "Oh, God!" as they gazed down at the motionless form below. "I'd 'ave sooner let 'im keep the damn purse than 'ave this 'appen," cried the distraught woman. With fear clutching his heart Percy pushed his way through the small crowd that had gathered and knelt at the edge of the drop.

Seeing his father lying twisted and still at the bottom

made him burst instantly into tears and before anyone could stop him he had scrambled down the barrel chute. He cried "Dad", over and over as he first shook his father's shoulder, then tried to straighten his body from the awkward position in which it had landed. The man who had been working below stacking the consigment pulled Percy gently away. "Leave 'im to us, lad," he said tenderly, as the other drayman climbed into the cellar and lifted the distressed child within reach of the eager hands from the people above.

After being padded with a folded canvas Horace was also lifted out to the street, where he gained a degree of consciousness and began muttering incoherently.

The onlookers were silent as Percy knelt beside his father pleading with him to get up and come home. "Can you 'elp me get 'im up?" he pleaded to the crowd. "I'll be able to manage 'im like I always do, then."

As everyone there knew this to be impossible no one moved until the poor lad attempted to get his father's arm around his shoulder in order to lift him.

Then the woman involved in the incident gently pulled Percy to his feet and clutched him to her.

"Poor little wretch," she said. "'E's 'urt bad, son, and will 'ave to go in the ambulance. But they'll fix 'im up, don't you fret, lad."

Along with the ambulance came a policeman who took Percy home after his father was taken away shouting, "Bloody rapscallions!"

In spite of the disregard Horace displayed for Lucy and the children, the gloom over the house was unmistakeable.

Lucy had hardly been back an hour after visiting her delirious husband when the same policeman who had brought

Percy home called again to notify her that Horace had died.

Her grlef was as if his role as a partner had been exemplary. Her drawn face took on an extra pallor that would not have been thought possible by anyone who knew her, and her battered spirit was in the lap of the gods as she strove desperately to avoid a complete breakdown.

A man, who was considered by the family to be very kind, called and presented a cheque for twenty-five pounds to Lucy, just for her signature exonerating the brewery from responsibility concerning the fatality. Had Horace been a provider, the money would have been a criminal pittance, but as things were it was a heaven-sent bonus.

With the kind attendance of neighbours and the love of her children, Lucy was drawn out of the initial shock and settled into a calm acceptance of her bereavement.

Everyone acquainted with the family's misery when Horace had been alive looked upon his demise as a blessing in disguise. And although Lucy's thoughts never strayed for a moment in this direction she did feel that a disgusting oppression had been lifted from the family.

TWO
Honey Dowset

It was an hour before dusk on a lovely summer evening as Percy, now fourteen years old, and his friend George Goble left the beach and ambled along the promenade. They had been for a swim after school and were joking and laughing as they made their way homeward. As they passed some tennis courts a ball came over the high perimeter fence, and there followed calls from two girl players within, to return it. Percy was struck by the culture of their voices and knew that their education was from a source other than a council school such as he and his kind attended.

"'Ark at that, George, aint that nice?" he remarked at the refined manner with which the girls requested the ball's return. "Proper luvly," agreed George as he threw the ball to Percy who then headed it back to him.

The girls watched somewhat exasperated as the two youths tossed the ball back and forth to each other.

"Throw it back immediately, you rascals," one of the girls demanded, pushing her golden hair from her face as she approached the fence. Percy, impressed by her loveliness as she came closer, was momentarily transfixed.

"What are you staring at ?" she snapped.

"A lovely tart," replied Percy.

"Cheeky young swine," she said as she made her way back to her friend in the centre of the court. A short whispered discussion went on between them and at the end the boys were asked if they would like some chocolate.

George inquired if it was milk or plain, and set Percy giggling. After another short confab the girls sprinted through the gate and by taking opposite directions around the outside pathway, trapped the two boys.

"Now what have you to say for yourselves?" leered the blonde as she grabbed Percy's shoulders. Her friend tried to do the same to George, but he fell backwards and pulled the girl on top of him.

"Please miss, I didn't mean it, miss," wailed Percy jokingly as if she were one of his teachers. Meanwhile George's captor lay spreadeagled over him with the hem of her pleated tennis skirt up around her waist, which presented a very pleasant view indeed to Percy.

"Cor, you ought ta see 'er frilly knickers, George," he shouted. But part of her skirt was covering George's face and he shouted back that he could see nothing.

"Cor, it's luvly," chuckled Percy.

"Filthy toad," said the blonde as she tried to box his ears. It turned into a wrestling match, and being a few years younger and just a mite smaller, and considering that she was a girl, Percy was soon in the same position beneath her as George was under her friend.

"What's mine look like?" he shouted to George, who intimated that he could not be bothered to look, as he had now focussed his eyes sufficiently under the skirt for it to prove interesting. This made the girl snatch the garment from his face and stow it away between her legs.

After the pretence of spluttering and coughing George began describing how the blonde looked.

"Oh, she's lovely too, Perce, pink knickers on a luvly round bum."

"You cheeky blighter," she said, "Box his ears, Irene, and hard — they deserve a lesson."

Amidst their chortles the boys squeaked and moaned as if they were in the grip of a beating, but none of the blows bore any intent to harm.

"I wanna go 'ome now," said George, as Irene stopped slapping at him.

"I've gotta get my Dad's supper."

"Can't your mother get it?" inquired the girl.

"'Corse she can't, that's why, now get orf," went on George.

"I won't, you'll just stay there until you tell me," she replied stubbornly, as the lad struggled in vain to free himself from beneath her. "Let 'im go, you can both share me," said Percy cheekily.

"No I won't, not until he tells me," said Irene.

"What shall we do, Perce?" asked George.

"What will you do, you mean. I like it where I am," chuckled Percy.

"Aw right, what shall I do?" George said, somewhat annoyed.

"You might as well enjoy it while you're 'ere, you may not get the chance again, so start doing this," said Percy as he began to jerk the lower part of his torso between the thighs of the girl who had him pinned down.

"Now you just stop that," said the blonde firmly, but Percy ignored her and carried on with the exercise.

"Keep still, you horrible boy," shouted Irene as George copied his friend's suggestive movements.

In an attempt to restrict the action and flatten him to the ground, the blonde shifted her weight from her knees and held herself heavily against her captive. This action compromised her even further, for now she was moving in harmony with him. Freeing one of his hands in order to slap his face, gave Percy the opportunity of locking an arm around her waist and hugging her to him. Letting go of his other hand, which he clamped around her neck, she clawed at his face and hair.

"Let me go you little beast," she cried angrily.

"No fear, I like it," said Percy as he began kissing the struggling girl's cheek.

Meanwhile, Irene had freed George from her clutches and he started to pull the blonde from his friend, until he was asked whose side he was on. As he stood back in confusion, Irene pulled at Percy's hands in an attempt to free her friend.

"Stop 'er, yer bloody fool," shouted Percy.

"What'cha mean, don't yer wanna get 'er orf?" George asked, looking puzzled.

"Not partically, they started it didn't they?" went on Percy, so George threw himself back into the serio-comical melee with the result that he was once again beneath the body of Irene, who thought it a less embarassing position than having him on top of her. He was beginning to enjoy it and although he had not forgotten about his father's supper he was willing to take the consequences for not preparing it.

The blonde stopped clawing at Percy and just lay panting with her cheek against his. Mustering some composure she asked him to let go of her and he asked what she would give him if he did. A bar of chocolate, was her reply, to which she was asked if it was one each for himself and George or one between the two of them. "I'm not giving them mine," chipped in Irene, so the blonde said it would only be one bar. "That alright wiv you, George ?" asked Percy, but George said he did not want any and preferred to stay where he was. Irene too began to feel compulsive about her position even though involuntary. She bore herself down heavily on George's lower trunk, in natural response to the swelling that had become noticeable to her in that vicinity.

"The chocolate is in the changing hut if you want it," the blonde told Percy, but he said she could keep it, as he too would stay where he was.

"I've just come out of hospital from an appendix operation," she pleaded, "and I think I've pulled the stitches."

Succumbing to the concern in her voice, he released his hold around her neck and waist, whereupon she shot to her feet, laughing. "Ever been had?" she jeered as Percy grabbed his towel to cover the slight bulge in the front of his trousers as he got to his feet.

Meanwhile George and Irene were embracing and kissing in quiet concentration of their position, and when it came to parting them they were both reluctant to let go of each other.

The blonde pointed out that they were out in the open even though it was nearly dark. She also reminded George that his father would be waiting for his supper. As neither reason had any effect on the pair she said a policeman was coming and they were on their feet in a flash. Percy noted the way white lies rolled off her tonguee and surmised that she could be a bit of a mischief when the mood took her.

"Don't suppose we'll get the choclit eiver," went on George as he stood in the manner of Percy with his towel obscuring the bulge in his trousers.

But Irene was quick to reassure the boys that they would, to the surprise in the form of an inquiring look from her friend.

Pointing to some changing huts at the edge of the promenade, Irene bade the boys go to them and wait, which they did in silent anticipation of something that had never happened to them before outside of the obscure dreams associated with their age.

"Let's do it with them," said Irene eagerly, when the lads were out of earshot.

Her friend thought she was mad and told her so. "They can't be any more than fourteen," she said. "Besides, they're destitutes from some council estate. Do remember who you are and have a little decorum."

"I'm not keen on older boys, they frighten me," explained Irene.

"Only since your uncle took you out in his boat and...!"

"Yes," snapped Irene, cutting her short, "and how much decorum are we supposed to have? My father's a hotel keeper and yours an estate agent. That doesn't make us royalty."

"They're coarse and grubby," argued the blonde, "they probably keep old bicycles in their hallway and coal in the bath."

"They can't be grubby at the moment, can they, considering they've been swimming?" reasoned Irene.

"Honestly, how can you degrade yourself in this way, Irene ?" pleaded her friend.

"Oh, don't be so pompous, Honey," pleaded Irene.

"Come on, for the devil of it, they're not bad looking, are they? Besides, if you had left us for just another minute I would have got the sensation and there would be no need to associate further with them."

"Well, you go with George then, or whatever his name is, but I don't want the other one any more," said Honey.

"Any more?" burst out Irene, surprised. "Any more?" Quieting down she looked suspiciously at her friend for a few seconds and then soliciting her confidence she said quietly, "You've had the sensation, haven't you?"

Honey remained silent and looked away. Knowing her as she did, this, to Irene, was an admission.

"Well, aren't you the devious one? Blow you, Aggy, I've popped my cork, aye," went on Irene. "Right, you know what you can do the next time you want me to keep some lobster occupied while you meditate with 'is friend."

"He's not a lobster," snapped Honey, in quick defence of Percy.

"Indeed he's not, so what's wrong with stoking up again?" coaxed Irene. While the girls haggled, Percy and George discussed the event with understandable excitement.

"She had 'er wicked way wiv me somehow," Percy said with matter of fact nodding.

"'Ow d'yer mean?" asked George.

"Well, one minute she was 'ugging me, then nothing," complained Percy.

"That Irene nearly snapped my knob off, 'cause it wasn't laying flat on me belly," went on George. "I still enjoyed it though, didn't you, Perce."

In a non-committal way Percy shrugged and his reply of "Alright!" lacked the exuberance that George expected.

"What's up, then Perce?" he said, studying his friend. "Don't yer like 'er much."

"I'd rather 'ave that Irene, she's got a lovely arse."

"So's the one you 'ad," went on George.

"I couldn't see 'ers as well, could I? That Irene gave me the 'orn," Percy confessed.

"Watcha fink they got in mind then?" asked George eagerly. "'Ard ta say, aint it? Yours is keen and mine aint," said Percy, turning his gaze towards the girls. "That blonde's a right cow."

"Wot's wrong wiv 'er?" asked George.

"I fink she is a teaser. Yer don't know where yer stand wiv such a mischievous bitch," warned Percy. "That Linda Beck tried that wiv Joey King, didn't she, and 'e sloshed 'er."

"'Ere, she was the one that 'ad a baby wivout bein' married wasn't she," chipped in George.

"Oh yeah, that's right," Percy said with surprised realisation. "Bloody sod for doing that to 'er."

"Well, make yer mind up. First yer say she deserved a clout, then yer get narked at the bloke for giving 'er one," said George, giving his friend a nudge.

"I didn't say I agreed wiv 'im bashing 'er did I ?" Percy said, with a degree of annoyance. "I got no time for blokes knockin' women about or don't bother to look after 'em when they gets their oats. I'd do 'em if I 'ad the chance."

"Not Joey King you wouldn't 'e's practicly eighteen now," said George as he leaned towards Percy to deliver the warning.

"Come a few years and the age gap won't make no difference. Then 'is sort better keep clear of me." George noted the strong conviction in his friend's voice and pitied anyone big or small, strong or weak, whose folly of ill-treating women ever came within Percy's reach to avenge.

One way or another the girls had come to a decision and casually approached the two youths.

"Tuk yer shirt in, slick yer 'air down and do yer flies up, they're comin' ta finish you off, George."

"Gawd, I can't stop shaking, " George whispered.

"Nor me, they're the sort that not many buggers of our age can get within a mile of."

"I don't care if the ol' man does gi' me the strap, it'll be werf it, Perc."

"We 'ope," said Percy.

"And what might your name be, young man?" demanded Irene, addressing George and prodding him gently in the midriff with her tennis racket.

"It's George, you know it is, you 'eard 'im call me George. An' your name's Irene ain't it ?"

"Er, yes, quite," she said, resting her racket on her shoulder, "but what's your other name?"

"Goble! an' what's 'er name?" he snapped, nodding as he did so towards Honey.

Ignoring his question Irene asked her friend if they were acquainted with any Gobles, and after a few moments' deliberation from Honey, apart from the "greengrocer", the answer was no.

"Does pater sell potatoes?" Honey asked sarcastically.

"Do what?" asked George, looking somewhat perplexed.

"Does yer ol' man sell taters," chipped in Percy, who then answered for his friend and said "No, 'e don't."

Honey looked Percy up and down, then spoke as if he

were applying for the job of butler. "And you are ?"

"Percival Longpre, my lady'" said Percy sarcastically, touching his fore-head with his forefinger in the manner of a menial servant.

"We calls him Percy Longprong," chuckled George. "Don't ask me why though, will yer?" he continued.

To cover her embarrassment Honey took on a polite attitude as she asked Percy if he was of French extraction. His answer of "As English as they come," sent George into a fit of sniggering which brought a disapproving glare from Honey, along with a request for him to "Shut up."

"Yeah, shut up, George. Don't get stupid jus' when they're gettin' friendly," added Percy. Sensing she and Irene were being inadvertently compromised prompted Honey to give Percy a curt "Thank you."

Being aware that she was liable to walk away at the drop of a hat, Irene smiled at the boys and bade Honey to stay benign. "This is Honey Dowset and I'm Irene Meadow," she said good naturedly.

"Pleased to meecha," said George, sticking a hand out and having it nearly snatched off.

Percy managed a tenuous "Yeah! Same 'ere," but kept one hand in his trousers pocket and the other on the end of the towel that hung over his shoulder. His nonchalance intrigued Honey and aroused a glow of interest within her.

"Either of you play tennis?" she asked brightly.

Not only the friendliness of her manner but the question itself made the two boys look inquiringly at each other.

"Is that all you've 'ung us about for? A game of tennis?" asked George with unmistakeable disappointment.

"Certainly not," said Irene. "She is only joking. Tennis

is over for the day. Now it's time to relax and eat some chocolate." So saying she took George by the arm and bundled him inside one of the huts. Her directness brought a look of awe to his face, and his reassurance to her inquiry as to whether he had been "right in the sea," was hardly audible as the door slammed shut.

For a few moments Percy's thoughts dwelt on how lucky he thought his friend was to be rushed into an out of sight place by a girl like Irene. Not that he thought Honey unattractive, for her looks bordered on the beautiful, but her devious manner he thought showed a selfish streak. And although he did not fear her he felt she could be a source of danger. Her enigmatic nature showed a boredom for the ordinary and commonplace and was not the type of personality that Percy could feel at ease with.

Yet at his age the looks of a person was the important and decisive quality. So in the efforts to bolster their ego and impress others, boys and girls alike have saddled themselves with untold torment from the world's Helens and Adonises. Not that Percy conjured up any thoughts of long term fruition with the lovely Honey Dowset. He knew she must have many admirers far more interesting to a girl of her age than he could be at that time. However, he had felt her breasts and thighs pressing hard against him and had smelled the fresh perspiration of her warm body, and his enthusiasm to experience an orgasm while embracing her was overpowering.

He felt that waiting for her to take the initiative as Irene had with George was a waste of time.

"Where's, my choclit then?" he asked cheerfully , although as fond of it as he was he was not that interested, but it was just something to say.

"In the hut," replied Honey, "but we can't get to it at the moment, can we?"

"Why not ?" Percy asked with a realisation that she was beginning to turn hostile again.

"Because it's occupied, isn't it," was the reply.

"'Aven't you got one fer yerself?" he asked with surprise.

"No, we always share one," she said casually.

"Well, wot's wrong wiv that one there? That's empty," said Percy, pointing to a hut.

Honey went all matter of fact as she told him the chocolate was not in there. She knew it was only the talking point and sought to embarass and frustrate the beated youth into making his desires plain to her.

"Let's go in there, anyway," he suggested, fully aware of Honey's antagonistic mood.

Like a maid of chaste innocence she asked, "Whatever for?" and Percy, nodding towards the hut occupied by George and Irene, answered, "Same as them."

"And how do you know what that is?" she argued.

"Well, they're not 'aving a muvver's meeting are they? P'raps a mum and dad's meeting though, eh? I'll go and 'ave a look." So saying he went to the hut and disregarding Honey's warning that he should not, he pushed the door open before she could stop him. It did not open fully as it was checked by two bodies, one on top of the other, and in the tangle of limbs Percy could not for the moment distinguish which belonged to whom.

Then he recognised George by the swimming trunks around his calves, and the fact that the hands clasping the buttocks were too clean and well kept to have belonged to anyone other than Irene in that circumstance.

In this embrace George was on top of Irene. Their position was more in keeping with the idea held by the majority of how a union between male and female should be. It certainly went through Percy's mind as he stood somewhat aghast at a sight that is rarely seen by people of any age in life or times.

Envy consumed him as he watched his friend sampling the pinnacle of desire, while he suffered the frustration of Honey's antagonism. And the fact that he fancied Irene very strongly himself only gave further rise to his feeling of disappointment, that it had been Honey who had pounced on him initially.

Considering that it was he who had introduced the element of sexual play into the proceedings Percy could not help a slight feeling of enmity towards George. After all he did need prompting into small adventures and yet here he was experiencing the big one that Percy always thought he would lead the way in an example to George.

He could beat him at fighting, football, swimming and most other energetic displays connected to their age. Yet there before his eyes lay George, getting splinters in the toes of his plimsolls from the hut floor as he heaved between the legs of what to both of them was not a giggling, uneventful girl of their own age but a mature young woman. She came in the category of other boys' "mums" and older sisters as a subject of masturbation, which was no light matter in the order of things.

Of course he could always brag amongst his chums about being first or no doubt the only one to observe at close hand a male and female locked in seduction. Although George, of course, would not be amongst the number of those impressed by the boast.

The sight flabbergasted Percy, for expectation is one thing but reality another. George was similarly astonished as he wallowed bodily in the ecstasy of life, expecting any second to awaken to the spasm of a wet dream. Both he and Irene were panting heavily, she emitting groans of pleasure which were at first mistaken by Percy to be the results of some hidden brutality on the part of George. For by this time no doubt all the hitherto secrets of command and satisfaction had been opened to him. And here he was gluttonizing at his initiation, thought Percy, in more primitive terms.

Honey had gone to pull him from the doorway and she too stood spellbound momentarily at the sight. One of the hands stopped caressing George's buttocks, and the hut door slammed into Percy's nose, causing it to bleed profusely. Cupping a hand over his nose he turned to Honey for some light consolation, but was not surprised at the "Serves you right" she gave him as she turned away with an air of indifference.

The superficial injury did little to dampen Percy's ardour, especially after the sight he had just witnessed. What he had seen of George looked forthright and dominant, and he was determined to bring about the same situation between himself and Honey. Providing of course that it did not involve any distress to her, which by her attitude of looking down her nose at him was going to prove difficult. But she too felt the effect of the unexpected sight, and try as she may to treat it as inconsequential, a passion was revived in her, much to her annoyance.

Percy thought she was talking to someone else when she bade him to follow her as she entered the vacant hut adjoining the one being enjoyed by Irene and George. Here indeed, he thought, was a female of record changing temperaments.

He was jerked out of his pondering by Honey telling him to make haste if he wanted her to help stop his nose bleeding. Whether it was for this reason or a more pleasing one that she summoned him, at that moment he desperately desired to be near her, whatever the circumstances.

He had barely cleared the door when Honey slammed it shut and told him to lie on his back, which in silent obedience he did. She knelt beside him and took the rolled towel that Percy had clutched to his chest, then placed it under his neck. With her hand gently under his chin, she eased his head back and he gazed into her lovely face, the countenance of which now plainly changed from tormentor to seductive lover.

With mixed feelings of a hero being ministered to by an angelic nurse, and a young man on his wedding night, he was sure that Honey could hear his heart pounding excitedly within his chest. Nevertheless, in spite of the subtle liaison that existed between them, he could not discount entirely the fact that at any moment she might tear the tail off his shirt, and tie his nose up in a sling. She spoke to him in soft, soothing tones, wonderfully acted, he thought, as she reassured him that the bleeding had now stopped, and he should not worry. With all the boyish skirmishes and clobbering resulting in split lips, black eyes, and an assortment of bruising he had come to experience in his young life, the damage to his nose was of little consequence. However, he did realise that it was a focal point on which to re-establish contact.

But merely lying on his back with Honey just caressing his chin and head was nowhere near enough for Percy, even had he not seen his friend George gorging to his contentment. Yet how to manoeuvre the situation to that ultimate desire of most adolescents was the problem he struggled with. He certainly could not employ the tactics of their previous encounter for fear of breaking their fragile comradeship. His quandary was short lived when Honey, in the pretence of adjusting the towel beneath his neck, casually rearranged her kneeling position, with the result that Percy's right hand now lay between her legs.

However perplexing the situation had been, Honey's action confused him further by her behaviour of undeniable cooperation when none was expected.

He lay for a while as would the wounded hero, too honourable to flex a finger in case it caused a feeling of violation towards the ministering angel.

Once again Honey took the initiative, and without pretext of any kind she lowered herself on to Percy's hand. Her actions were encouraging, and worthy, he thought, of a display of boldness on his part. But his hand was trapped palm down and incapable of movement until Honey eased herself up a fraction to allow him to manoeuvre it to a more convenient position between her legs. This, to Percy, seemed a definite committal, an insistent invitation to touch her most private and aluring part. A sign indeed of being minutes away from mutual pleasure.

Daylight had gone, and all that lit the hut was the glow from the tall promenade lights that filtered on the scene through the frosted glass windows at the top of the door.

An ideal setting, thought Percy, for the rough and tumble of first love. Honey had his undivided attention and he was oblivious of the bare floorboards upon which he lay.

With the confidence of an accustomed lover he began caressing her through her underwear. The feel of the silk sliding over the pubic hair combined with the moist warmth made an adjustment to his trousers front necessary to accommodate the swelling within. Honey, breathing heavily, closed her eyes in ecstasy as she began to move in harmony with Percy's manipulation. Her hand groped excitedly to his trousers, and dispensing with the courtesy of undoing them properly, tore them open, causing two of the buttons to pop off and ricochet around the hut.

The abusive manner with which his erection was clawed free from the encumbrance of its cover caused him to both gasp and wince.

His experience was certainly being enriched, but not in the way he expected. He now knew how it felt to be practically dismembered and it did not fit in with the scheme of things as he had imagined them to be in such a circumstance. In fact the whole situation bore little or no resemblance to his anticipations, not only of his introduction to the act but at future times of familiarity.

It was no way for any girl to act, let alone one of her class, he thought. Prompted by the enchantment of the moment, he would have uncovered himself had she waited.

Sensing that her eagerness had aroused a slight disdain in Percy, she bade him "Hush!" and kissed him ravenously on the mouth. Not only did it compensate, but gave new vigour to his confidence. This resulted in the elastic on one leg of Honey's drawers being dispensed with in a similar manner to Percy's fly buttons. But he did not snatch at her bareness with the same impetuosity she had applied to him.

She groaned passionately, and wriggled on his hand as one of his fingers slipped into her. Breaking off the kiss she glanced at his nakedness which she momentarily freed from her grasp.

"Oh my God," she sighed, "No wonder they call you Longprong.

Clutching his erection again, she closed her eyes, laid her head back and was engulfed in responding to the occasion. It was her intention to reach a climax from that position, but Percy interrupted her concentration by moving his hand from her crotch and lifting her leg sufficiently to slide himself beneath her.

"No, you mustn't," she whispered with alarm as she quickly removed herself from him. For a moment his spirit plummetted to despair. To be so close in reality to any man's dream, be he youthful or middle-aged, only to have the near certainty shattered at a crucial time, was soul destroying.

Obviously at a point of frustration also, Honey sat back on her heels and closed her eyes. Her breathing was fast, heavy and spasmodically delivered a sigh.

Sensing that all was not lost, Percy reached up and curling an arm around her shoulders, pulled her to him again and started kissing her neck.

"Oh, God, no," she murmured in the manner of being on the brink of submission, while at the same time stretching full length beside the youth.

"Oh, you can't, you mustn't," she said, in almost a whisper, but her voice rose to a quiet frenzy as she climbed astride him. "Oh, you devil, oh, my God, you are." She arched her back momentarily to pull her underwear down around her legs, then settled back to make contact with Percy's member. Intent on an insertion, his hand groped nervously past their two abdomens, but was firmly pulled away and placed around her waist. "Not right in you're not, so there," she said sternly, and he knew that disregarding the warning in her voice would lose him the girl.

His obedience gave her confidence to work her body with unashamed gusto at him, and he realised that he must join her rhythm or be left high and dry.

With one arm around her waist and the other around her neck, holding her lovely mouth to his, he rocked against her with equal zest.

Overwhelmed by the ecstasy of such an advanced experience, it was not long before his thrusts became faster in the preliminary of ejection. Honey, knowing in her superior wisdom what the change in his tempo meant, broke off the kiss and amidst moans and groans of pleasure (the similarity of which Percy likened to those uttered by Irene) mixed with pronouncing him "A lovely swine, a devilish boy, and masterful to boot," her excitement overflowed simultaneously with his.

Locked in each other's arms brought moments of indescribable beauty to Percy. He had found it as fulfilling as an insertion could have been. His envy at whatever George might have enjoyed was gone, for he felt accomplished.

As the two infatuated boys hurried home, chattering excitedly about their unbelievable good luck, they trembled slightly, due to the chill of the late evening, and the very unusual events in which they had participated.

George was ready to receive his father's fury for not preparing his meal. Irene had been well worth having his ears boxed for.

Now that they had such refined and mature girl friends (for arrangements had been made to meet them the following evening) and even though they did not consider themselves betrothed, they did feel that the familiarity so swiftly achieved gave them, to a degree, a claim on several more occasions of intimacy.

Believing themselves to be on the threshold of manhood, they voiced their resolve to give up masturbating as a token of faithfulness to Irene and Honey.

George's house was but a few steps away and Percy wished his friend good luck as he turned through the gateway and approached the front door. Gone was his manner of disregard for his father's meal. His countenance was anxious and expectant of a good wallop as he timidly knocked the door.

Glancing back, Percy saw the door open and an arm emerge, which grabbed George and dragged him in simultaneously to a gruff voice asking, "Where the bloody 'ell you bin?" followed quickly by the sound of a slap and George shouting "OH.!"

Compared with his late father, Percy did not consider George's dad to be a beast. Everyone knew he had a lot to put up with, bringing the boy up alone since his wife was committed to an asylum for the insane. He was a navvy and worked hard. He did his best for the lad, and the anger Percy witnessed was through the concern for George's whereabouts rather than the absence of any supper.

That was something Percy had never come up against. Not that his mother was callous or unfeeling, but she never showed any anxiety as to what might befall him on his boyish excursions. He remembered quite a few occasions when it was touch and go whether there would be a knock on her door to inform her of an accident to him. One particular instance was when he fell into the harbour while unable to swim. He would have drowned for sure had not a youth descended one of the fixed ladders at the quayside and pulled him out. It was as if his mother had a steadfast confidence in his capability to look after himself.

It was because of this and other attitudes to different things, that Percy looked upon her as being somewhat naive where the many hazards of the world were concerned. Not that he himself had knowledge of a great deal outside his sphere of wanderings, nevertheless the experience of having the father he had, was the nucleus itself of education in respect of the world's pitfalls.

Keeping their part of the bargain, the following evening had the two eager lads perched on the low promenade wall overlooking the tennis courts where Honey and Irene were once again playing.

It was not the intention of the boys to go swimming that evening, so they had not brought towels or bathers. But owing to the insistence of their girl-friends that they should bathe, swim suits or not, or there would be no fraternising, there was no alternative than for the ardent pair to take the plunge in their underpants, then dry off as best they could in the warm breeze.

"Expect they think we got crabs or summink, eh, Perc?" said George, seriously.

"Sounds like it, don't it ? Druids drip and Ploughman's pimple as well, I shouldn't wonder," answered Percy casually.

An air of impatience came upon Percy. Irene kept waving to George, but the only time Honey moved her arm was when she hit the ball. Percy had a premonition that all was not well with the arrangement as far as she was concerned, for she was plainly ignoring him since his return from the beach.

When the girls had finished their game, the boys half scrambled, half fell down the wall to meet them.

It came as no surprise to Percy when Honey said she could not stay but had to hurry home to change for an important engagement.

"Aint I important?" asked Percy, but his question was ignored.

She stepped into one of the huts and attempted to close the door, but was prevented by Percy barging in after her.

"I could 'ave gone to see Laurel an' 'Ardy to-night," he said.

"Why didn't you then," she snapped.

"'Cause we arranged ta meet, that's why," he reasoned.

"Well we'll just have to postpone it until another time, won't we ?" she said, in a manner that was meant to have a pacifying effect on the lad, yet lacked all conviction.

Percy knew he was being humoured and that she was likely to promise anything to get rid of him. She made him feel like a child who had been expecting a treat from an adult, and then let down with no grounds for redress.

The subject of the matter involved however, was not the pastime of children, even though they are begot by it, and at the impressionable age he was, Percy, through no fault of his own, was past being pacified as one where the instinct of mating was concerned.

He saw no alternative to pursuing his purpose and put forth good reasons why the arrangement should be honoured. "You promised yesterday," was one, and "You could 'ave told me as soon as I come down," was another. "An' I'm all wet underneaf fru swimmin' in me pants," he went on, but all to no avail. Pleading for a ten minute roll about was also rejected, and when he caught hold of her, in an attempt to cuddle a little affection into her, he received a stinging slap on each side of his face.

The force of their delivery convinced him that whatever affection he had enjoyed before was not forthcoming that day, or if ever again, from her. She was a locked and bolted door.

Anger welled up inside him and he felt like striking her back. He could well understand now how some women had brought about attacks upon themselves even if they had acted only half as hateful as Honey had turned out to be.

"Get out, you despicable little toad, and don't come near me again, or you'll get what for," she shouted, as she gave him a vicious push from the hut, causing him to land on his back. At that moment the front wheel of a bicycle came close to his head, and he half expected to see a policeman glowering at him as he looked up, but thankfully it was not.

"Having trouble?" asked the young man who was about the same age as Honey. He was Carvel Ralling, a councillor's son.

"Nothing I can't handle," she said, dusting her hands off.

"Are you ready then?" he asked as he looked inquiringly at Percy and Honey, in turn..

"Won't be a sec now, Carv, just tidying up," she said.

"You goin' wiv 'im, then ?" asked Percy, picking himself up off the ground.

"What's it got to do with you?" asked Carvel, as he looked the inquirer up and down.

A feeling of mischief descended on Percy, along with the remembered words of wisdom given to him by his friend George's father. "If a woman's heartlessness threatens to separate you from your sanity, beatings are futile, for there are other means to settle your anger of her."

The thought struck him for a moment that perhaps George's mum had tried to drive his dad mad, and he had reversed the consequence, resulting in her being certified.

Here then, somewhere, was the solace to his downtrodden and frustrated emotions, and he would seek them out, then use them past the hilt.

"You one of her boy-friends?" Percy asked, with a casual calmness that hardly suited the hostile circumstance. Carvel gave a mystified look to Honey before settling his gaze upon Percy in what seemed an attempt to understand his impertinence.

"Bit of alright ain't she ?" Percy continued. "Best one I've ever 'ad."

He spoke as if in mutual admiration for a cricket bat or an obedient retriever.

Carvel's mouth gaped in surprise and disbelief, but Honey leapt at their tormentor and Percy had to duck and dodge from the flaying of her arms.

"You impudent young swine, if you don't go away I'll get Carvel to give you a good thrashing," she shrieked.

"Oh, don't say that," he cried, feigning despair. "We're mates, aren't we, Carve? Does she tear your fly buttons off too?"

Flabbergasted, Honey looked guiltily at Carvel. She was shaking her head and attempting to speak, but a denial of Percy's inference never passed her lips.

Carvel let his bicycle drop to the ground, and in his eager haste to get at Percy, tripped over it, put a foot through the spokes, then landed, face first, on the grass. The situation deteriorated further than Percy intended. Not only was the young man after him for his insults to Honey, but for damage, and perhaps injury as well, now. For what it was worth he would have to solicit George's aid to deal with the enraged Carvel, who would be forced to think twice about taking on two lively fourteen year olds.

But on glancing frantically around, neither George nor Irene were anywhere to be seen. Desperately he put the survival index of his brain to work. What had his father told him about combatting a bigger and stronger man? That's it, got it, he thought.

"Go for their bollocks, boy. That'll stop the biggest of 'em. But remember this, you only get one chance, an' if yer mess it up by missing, you'll probably get maimed." Further, it came to his mind that it was necessary to take a few wallops at first to put the adversary off his guard.

The information was of little help to Percy, for he could only commit such an act on a man who aroused deep hatred in him, and he did not even dislike Carvel.

Summing up the situation, the only option open to him was to do a bunk.

Honey had been belittled by the way he had spoken to her boy friend, then he had come a cropper in an attempt to defend her character. It took the edge from Percy's anger, but just as he turned to leave, Honey leapt upon him and pulled him to the ground. "Hold him," Carvel shouted, as he dragged his foot free of the spokes and scampered along on all fours to her aid. He held one of Percy's arms to the ground while Honey held the other.

Carvel's headlong fall had made his nose bleed, and Percy was receiving the drips, as his captor leaned over him. He began spluttering, then spitting out the blood that had dropped on his mouth, and telling Carvel to get off as he was drowning him, but Honey slapped his face and said it was no more than he deserved.

"Move yer 'ead over then," he shouted, "so's the rotten

stuff don't keep droppin' on me." Again Honey slapped him around the face and head. "Serves you right, you young horror," she said, struggling to keep hold of his arm.

"Why don'cha let 'er stop the bleedin', Carv?" Percy said good humouredly.

"She snatches yer flies open while she's doin' it though, but it aint bad."

Honey almost choked with anger. She let go of Percy's arm and began pummelling his face and chest to the extent that Carvel had to lean over him to protect him further.

He told Honey to calm herself but she pushed and pulled at him until he was dislodged. As she heaved him away she fell across Percy and presented him with the opportunity of getting back at her in the way she would hate most of all. He thrust a hand between her legs, locked an arm around her neck, and before she could gasp, he was kissing her on the mouth. His grip on her was vice-like, and was not relaxed until he had kissed and groped her for some ten seconds.

Carvel could not believe his eyes and glanced about nervously to see if anyone on the promenade or the perimeter path was looking.

On being released, Honey scrambled to her feet and stood silently staring down at Percy as if seeing him for the first time. She looked dazed and bewildered over the tactics he had used.

Snapping out of her perplexity, she asked Carvel twice, in quick succession, if he had seen what Percy did, knowing full well he had, then demanding that he did something about it.

"You've done enough yourself, look at his face," he said. His tone held sympathy for Percy, yet at the same time placed guilt upon Honey for her brutality. She knew he was right, but being the last in a million to admit it, she insisted that he deserved every bit, and more, of what he got.

Percy sat up and felt the lumps and bumps of his bruised and bloodied face.

As strange as it may seem, he considered he was half way to subduing the evening's frustrations and getting even with Honey.

"My ol' lady will take me to the police station wiv this now," he said, unhappily, pointing to his face.

"Who will take you where?" snapped Honey.

"My mum, to the cop shop," he replied.

"I should have thought the hospital would have been more appropriate," she said drily.

"She'll make me tell 'em everyfing," he said, almost sobbing.

"What do you mean?" she asked, becoming aware that something unpleasant was about to emerge.

"I'm a minor, aint I?" he blurted.

Making out that she thought he was referring to an association with coal, Honey remarked that she would never have guessed, as he looked so clean. Her flippancy was an attempt to minimise the serious implications in what he had said.

Carvel strolled the few steps to his bicycle, stood it up and began examining the damaged back wheel his foot had gone through.

Honey stepped over to him and with her back to Percy, she asked quietly if they should leave.

Carvel said he was going to mend his bicycle as he needed it to get to work the following morning. He advised

Honey for her own good, to stay with Percy for a while, and get him to change his opinion about who he was going to lay the responsibility on for his bruises and anything else he had in mind.

The suggestion brought indignation and an outburst of contempt at the idea of humiliating herself to Percy. She refused to stay, saying that Carvel was implicated also, and if he was leaving the scene, then so was she.

"After all, you held him, didn't you?" she cautioned.

"I didn't hit him though, did I? I can't afford to get involved in what you've stirred up, my father will skin me alive."

"Oh yes," she said sarcastically. "Councillor Ralling's son must be beyond reproach for anything, in case it should reflect on Daddy. Well, it won't work, if he splits on me, I'll involve you, so you had better help me."

Although Percy could not hear what was being said, it was obvious that the pair were worried. And he intended keeping them that way until he got what he came for.

The amicable manner with which the couple now approached him was barely credible. Carvel held out a florin, "For a treat at the pictures and some sweets," he said nervously.

Honey, now mild and ladylike, with eyes lowered, was full of apologies for the bruises she had inflicted, and promised to meet Percy two nights, hence. But he replied that owing to the way he felt, he would probably be in hospital and she arrested by that time, as his "Mum" would go mad when she saw the state he was in.

The blood drained from Honey's face as she gave Carvel a worried look. Falling for Percy's act, Carvel tried to cheer him up by telling him he did not look too bad.

"You don't know 'ow I feel though do you?" Anyway it's nuffin' ta do wiv you is it? You never 'it me did yer? Or took advantage of me?"

"I should say not, I wouldn't do that to a youngster like you," he said, with cheerful relief at being relinquished for his part in the fracas. Nevertheless, he was somewhat uneasy as to what was meant about Percy being taken advantage of. However, he did not pursue the issue. The look that Honey gave her friend spoke volumes as to the contempt she held him in at being let off, especially when he asked Percy if it was alright for him to get home and mend his bicycle, and was graciously given a "Course yer can, Carve," as consent.

It was a pleasing sight to Percy as he watched Carvel wheeling his machine away with the damaged back wheel held off the ground. "Fanks fer the two bob," he yelled to him, before he was out of range.

Honey knew she was being compromised when Percy asked her to take him to the hut and "Nurse me better," as he put it. She whimpered, pleaded and promised, all falsely, but to no avail, for he had suffered a deep disappointment and had no more compassion for her than, by her demonstrations, she had lavished on him.

Yesterday and up to the time she put the first scar upon his heart, he had loved her, been the slave of infatuation, or whatever the term should be when one person is overwhelmingly consumed with the company of another.

Now he was eager to implement his instinct on a purely base arrangement, for he did not even like her. It was one of life's situations that, like hosts to come, he would not have thought possible. It was inconceivable that two people with an obvious dislike of each other could exercise the pinnacle of intimacy, and it was not long before he realized that Nature does not rely solely on harmonious relationships to propagate offspring.

In the hut, Honey ruefully asked what was expected of her, adding with a hint of composure that what they did the previous evening would be alright with her. Percy, however, told her quite frankly that he wanted from her what George had had with Irene, and in the same way, with her lying down and him on top.

Barely had she finished telling Percy what a cheeky toad he was, and he could jolly well go on wanting, when she was pulling him back inside the doorway as he attempted to leave.

"You contemptible little swine, you would go and report me, wouldn't you," she gasped breathlessly.

Percy never answered, but relied on the look of impatience and anger he gave her as an affirmative reply. For some ten seconds they stood in silence, glaring at each other, before Honey gave a resigned sigh and said, "Oh, very well, you win."

Her capitulation was meant to sound calamitous, but was only convincing enough to revive and emulate Percy's lust of the evening before.

The feeling of dominance revitalised his ego and with every confidence, he removed his trousers, pants and shoes.

Caught up in the mood of the situation in which she saw no alternative, Honey readily removed her panties in eager preparation of the pleasure about to be forced upon her.

Noting her contribution to the preliminaries, which saved the need of Percy dragging them off, which would have been none too ceremoniously, he took off his shirt, and spread it on the floor for her to lie on, which she did at his gesticulation.

Clad only in his socks with a big toe protruding from each, yet neither with anything like the prominent audacity of his erection, he got down beside her. The sight of his male feature poised to perform chained her so passionately to desire that she would have fought tooth and nail against any chance of opting out.

As they laid hands upon one another the primitiveness prompted a mild crudity from Honey. Referring to Percy affectionately as a horny beast she asked how he came to be so big, but not knowing what to say, he did not answer.

"Hand reared, I expect," she panted. "Boys who toss off a lot do get terribly big," she went on casually.

Percy was somewhat surprised at her knowledge of what boys did. He was sure his sister was unaware of such things.

Normally he would have been embarrassed if a girl said anything like that to him, but Honey's manner of accepting it for the way of life it undoubtedly was, put him at ease.

Assuming she was ready, and with the stimulation connected to just such anticipation, he moved on top of her and lay between her legs. His excited fumbling made an insertion unsuccessful until Honey pulled his hand away and brought about the introduction. Contact completed, she heightened the mood by telling him how very naughty he was to go around forcing girls to do such things. She supposed he would keep forcing her whenever he came across her now that he had had his wicked way.

Her words trickled off to moans of rapture as she lunged so greedily at him that he could not get in rhythm until he told her she was going too fast.

He expected the ceremony to be at the pace he desired, which at that time was slow and leisurely to enable him, at this magical milestone of initiation, to take as much in as possible.

But it was not in Honey's make-up to be languid on such an occasion, and hugging Percy to her with a force that nearly stopped him breathing, she thrust back and forth at him in pursuit of a climax.

Realising that he was in the clutches of an experienced performer he ceased trying to co-ordinate and let her movement serve him also. At the point of culmination, his intention was to withdraw as this was what unweds were supposed to do, but Honey, aware of the time of the month, locked her legs around his torso and kept him in.

Had his moment of pleasure not come seconds before hers he would have had them spoilt, but his passion was safely away when she clawed his back while herself in the throes of extreme delight. Giving herself fully to the influence diminished her sense of propriety, for bad language became coupled to her quivering.

He had not kissed her for somehow he did not want to, but his cheek had been pressed against hers, and that side of her face was quite messy, not only from his still bleeding lip, but the blood that had dripped and dried on him from Carvel's nose.

Looking at herself in the hut mirror, while Percy was dressing, she complained of the mess he had made of her and how mad her father would be if he saw her in that state. The annoyance and the hint of her father seeking vengeance against a mistaken culprit however, was quelled when Percy made a contribution to the complaints by reminding her of how furious his mother would be if he let the cat out of the bag.

Once more she became amicable, even to the extent of hastening out of the hut and returning with a wet handkerchief with which she gently washed his face, not unlike the way his mother used to.

"There you are, Master Longprong," she said brightly as she patted him dry with her knickers.

"A fitting end to a comedy of errors. Now pray tell me, is there anything else you desire of me before we tear ourselves away from one another.

Expecting a "No fanks," or a shake of the head, the answer of "'ave yer got any choclit?" almost brought tears to her eyes.

He stood before her tucking his shirt in and brushing his fair hair from his eyes, and casually asked for chocolate as if he were off with a few scraps of food on a Sunday school treat. He had been the victim of seduction rather than the villain and pity joined in her heart the momentary quenched lust for his body.

She threw her arms around him and hugged him to her in the sparsely known purity and innocence of one human being for another.

Their departure from each other saw Honey waving from the promenade to Percy who was wading up to his waist in the sea, eating chocolate.

THREE
First Reckoning

As Percy's sexual prowess happened a full day following that of his friend, he was weighed down with anxiety for that same period of time worrying whether or not sores would appear on his penis as they had on George's.

Three days after his initiation to intercourse with Irene, he confided in Percy about the unusual blemish on his person. Other boys were in the toilets when George was showing his mysterious wound and it was not long before most of the school, who had heard through the bragging about his gorgeous conquest, were tormenting him regarding the consequences of what he now looked upon as his folly.

"Poxy Goble," some shouted, while others chanted "Georgy's got a dose, Georgy's got a dose, serves him bloody right. Longprong will be next, Longprong will be next!"

The two boys felt they were tied to a stake waiting for the faggots to be lit while their companions gleefully watched their torment. The prospects of having to submit to the umbrella, an instrument which, after being inserted into the penis, opened up on extraction, dragging scabs and matter to clear the passage, terrified them.

In truth they knew very little about the ailment in question and the smattering of information they had was based tenuously on boyish tales and hearsay.

The twenty-four hours passed in which time whatever had befallen George could, by remate theory, have settled on Percy also, yet, by any stretch of imagination or expectancy, his privates remained untarnished.

This perhaps, he told George, was due to the fact that he went back in the sea immediately after his session with Honey. It seemed so unfair to George, for out of the two he considered Irene to be the soul of purity, and if any sticky wickets were passed around, Honey would have been a more likely distributor.

A further week passed without change in either boy's condition, and a visit to the library was made as a discreet way of gathering somewhere near correct information on George's embarrassing blotches.

As the pair sat in the reference section with their attenti on fully devoted in the pages of a large medical encyclopaedia, a dignified looking man of middle age stood in the doorway and was taking great interest in them.

It was Mr. Quomby, their headmaster, who, knowing the two as he did, would have been greatly surprised if they had been there to improve their level of education. Percy spoke excitedly as he pointed to a section of the page they were studying.

"There yer are, George, six weeks after yer get spots come up, not free days, you aint got it mate, well, not yet anyway."

"That don't let you out, then, do it ?" said George, looking at Percy as if he were a first class candidate through going with Honey.

"Bugger me, no it don't, do it," he said thoughtfully,

turning somewhat pale.

"Ah, ha, so it's true then?" said Mr Quomby, who had crept up on them and now had his head placed just above theirs and was studying the item of their interest.

Percy attempted to slam the book closed but the man's hand shot forward and prevented it. While he sat down and intently studied the page, the boys stood and looked nervously at each other.

Having read enough, he turned to them, shaking his head sadly in disbelief.

He told them of the gossip in the school playgound that had brought the matter to his attention and what he had just witnessed confirmed his suspicion.

"For two such fine lads as you to go with women of disrepute is bad enough, but perhaps to have contracted a disease which could threaten the whole school has to be gone into, you understand?" he said sympathetically, to which the boys timidly answered "Yes, Sir."

He told them both to stay away from school until further notice and that their parents would be contacted.

On the way home George became very upset and no matter how Percy tried to convince him that there was nothing wrong with either of them, the fact of the headmaster interposing in the matter seemed to put the seal of doom on the whole affair.

George began sobbing and said he did not want to go home as his father would half kill him when he found out what had happened, to which Percy replied that his mum would be none too pleased either.

"Wot ever happens, don't give the girls away," said Percy. "Uvverwise they won't arf be for it as we're minors."

"'Oo we gonna say we got it off then?" said George angrily.

"I keep tellin' yer, we ain't got nuthin' from no one," said Percy with a touch of exasperation in his voice.

"My dad'll make me show 'im me nob and 'e'll know I bin doing summink sides tossin', and I've even bin frightened to do that since," he complained.

"Look, George, if we 'ave to blame someone, we'll say we give Daisy Oxford a couple a bob for both of us, eh? But I don't fink we'll 'ave to. We can say we was just spinnin' yarns as usual."

"Oh yeah ! And wot about me spotted nob that might be like the top of a pepper pot, later, is anybody gonna fink that's a yarn?" he moaned.

Percy was worried over his friend. Never before had he seen him in such a state of mental stress. He had noticed the anxiety mounting over the past week, but now he seemed at the end of his tether.

Knowing how much George liked Sylvia, Percy asked him in when they reached his house, saying that his sister would get them tea and biscuits to cheer them both up.

However, as she smilingly approached them with the tray of refreshment, tears welled up in George's eyes and began rolling down his cheeks, then, before she could inquire as to their cause, he got up from the sofa and ran from the house, crying his heart out.

Pushed for an explanation, Percy said it was because he was behind with his homework and the headmaster was after him. He added that George was in love with someone he could not get to see. This part of the excuse held more truth than he knew, for George loved Sylvia and had since he was twelve when he first came knocking on Percy's door and she answered it.

Knocks on the door after half-past ten at night were common enough when Horace was alive and Lucy answered them to the familiar scene of her sagging husband being propped up by her son. But since she had been widowed, any summons to the door after nine-thirty in the evening was considered to be an occasion. Therefore, when around the hour of eleven, just as they were settling down for sleep, loud and commanding knocks came, it could have been nothing but an emergency.

George's father was at the door inquiring as to the whereabouts of his son, whom we had not seen since breakfast time. Percy was called from bed by his mother but could tell his friend's father nothing more than that George went home, or so was thought, at about five o'clock that afternoon.

In spite of the headmaster's order, Percy went to school the following day, and in the late evening, news came that he had been found dead, floating in the harbour, minus his trousers.

The whole neighbourhood was shocked over the tragedy and pronounced it as being the result of a disturbed mind inherited from his mother, as did the coroner. Percy was required at the inquest to throw some small light on the sad circumstance. They explained to him what was meant by non-committal evidence which eased his mind somewhat for he was prepared to diminish and stretch the capacity of his tongue to protect Irene and Honey, whom he felt in his heart were not wanting in cleanliness.

Although it could not be hidden that the tragedy was due to an incapacity to cope with a problem of this nature, as the coroner put it, an examination of George established that he was not infected by any disease of promiscuous intercourse. His rash had been caused by sand being manipulated into the pores, which, according to the medical evidence given in court, was quite common in the summer months when sea bathing was popular.

Unbeknown to anyone, George's condition had been aggravated further by an ointment that his father used for the cement poison on his hands. As well as applying the medication to himself he had rubbed in particles of cement that had passed from his father's fingers into the jar.

No sooner had the coroner closed the case than Percy was quietly questioned by a policeman who was endeavouring to obtain information that might enable him to nab someone or another for offences against minors. Like policemen have to be, he was tricky and patronising. He appealed to Percy's sense of duty to tell him who the hussy was that George had been bragging about prior to his death. Even without remembering his father's warning against having any truck with policemen, his mind was closed against the answers the officer wanted.

After receiving a short sermon on the damning demands of the flesh, which sounded more alluring than dangerous, he was allowed to go home.

FOUR
At First The Yoke Seems Easy

In view of the stigma, Percy was pressured into leaving school in October instead of at the Christmas break. Too many complaints came in from parents, some of whom threatened to keep their children away if the bad influence and affront to decency were not removed from the school. Therefore, even though reluctantly and with long deliberation, it became expedient to end his tuition.

Percy, for his own part, was not put out by the decision, but was somewhat concerned for any degradation his mother might feel. However, as she did not gossip and so had little or nothing to do with the neighbours, the task of making embarrassing excuses and explanations to them did not arise.

Along with the bulk of his generation the measure of his education was unspectacular. He could read, write and count well enough to serve the menial occupations open to him and his kind, and a few weeks more or less would have changed nothing.

He was taken on as a bake-house boy by the Co-op. It was a pleasant enough job within easy walking distance of his home. He was set to greasing cake tins, weighing the mixes, cleaning the ovens, keeping the flour bins topped up, washing up, to mention but a few of his routine tasks. He earned about five pounds a week but was only paid ten shillings, for all labour was underpaid at that time and it was many years hence before the extreme became reversed.

From his very first day in the bake-house he plundered the cakes and was continuously told by the kindly foreman that he could only eat the broken ones. Consequently, when packing them in the trays some slight accident always occurred to one or two of his favourites to make them unsaleable. Moreover, as he settled into the routine, his intake of meat pies, a variety of fancy cakes and gateaux, and peaches dipped in huge tins of cream made it unnecessary, except at weekends, for his mother to provide him with meals.

Also employed in the same establishment was a youth of seventeen years, who was learning the art of confectionery. His name was Ken Edwards. He was six feet tall, perfectly proportioned, and had thick, well groomed fair hair. Through his good manners, respect and self assurance, the pleasant young man was liked by everyone, especially Percy who he took under his wing like a younger brother, and referred to as "Nipper".

In spare moments Ken would chase Percy around with a wet flannel which he would squeeze down his neck when he was caught. In turn Percy would throw odd bits of dough at Ken as he staggered along with a hundredweight sack of flour under each arm.

Added to the ample supply of food, the like of which had been well beyond his mother's means to afford, and the congeniality of his fellow workers, especially Ken, were three quite attractive young women who took Percy's fancy most strongly.

As Percy's bottom received pats and squeezes each time

a certain two male patissiers had occasion to pass near him, he thought he would try his luck in the same way on the girls to see what could be accomplished. They worked side by side shaping out the pastry for the meat pies on hand operated machines. Each time their hands went up to grab the lever, so their skirts rose, and at odd times Percy would stand transfixed as each gave a tantalising glimpse of suspenders and stocking tops. Two or three of the bakers would find the same spot an ideal position to stoop down and tie their shoelaces, and Percy thought how clever they were to accomplish it while looking in the direction of the girls.

Being only too well aware that fondling the opposite sex was not always received as complimentary, and that in some circumstances it could be downright dangerous, he decided to sound all three out simultaneously. This way would, he thought, minimise any grievance by making it less personal. He was on friendly terms with them and often joked about taking them out, even though they were four or five years older than him, but he had never laid a hand on them, even though he yearned to stroke their silky legs.

He was forever tying his apron tighter, in an attempt to keep down the expansion in his trousers. Unfortunately the more pressure he applied the worse the problem became, and at times he found it necessary to hold a small baking tray at his front to cover his embarrassing bulge.

On the day that he decided to perform the triple touch, he stood watching them from a corner as a matador watches, from behind the safety barrier, the movements of a bull he is about to challenge. He made three negative journeys around them but seemed powerless to move a hand.

Plainly the girls sensed that something unusual was

about to occur, and watched him all the way round on his third attempt. They smiled at him and looked at one another with inquiring frowns, over the off-putting behaviour.

There was naught for it but to leave the scene for a moment, which he did through a door at the far end of the bake-house. But once in the yard he sprinted quickly to a side door and re-entered behind the girls who were still glancing inconsequentially at the door through which he had just made an exit. Overcome more now by mischief than sexual coercion he pounced and in two seconds the bottoms of the three girls had been audaciously and affectionately squeezed.

Betty Moon, a five and a half foot sturdy girl with a pixie face and chestnut curls, gave a quick shriek and then began giggling. Cathy Truebridge, next to her, an older version of Honey Dowset, but with her hair in page-boy fashion, gave out with a startled "Oh!" and with obvious annoyance called Percy a cheeky young sod.

Mary Earl, a tall slow walking girl, well built, and with dark brown shoulder length hair, and a face that Percy likened to a Spanish beauty he had seen in a film, just gave a 'Whoops!" and laughed shyly. She had a quiet, gentle nature and took not the slightest offence at the unsolicited fondling. Indeed it was her understanding that was instrumental in talking Cathy out of reporting the incident to the foreman.

The following afternoon while in the cellar where he had been sent to bring up a tin of frozen eggs, the light was switched off. Then he heard the footsteps of two or three people descending the stone steps. They were preceded by a spear of light from a small torch that was turned on to his face, completely dazzling him, as the intruders entered.

Each of his arms was gripped and he was pulled to the

floor where someone pinned his legs down also. Getting over his initial fright in which he was silent, he swore and wriggled vigorously as another unseen assailant began undoing his trousers. He expected to be stripped of them but they were only pulled down to his knees.

Nothing happened for a few seconds and then a hand which he recognised to be female began applying a sticky concoction over his penis and testicles. He nearly broke from those who held his arms as they rocked with suppressed laughter. He knew they were men by the force with which they held him and the smell of the Fields brilliantine that was used on the hair of a particular baker named Chaxley Gossling. He recognised too the wheezy breathing of Ron Budgin, and the tobacco smelling breath of Tom Penrose. Furthermore, the distinct aroma of Evening in Paris showed it to be none other than the affronted Cathy who was now smearing his privates with he knew not what. However, he had to admit, her manner was gentle to the point of almost making it pleasurable, if the rubbish she was massaging on, and the men, were missing.

With whispers of "Come on," "That's enough," and "That'll teach him," they left in the same fashion by which they had arrived, with the torch still dazzling his eyes. He was about to cry out that he knew who they were, but thought better of it in case it provoked one of them into giving him a clout.

By touching that part of himself upon which Cathy had concentrated, he established the substance to be treacle. As he sat up in the dark wondering how best to rid himself of it, the light came on and at the end of the footsteps descending the steps, Mary appeared. Percy made no attempt to cover himself, but just leaned back on his hands. Though it was plain she hardly believed her eyes, she smiled encouragingly at Percy before excusing herself, then returning with a bucket of warm water and a cloth. In the meantime Percy had removed his trousers and underwear and stood with an erection before her. He asked her to wait and keep anyone from entering while he cleaned himself up, and she sat on the bottom step.

Her position enflamed Percy further, for he could see between her legs right to her drawers, and the gap of flesh at the top of her stockings drove his passion to breaking point. Without a care for who might come down the steps or whether the room was full of people, he thrust himself between her silk-clad legs and within ten lunges, before she hardly realised fully what he was doing, and being too sympathetic to stop him anyway, his passion was relieved.

As he stood back from her it was like the awakenig from a dream and he felt ashamed. He apologised and said he expected the sack for his terrible action.

He rushed to the bucket and wrung the cloth out, then approached her to wipe the sperm from her underwear, but she took over the task and asked him if he had been hurt by the others.

Her manner surprised him. She was entitled to be very angry to say the least, yet here she stood wiping away his mess and showing concern for his well-being. Seeing her standing before him with her skirt up, not minding if he gazed upon her, made him feel like her accepted lover, and he wanted her again.

In the midst of trying with little success to control his freshly aroused lustful desire, the voice of Harry Stone came bellowing from the top of the cellar stairs, as he requested, none too politely, to know when the bloody eggs would be arriving.

The incident with Mary in the cellar was fixed more firmly in Percy's heart and mind than was his experience of entirety with Honey. Yet all his attempts to promote any further association along the same lines were met with gentle but frustrating rebuke.

Mary liked him well enough for he appealed to the randy side of her, but his age made any association, outside of looking upon him as a younger brother, out of the question. At Christmas, as well as having his bottom and penis grabbed at five or six times by the two patissiers in the spirit of celebration, Mary gave him a kiss. But it was not in an out of the way location whereby he could have taken advantage of her kind understanding again. Nor was he the only one for she kissed all but two of the men in the bakehouse, and Ken hung on for at least fifteen seconds and he was not even in love with her, or so he said. But he did the same with Cathy and Betty, so perhaps he was telling the truth, thought Percy.

Nothing in the way of festivity was laid on by the management, and so it was left to the spontaneous off the record devices of the workforce to fit in a responsible celebration with their tasks. Not that there was much to be done in a bakery on the afternoon of Christmas Eve. All that had been ordered had long since been despatched, and the plant was ready to shut down for the occasion.

Bottles of beer that had been brought in during the lunch break were opened, along with two bottles of whiskey and rum, that someone had won in a raffle. Ken and Percy shared a milk bottle three parts full of a mixture, two large gulps of which started the bakehouse swaying for Percy.

Generous amounts were poured into cups from the mess room and given to the girls. They coughed and spluttered and fanned their mouths with their hands over the strength of their beverage. Playfully protesting, Betty was coaxed into the boiler house by Ron Budgin and Harry Stone. Once inside, the light was switched off and an excited female squeal was quickly stifled.

Percy was overwhelmed by a feeling of adventure and daring. He understood, on that first occasion of alcoholic intoxication, how they got troops to advance openly on the enemy, for if called upon at that moment he would have charged out of a trench single handed at an army.

Mary stood holding on to the cake rack to steady herself as she giggled with Cathy over Betty's plight, and Percy was prepared to sweep all before him in his compulsion to fondle her again. He turned to Ken for another swig from the bottle in order to heighten his feeling of bravado, but on returning his attention to Mary, he saw that both she and Cathy had been pounced upon by two lusty drivers from despatch.

The newcomers had the two girls locked in an embrace as they kissed them. Percy's mouth dropped open in surprise.

"Cheeky buggers," said Ken indignantly, "they're nothing to do with our department." He was about to remonstrate with them but was stopped by Percy who, after giving him a wink, crept up behind the one cuddling Cathy and placing a hand stealthily between his slightly parted legs, grabbed her inside thigh, then ran back to Ken.

In Cathy's drunken state she assumed the offending hand belonged to the one caressing her, even though he had one arm round her neck and the other around her waist. She struggled free, called him a filthy sod and slapped his face.

A look of utter surprise came upon his countenance as he asked what he had done, and denied most strongly the accusation of being too handy, as Cathy put it. He tried to get back to the position before the outburst, but she was much too annoyed and told him to "Bugger off."

As he still persisted, Percy rushed at him and pulling at his jacket told him to leave their girls alone. Telling him to "Hoppit before he got hurt", the man sent him tumbling across the floor upon which action Ken rushed in and pinned the intruder's arms to his sides. As he struggled to manhandle him to the door he was leapt upon by the man's companion and all three fell to the floor.

Calling them "Rotten sods", Cathy bent over and started pulling their hair, while at the same time giving Percy an excellent view of her underwear. This being the proverbial red rag to a bull, he purposely tripped on his headlong dash to join the fray and dragged the staggering Cathy down on top of himself.

She was totally unaware that her attempts to scramble clear were being thwarted by Percy. He had her overall gripped tightly in one hand while the other groped her leg in a supposed attempt to move it from his crotch where he feigned with groans and winces that it was causing him discomfort.

Completely enthralled by the feel of her writhing legs against his, he became almost oblivious to the blows that came to his head and shoulders as Ken battled with the two beneath him. Cathy wriggled, pushed, swore, and intermittently apologised to Percy for distressing him as she strove to unravel herself from the contorting bodies.

However disturbing the scene of conflict might have seemed to others, it was not recognised as such by Mary. She sat cross-legged on the floor and rocked with a laughter that almost became hysterical, as the rest of the workers returned from a drinking bout in the mess room singing "O! Come All Ye Faithful". Fortunately she did not observe Betty leaving the boiler house with her overall and skirt haphazardly tucked in her drawers. Or the guilty look upon Harry and Ken as they followed her out and dispersed in different directions around the bakehouse, for she might have convulsed!

Mary's mirth was infectious and almost everyone around, including Ken and his combatants, joined in the laughter. Percy and Cathy, however, seemed to be on a plane apart and battling with different problems, for she was hell bent on pulling her clothes back down to cover her legs while he struggled to concentrate on an excitement while she still had them around her waist.

He was forced to let her go when the foreman came on the scene and told everyone they could knock off. There was a bustle of shaking hands and kissing, amidst seasonal well wishing.

Along with affectionate pats on the head, three of the bakers each gave Percy a florin and Ken gave him a bar of chocolate, then all too soon everyone drifted away. It had been his first taste of the party spirit and jollity, and he felt lonely in the silence.

He could not leave with the others for he had yet to clean the big mixing bowls, whisks and scoops. The large stone sink was partly surrounded at the sides and above by glazed tiles upon which hundreds of flies settled in numerous batches. Usually it was a pastime of Percy's to stand back and throw a wet cloth to see how many he could kill with each strike. But that afternoon his concentration was fully taken by the washing up, for he was eager to get home.

As the water gurgled noisily from the sink and he was

deafened to any reasonable sound roundabout, a hand touched his arm and almost scared him out of his wits. Turning in a flash he found it to be Freddie Hubbard, a little gnome of a man with massive lenses in his horn-rimmed spectacles.

He stood holding a bucket, cloth and scraper, and had come for some water to wash the floors which usually took him a full eight and a half hour shift daily to do the lot. He could not hear too well and Percy had to shout when telling him of the frivolity that had taken place an hour before. After five minutes of chatting, and smoking one of Fred's Woodbines, the lad wished him a Merry Christmas, then ran upstairs to put his apron away and don his jacket.

Even though there was a pungent aroma of Evening in Paris on the stairs, Percy was still surprised and somewhat worried to see Cathy sitting inside when he entered the mess room.

Quite impassively she said she had returned in respect of what had taken place that afternoon. His contented disposition plummeted, and swallowing hard, he prepared himself for a verbal onslaught if not a physical one. Evidently on sobering up she had come to realise that he had been taking liberties with her again and had returned for another measure of revenge.

With discipline in her voice she bade him sit next to her, which nervously he did, and the arm she placed across his shoulders was, he thought, a preparation to strangle him.

"I thought the way you acted this afternoon," she said seriously, and with hesitation that made him hold his breath, "was absolutely marvellous," she continued.

Relief flooded over Percy and turned to pride as she applauded his protective spirit towards her. It pleased her no end to have been referred to as "one of their girls", as if she were part of a respectable harem. She cupped his face in her hands and kissed him on the lips and then told him to put his arms around her, which he did, after first putting his presents of money and chocolate on the table.

"Who's the chocolate for, your sweetheart?" she inquired playfully.

"My Mum," he answered proudly.

"I was right then, wasn't I?" she said. "Anyway you look as if you've got enough money for a good night out tonight."

"That's to 'elp wiv my sister's new coat," he said. "She's got a boy friend and me Mum says she's got ta look a bit decent for 'im."

Cathy looked at him in silence for a few moments. She had already begun to like him but the simplicity of his unselfishness brought pity to her heart, and she found him lovable. Tears of shame trickled down her cheeks as she thought of how mean she had treated him in the cellar over such a petty act. Furthermore, he had received a fat lip and a bruised eye through trying to protect her, and she took him in her arms and hugged him.

Still under the influence of alcohol, the inhibitions she had previously cherished were disregarded, and as well as wanting to elate a brief moment in Percy's life, she too had a need for a fulfilling relationship. Neither was he anywhere near sober. But when Cathy said that she had something of immense importance to talk about, but if he told her he was under sixteen she would have to leave, he understood the situation perfectly.

When, looking him straight in the eyes and receiving

the answer of "No", when she asked him if he were sixteen, she sighed sadly until after a lapse of a few seconds he added "I'm seventeen."

Her face lit up, she hugged him tightly again and whispered in his ear that she was going to give him the best Christmas present he had ever had.

"But," she said as she looked with stern sincerity into his face, "If you ever tell a living soul I will never ever speak to you again, do you understand?"

He said he did and she embraced him yet again, but this time placing one of his hands under her dress, then sliding hers to the front of his trousers.

Within a minute they had moved up to the flour loft and Cathy gave him a contraceptive sheath from a packet that had belonged to her brother before he went with the army to Egypt.

After an unsuccessful attempt to roll the article on inside out and having to be corrected, he laid with her among the sacks of flour where preliminary fondlings were eagerly exchanged.

The feel of her hand upon him made him think of the last time she touched him and the incident that followed with Mary. His sensuality was at a peak and as it was his first experience with a preventative he wondered if he would burst out of it. She removed her black satin cami-knickers but he stopped her from taking her stockings off. In his opinion they made plain legs acceptable, but for beautiful legs like hers, it was an added touch to perfection. In all his thoughts of making love to her, her legs had always been sheathed in silk fascinatingly supported by suspenders, for to him, these were the epitome of female seductive apparel.

The combination of Cathy's tender embrace, and her Evening In Paris perfume in fusion with her sweet body fragrance, made it impossible for him to hold back from coming in under two minutes from the time they became interlocked. That he held out for so long was a feat in itself considering the beauty and allure of his accomplice. Nevertheless he did not feel ready to withdraw and remained connected, to Cathy's satisfaction, for two more orgasms.

Besides giving him an experience of indescribable beauty, her loving manner and lack of vulgarity restored his faith in how he thought love-making should be. Indeed she surpassed the ideals that his brief encounter with the unstable Honey had caused him to doubt.

He could not think what had suddenly made her take a liking to him when previously he had usually been looked upon as a source of annoyance. But having heard that it was unwise to look gift horses in the mouth he gave the matter no more thought, for he considered that only the unpleasant happenings needed looking into.

After both had gone to their individual cloakrooms to wash and tidy up, they crept through the bakehouse where Freddie Hubbard scraped, scrubbed and stretched his way monotonously across the floor. As they tiptoed silently behind him Percy felt a clutch of pity for the little man whose life, quite obviously, was past any such experience that he himself had just enjoyed, or if indeed, his artless make-up had ever at any time conjured up the necessary impudence to bring about a worthwhile mating exercise.

Before they left the building Cathy pulled him to one side of the door and embraced him again, then placing her forefinger gently across his lips she whispered, "Remember now, secrets."

He nodded, and they walked away together, for they lived in the same direction. Such was the feeling of the two for each other, that as much as a one-off occurrence the incident was thought to be at the time, it blossomed into a powerful love affair, more so through being clandestine. The meetings began by mere chance six months later outside a Brighton dance hall called Sherry's.

It was a popular spot for the racing fraternity and low life of the town, and whenever he could, Percy would for the price of threepence, sit on the balcony and watch the colourful array of dancers glide and shuffle around beneath him, and he longed for the time when his manner of dressing and his age would permit him to join them.

Leaving the premises one night he noticed two men trying to get an intoxicated young woman into a motor car aginst her will. He had taken some six steps past them when he recognized Cathy's voice as she protested as best she could, considering her condition, against being manhandled. With some urgency he retraced his steps and asked the two men who were, on one hand, using their voices in mild persuasion, while on the other, applying a considerable amount of physical pressure, what they were doing with his sister.

Still keeping a grip on her the two explained that she had had a drop too much to drink and they were going to see her safely home. Percy said he would go with them but was told he could not on account of a damaged spring that would not take the extra weight. In fear of how the pitiless looking pair would treat her he grabbed Cathy around the waist from behind and began pulling her from the man inside the car, saying that he would take her safely home.

He felt the velvet of her skirt sliding against her

undergarments and caught the scent of the perfume that he found so fascinating. He understood only too well that active males would chance their arm to the shoulder in an effort to seduce a girl with Cathy's allure. But second to the consideration for her welfare, was a scheme that if anyone was going to lie between her legs that night, he was prepared to go to some lengths to make sure it was him. After all he did carry a great affection for her.

By the way the man outside the car wrenched his arms from Cathy's waist Percy knew he was very detemined, and by the smell of his breath, intoxicated and therefore dangerous. Percy landed on the pavement with a thud but picked himself up in time to take advantage of the target that presented itself to him. The man with legs spreadeagled had almost got Cathy into the back of the car when Percy kicked him in the crotch from behind. At first he thought he had missed the mark for the man swung round and knocked him to the ground, where he lay fearfully looking up and waiting for the onslaught that his father had told him came about through kicking off target. Just as he was poised to deliver a vicious kick to Percy's head which would have certainly rendered the lad senseless the man let out an agonising wail, clutched his testicles and collapsed to the ground. Percy leaned up on an elbow and looked into the man's contorted face as he writhed with pain.

"My dad taught me that," he said proudly to his first victim. "An ol' solier he was."

The bully began to retch and Percy got to his feet so as to be out of range when the man spewed up his night's intake of alcohol, which he did within seconds of the lad leaving his side. This too was a lesson from Horace, but more by inadvertent demonstration then explanation.

Turning his attention back to the car Percy found the situation was a stalemate. Cathy lay face down with arms outstretched on the back seat with her legs sticking out of the door, while the man inside, although holding her captive, could pull her in no further. He was not too clear as to what had gone on between his companion and Percy, but realising he was now committing an offence on his own made him release Cathy as soon as her young rescuer began pulling her from him.

The strenuous training of half carrying his drunken father about when he was only a child made getting Cathy away from the scene comparatively easy. With his arm around her waist and her arm around his neck he hurried her through the back streets and alleys until he considered it safe enough to take to the main road. She had been mumbling and complaining continuously and could not comprehend who he was until, in need of a rest, he took her to one of the promenade shelters.

For a while she acted with mistrust and accused him of being an accomplice of the others, and that he had brought her to the shelter for mischievous purposes. He began to wonder whether she was as drunk as she seemed or if she was part acting in order to deny recognising him. Nevertheless, even with the possibility that she no longer liked him and regretted their act of intimacy, he had no intention of abandoning her to the hazards of the night. For no matter what her feelings were for him, he loved her unselfishly. Cuddling up to her he asked if she had any cigarettes, and after fumbling in her bag for a few seconds she gave him a packet, whereupon he placed one gently between her lips as well, to keep him company as he put it. Before he could throw the match down after lighting them she grabbed his wrist and held the minute illumination back near his face. Scrutinising him closely until the match burnt his fingers and he had to quickly discard it, she came to recognise who he was.

"Percy?" she inquired with genuine surprise. "Our Percy? My Percy? Percy Longprong? Oh no, it can't be, it's too good to be true," she said joyously. "Rescued twice in one lifetime by the same gallant young rascal."

She threw her arms around him and gave him the hug he had longed for ever since his exceptional Christmas present. There had been less contact between them after than there had been before, and had he not been so deeply impressed he would have forgotten it as if it had been a dream.

While they sat and smoked their cigarettes Cathy confessed to the strain she had been under through wanting him to make love to her again and yet afraid the association would come to light if she rekindled it.

"That's why I've been ignoring you," she said apologetically. "I didn't want to, but I was worried."

"You don't 'ave to worry over me, I won't let you down ever," he said adamantly, to which she replied that she already knew that by his silence over their secret which any amount of boys would have blabbed all over the place.

"I take this night as an omen that we are meant to be together," she said, then added, "well, for a while, anyway."

Leaving the shelter and making their way along the promenade in the direction of home Cathy began to whoop and sing happily at the top of her voice. Percy looked about them nervously and told her to be quiet in case the pair from whom he had snatched her were driving around looking for them.

"We don't want them finding us, do we?" she giggled.

"Not before you've had your reward anyway."

"Not ever if I can 'elp it," he said casually.

"How did you manage to get me away from that pair of ruffians then?" she inquired.

"Pure bloody fluke, that's 'ow," he said, puffing slightly as he hurried her along. "I'll probably 'ave bloody nightmares thinking 'ow close I come to getting me face smashed in."

"No you won't, because you'll be too busy dreaming about me," she ordered playfully. She began to sing quietly and do little dance steps as they went along. Percy could hardly believe that a girl like her could be as happy as she obviously was over someone like him. As elated as he felt, a minute thought flickered in his mind of how he would manage when the time came when, for one reason or another, he would lose her. For as much as she had told him in the shelter that she loved him, he knew it could not last even though he intended to give the affair all his endeavour.

They talked on all manner of inconsequential things until Cathy broached the subject of dancing. She said she would like him to go with her sometime and told him he could borrow her brother's suit when he pointed out that he was far too shabby for such a treat. Indeed, it was a wonder that he was allowed on the balcony at Sherry's.

Cathy suggested they should go on the beach and he manoeuvred her expertly down the steps that led there from the promenade. Once at the bottom she scrambled somewhat off balance down the shingle and squatted out of sight behind a groyne support, saying she must shed a tear for Nelson. Percy had never heard the expression before, but realising to what it referred, put a finger in each ear so as not to feel embarrassed at the undignified pose the sound of her act would conjure up in his mind. For he did not like connecting her with such mortal necessities.

When she returned to him she had sobered considerably and bore no comparison to the state she was in when he carried her away. They lay in the deep shadow of the promenade wall and enjoyed one another midst the agreeable sound of the calm sea lapping gently on the shore and the sighs and endearments that flowed from Cathy in spontaneous compliment to the occasion.

Because of the late hour at which he arrived home Percy was chastised by his mother for the anxiety he had caused her. Since George's death, while she had not been anything like overbearing towards her son, she did try to instil a sense of responsible conduct in him, and one of the rules she sought to lay down was that he should be home by eleven p.m. from evening gallivantings.

Not that he had been a rowdy or disrespectful boy at home in regard to his manner towards her or his sister. On the contrary, his attitude had always been considerate and protective. Nevertheless she recognised more than a trait of resourcefulness in him. It stemmed back beyond the incident with the chicken and suit, therefore she was justly concerned, at this time of approaching manhood, that he restricted his faculties to the realms of decency. But having no wish to dominate the boy, even if she had had the power, there was no choice but to rely on the consideration he had for her, and his good heart, to keep him out of trouble.

Even though bursting with curiosity, she made little comment regarding the source from which the suit came that Percy arrived home with one afternoon. Cathy had brought it to work that day in a carrier bag, and he could hardly wait to get home and try it on. It was olive green in colour and the jacket had a smart little half belt at the back with three small pleats leading from it. Even as he put it on he felt a portion of inferiority being cast from his soul, but when he looked in his mother's dressing table mirror, he was filled with emotion at the elegance the sight endowed him with. "This was the real thing," he thought to himself. No more would he go out evenings and week-ends in little more than what he wore to work. He had found another element.

Even though to the eye of the expert the garment had been made for a slightly bigger man who would have filled it out completely, the lad looked suave and anything but out of place.

When he came downstairs to show her, Lucy felt strangely reminiscent of the time Horace stood before her looking just as smart, comparatively speaking, in the suit Percy had acquired for him. But on that occasion a chicken came along with it and she jokingly inquired whether one was in the offing this time as well. Further, as it was only May, she mentioned that like Christmas, people evidently began preparing for Guy Fawkes night earlier each year and seemed to be adorning the Guys still in far better attire than many people walked about in.

Seeing how grown up the suit made him look and the expression of boyish pride on his pleasant face brought tears to her eyes, and to hide them she hugged him to her breast.

Not surprisingly, as his courtship with Cathy progressed, he could not keep to the hour his mother requested him to be home by. But apart from a gentle reminder in the form of a mild rebuke, she accepted the situation, for she remembered only too well how at his age she too had wanted to take leaps and bounds through the world. Instead she settled for chaperoned holidays and visits to the military hospital where years later she met Horace, who even by her high standards of loyalty, could be held up as nothing more than a bad example.

Over the weeks Cathy and Percy became familiar figures around the Brighton dance halls. Acquaintances at these haunts were encouraged to believe they were brother and sister, on account of the age difference. But the belief wore thin for some who noticed the unmistakable delight and affection between the pair, and guesses were quietly made as to whether they were unrelated lovers or merely incestuous.

Each time they went dancing there were always a few men who tried to force their company on Cathy. Besides buying them both drinks one or two gave Percy a ten shilling note to put in a favourable word with his supposed sister. In the event of a situation getting out of hand by way of a too persistent admirer, a prearranged conversation would be used to dampen their enthusiasm. Cathy would tell Percy to go and see whether their ill-tempered father was waiting outside and while he was absent, she would explain, with humane concern for the unwanted romantic, that her father was just out of prison where he had been serving three years for grievous bodily harm, but she was sure they could sneak out past him. Another spoof was to mention that the tough looking fellow on the saxophone would have to be put right for playing off key so much. After all they could not have their big brother letting the orchestra down.

Occasionally they danced with different partners and when they did, a watchful eye was kept by each in case the other was dancing too close. Fortunately there was never any dire emergency to mar the evening's pleasure and any incidents were usually a source of amusement to chatter about on their way home.

Not that Cathy was a burden on him financially for she always paid for herself, but keeping pace with the new lifestyle took more than the pocket money he was allowed from his bakery wages. Usually the week consisted of two visits to the cinema and four to different dance halls. This included a Sunday afternoon tea dance, after which the pair had a meal in a restaurant before going to the evening session.

To keep up the rounds of pleasure it was necessary for him to find an added income to subsidise them, and as most of the time was committed, it left only Saturday afternoon and Sunday morning in which to raise the extra funds. The only means he could find was that of caddie on the local golf course, and if he was lucky by way of the weather, he could get two rounds in on each of the half days and collect more than his full time job paid for the week. Sometimes several of the golfers he carried for, who took a special liking to him for one cause or another, paid him two or three times the rate for the job. He was aware that the generosity was meant more likely as a bribe to obligate him to homosexual attentions than an act of Christian charity, and was on his guard when out on the course with any such benefactors. The only incident near the category of suspicion concerned a player who regularly brought along a bottle of lemonade or Tizer especially for the caddie to drink on the round. Then on every occasion the caddie had to urinate, the golfer crept round the opposite side of the bushes to watch. But when Percy compared it to the behaviour he had to stave off at the bakery, it was insignificant.

The part time job was beneficial to him in more ways than money, for it brought a great deal more fresh air to his lungs than did the smoky dance halls and cinemas or the stuffy bakehouse. He was happy and healthy with few dull moments in his life. And on the two evenings a week that his mother insisted he stayed home to rest, he would compose letters of endearment to Cathy and slip them in her overall pocket the following day.

As high summer was upon them they curtailed some of their dancing and cinema going and instead took bus rides to little outlying country districts such as Bramber and Steyning. When they went to the Devil's Dyke it was on the little steam train that Percy used to ride free on not so long before, by jumping on the buffers of the guard's van. From the Dyke he and Cathy would walk over the downs to the Shepherd and Dog inn at Fulking. The path took them past the camp site where he had spent many a weekend when in the Scouts. He often wondered what the skipper would have said about being clean in thought, word, and deed if he knew that one of his scouts had copulated with a girl on the very spot upon which the renowned Bulldog, the flag tent of the camps, and veteran of numerous foreign jamborees, was usually pitched.

They only made love once at this location for it weakened their capacity for the exhaustive climb back up from the North side of the downs. Instead they spent their devotions in the long grass on the South descent where they could look down on the little station and be sure of not missing the last train home.

Because of their undisclosed courtship the pair were reliant on good weather to pursue their sexual pleasures, for they had no understanding friends who could lend them a couch and a roof when it rained. One evening while passing their place of employment, after being forced first to abandon the beach, then a promenade shelter, by driving wind and rain, they decided to go in and dry off. After hanging their coats in the boiler room, they made their way, unobserved by the night bakers, up to the flour loft. Then with all the confidence of their successful association, and as if they were in their own bedroom, they made love once more among the sacks of flour.

As a love nest the place was ideal and became a habit. It was always warm, dry and highly unlikely that a casual stroller would come upon them and ruin their concentration as a young man had when they lay at the foot of the cliffs at Rottingdean. Even though they were practically out of sight, tucked in a hollow beneath a cliff overhang, the youth knew they were there. He sat on the low sea wall and gazed at them continuously until, feeling uncomfortable and unable to give full attention to the matter in hand, Percy decided tbey should find somewhere else.

Cathy had not seen the intruder and doubted that one existed. So did Percy after climbing back on the path and seeing no one as he looked over to the now vacant wall. As they returned along the lower walk of the cliffs he glanced back two or three times but there was no sign of life other than the sea splashing over the promenade. They had turned the corner of a jutting cliff and so lost sight of the place they had just vacated. Otherwise they would have seen the massive overhang come crashing down, turning, had they still been there, their cradle of love into their unmarked grave.

Neither did their haven in the Co-op loft stay secret for long. The night storeman discovered the use they made of the place but did not report it.

Instead he made a hide amongst the sacks where he would masturbate while watching the pair in their throes of delight. They remained blissfully ignorant right to the time the peeper's wife called in one day to inquire why her husband had not returned from the night shift. As the loft was the only place he was likely to be a short search there found him trapped beneath eight hundredweight sacks of flour that had caved in on him during his despicable observation. The only damage he suffered was to his pride for he had no time to tuck his genitals away before he became pinned down and helpless. The embarrassing circumstance in which he was found became a source of puzzlement around the bakery, excepting of course to the two lovers. They saw the connection between his predicament and their activity immediately. Understandably the man never returned after that day, and as tempted as he was to inform the management of his discovery in the loft, he thought better of it. To have reported them would have been a confession of his shameful attendance.

It had always been a niggling worry that someone who knew them would give them away. But their personalities were such that those who knew of their connection together, and there were more than they imagined, would never have knowingly brought harm to them.

Their illicit association survived to the haven of Percy's sixteenth birthday. So far it had been an exciting adventure that seemed endless. He had completely forgotten the thoughts he had on the night of the rescue, of one day losing her.

Ever since Cathy had introduced Percy to contraceptives on their first intimacy together, he had never been without a packet in his pocket. There were times however, when she not only consented to, but insisted on, a flesh to flesh encounter. With a mixed reluctance he could only comply with her wishes and hope on each occasion, that her timing was accurate. He dreaded anything going wrong that would jeopardise the relationship. It seemed that no sooner had the worry about his age been put behind them when the thing that most active lovers dread, happened. — Cathy became pregnant.

Ironically it came about when rounding off his birthday celebrations with unchecked homage to Venus. Cathy made no pretence at being pleased and by her attitude caused Percy to have feelings of guilt, even though he had always been more than willing to wear a contraceptive. When advising caution he was told it was no good to keep bathing with his boots on.

For two days she ignored him. Not even a furtive wink, a smile, or the sight of her lips pursed in a kiss came his way. He was confused and plainly unhappy as he felt his pleasant existence crumbling away, and not knowing what to do to stop it. He wondered whether Cathy thought her problem would automatically dissolve if she stopped associating with him. It certainly seemed that way. People in the bakery noticed the absence of his happy go lucky ways and Mary in particular tried to give him words of cheer in the mess room during the tea break.

It had no effect on him at the time but caused Cathy to be waiting for him when he finished work. She seemd to be her old charming self apart from a subtle undercurrent of jealousy concerning Mary's interest in him. And her question of whether he was getting ready to set his cap at Mary was more in earnest than the playful way she asked it would have been believed.

They started back in the old routine with an evening at the cinema where they kissed and fondled in the back row. Afterwards there was no attempt at finding a place to make love. Beset by their anxiety their conversation homeward was sparse and their farewells curt when their paths separated to their individual homes.

A few days went by before they got down to discussing the situation. It only came about when on returning from the Gentlemen's cloakroom at a dance hall, he found Cathy missing from the table they had been sitting at. He sat waiting to see her come dancing round with some one or other, but she never appeared until the floor cleared, then with horror, he saw her sitting across the hall talking intently to a woman who had previously been pointed out to him as being an abortionist. He and Cathy walked past her house once. It lay inconspicuous and ashamed in the South-east corner of a Brighton square. It was rumoured that the woman's two sons went about putting married women in trouble so that their mother could charge a high fee for relieving them of it. Her presence in the dance hall was more for business than pleasure, for rarely did anyone ask her to dance.

When Cathy returned to the table a strong debate followed, resulting in a decision to have the baby and get married as soon as this was legally possible for Percy. They left the hall early and made their way to the romantic solace of the flour loft where, as a tribute to their secret pledge, they absorbed themselves in unsheathed passion until the small hours.

Percy was as excited about the prospect as any young man would be even though the engagement was a secret just between the two of them. He had wanted to tell one or two at work such as Ken, Mary and maybe a couple of the bakers, but was told it was far too early to start making announcements. Understandably Cathy wanted to put off being called a baby-snatcher for as long as possible. There was no point in leaving work before she had to.

Her enthusiasm over the situation was well below that of her beau. She would not even attend the wedding of his sister Sylvia when she married a young army corporal at the local church. Percy assured her he would not make the slightest gesture that would cause his mother to wonder whether they were anything more than just colleagues. Nevertheless, Cathy felt a degree of guilt and credited his parent with more observant power than he did.

As the fine weather deteriorated so his income from the golf course diminished. More often than not he would huddle, soaked through, against the club house wall, waiting for the rain to stop, then return home chilled to the marrow, with pockets as empty as when he left. A cough came upon him, he became feverish, but paid no heed to his mother's plea to lay up for a few days. He told her that although he shivered on his way to work, once in the warmth of the bakehouse, he felt considerably better.

Cathy too became anxious, not only over his probable state of influenza, but by his overall condition of distress through not having the means to prepare for the baby. It saddened her to see the strain of events weighing heavily upon him.

Quite obviously a youth of his tender years was not meant for such a burden.

She was aware of the deprived circumstances he had known since childhood through the conversations about his late father's antics. Percy used to talk about some of them as a source of humour but to Cathy they sounded deplorable and more a matter, at times, for tears.

Without thinking in any way that it might turn out to

be a case of, *like father like son*, but purely seeing the impossibility of their plans ever materialising to anything but a destitute existence on the wages that Percy could earn, she decided to end her pregnancy. Highly conscious of the opposition she would receive, resulting in things being left as they were, she never told him of her intentions.

Keeping their habit of several months they went to the Sunday tea dance at Sherry's. She normally hugged him close to her in the slow, shuffle tunes, but on this occasion she was demonstrative to the point where he could hardly breathe comfortably. It was, he thought, as if she were apologising for something, or, he hated to consider it, saying "Goodbye." The feeling was intensified when at the end of the dancing session she said she was unable to accompany him to the little cafe where they usually had tea.

She refused to tell him where she was going and became annoyed when he started to insist on a reason for breaking the routine. Ordinarily she treated him as an equal in any discussions and masterful when making love, but her present manner made him submissive to her superior years. Consequently, when she told him to go home, he did not argue further.

As inconceivable as it once seemed that she would go back on her promise to have the baby, a terrible fear clutched at Percy as Cathy walked away and was lost from his sight amongst the early evening crowd. With heart pounding frantically he sprinted away in the opposite direction and arrived panting at the square in which the abortionist lived. Taking up an advantageous position to watch the dwelling without being too conspicuous himself, he had not long to wait before Cathy came into the square from the North side and approached the house of infamy.

Even though his guess at her destination had been right he was flabbergasted at seeing her there. For long moments he was tongue-tied and rooted to the spot, and she was inside the house and out of earshot by the time he was able to call to her. Hesitating no longer he ran to the house and knocked at the shabby door. Getting no reply he started banging and kicking it until the rotting wood began to splinter.

Soon a dim light came on in the hallway and threw a shadow on the glass of the front door, which within seconds was snatched open by an angry young man. He was Eddie Pope the elder son of Rachel, the abortionist. Giving Percy a push he demanded heatedly to know what he thought he was doing. Percy asked to see his sister who he said had just entered, and was told he was mistaken, as she was not there.

Percy was ordered to go away when he leaned around Eddie and began calling to Cathy though the open door. Refusing to do so he received a sharp slap on his face in quick succession to a blow to his chest, which declared the fight to be on. Expecting a mild form of retaliation, Eddie put up his fists and stood with his feet apart for the balance of the fighting stance. For a few seconds he was at a complete loss to know where the blow had come from as he lay writhing on the ground and wondered whether it was seizure due to an excess of sexual activity. Percy indulged momentarily in self satisfaction over his capability to protect himself from a full grown, aware man, who was neither drunk nor had his back turned.

Concentrating once more on his purpose he stepped into the dingy hallway and began calling loudly for Cathy, but Jimmy, Eddie's twenty-two year old brother, came pounding down the stairs. Eddie meanwhile having dragged himself to his feet, staggered back into the hallway and shouted a warning to his brother, "Watch out for his feet, Jim, the little bastard's a kicker."

That his bold brother had been toppled by a mere teenager, brought a look of disbelief and dismay to the newcomer's face. He stood looking at Percy as would a cobra when confronted by a mongoose. Although they looked upon him now as an unknown quantity and perhaps a veritable champion with modest composure who could deliver crippling blows with conjusto, he knew he was in for a hiding. He would not have attempted to make a run for it even if Eddie had not closed the door, he was too set on getting Cathy out at any cost.

"What's 'e want?" asked Jimmy nervously.

"Guess," said Eddie, knowing full well his brother knew the answer,

"Who is 'e?" inquired Jimmy, looking alternately between Eddie and Percy.

"Says she's 'is sister," was the reply.

"Is that right?" said Jimmy, looking and sounding unmistakably worried.

"Course it aint, you prick," Eddie replied somewhat angrily. "No more than she's yours. Christ, don't you recognise 'im? You've seen 'em dancin' together often enough, aint yer? An' 'ow many times you said, Christ, what a waste?"

"Oh yeah," said Jimmy with realisation, "Course I 'ave."

"And you can bet 'e's responsible an' all," went on Eddie. "More 'idden talents than what you'd credit the young bastard wiv' 'aving."

Percy began shouting for Cathy at the top of his voice.

If she heard him and came on the scene, he could perhaps talk her out of her intention and in turn she could save him from a thrashing.

"What's the matter wiv' you, you bloody idiot, we're doin' you a favour," said Eddie, but Percy carried on calling.

"We'd better shut 'im up or we'll get done out of a goose. Not that I'm in the mood for one at the moment," Eddie said gloomily.

"I am though, especially wiv 'er," Jimmy replied eagerly. "Fancied that fer ages aint I ?"

Their conversation horrified Percy. It was as cold and calculating as if he were not there, with neither malice or consideration intended. He was not being taunted or teased but merely a witness to a discussion that, apart from Eddie's pain-wracked testicles as evidence of his presence, he might have been on the other side of the world.

Evidently, not only was Cathy going to subject herself to a dangerous and illegal operation that would deprive him of an early fatherhood, but would be cajoled by some means into submitting to lustful abuse in the process.

Incensed with rage he rushed at Jimmy and butted him in the stomach with his head but took a hard punch in the eye before he could back away. Again he charged and caught Jimmy in the same way but the blow he received on the side of his head in return made him dizzy.

"You've got the bastard, now do 'im," shouted Eddie excitedly, but Jimmy had been knocked back on to the stairs and could not take advantage of the situation.

Percy rallied first and smashed his adversary in the face as he attempted to push himself up from the stairs, and blood spattered over the pair of them. Then while attempting to deliver the coup by way of a punch to the man's crotch, Eddie jumped on his back and he was sandwiched between the two as he was brought down. Throwing his head back sharply he felt it connect with his assailant's face and then blows fell upon him, it seemed, from every direction, as the aggrieved pair took their revenge. He was still almost rolled up in a ball with his head touching his knees and his hands clutched steel-like in protection of his own tender parts as they dragged him to the door and tumbled him down the steps. In spite of repeated attempts to return the crippling blow he had received, Eddie could not find an opening and had taken two blows in the face while trying to break the grip.

Some minutes later Rachel Pope came down the stairs with Cathy and could not believe her eyes at the state her two sons were in. They sat mournfully at the bottom of the stairs. Both had bloody faces and torn shirts, and Jimmy was still coughing over a pool of vomit. Strongly sensing Percy's hand in the affair, Cathy wondered if he had come charging in with an axe or the like.

Hurrying through the Northern exit to the square she heard her name called. It was more like a groaning croak than a human voice. Looking in the direction of the sound she saw a figure huddled in the shadow of a porch. Approaching cautiously even though knowing it to be Percy, she was confused and in sheer dread of being about to find out just what had taken place.

"What on earth are you doing there?" she asked desperately.

"Waitin' fer you o' course," he croaked. "You aint done it 'ave yer? Me an' my Mum'll look after it if it'll be too much for yer. Oh say you aint done it, after all, Cath, oh, please say you aint done it," he pleaded, as he began crying bitterly. "I'd started to love it already," he went on. "I'd 'ave looked after it alright and wouldn't 'ave caused yer no trouble, honest. Say ya changed ya mind, Cath, please."

Being at a loss to know what to say she bent forward and got hold of his arm to lift him up. "Come on, let's go home," she said gently. With a sharp intake of breath he stood up and limped out of the shadow whereupon seeing him only in the street lighting made her gasp and clutch at her mouth with shock.

His face was smeared with blood. Some had dried and caked around his almost closed eyelids. His mouth was so raw and swollen that he dare not close it, for fear his lips would weld together. Both lapels were ripped and hanging from his jacket, the back of which was rent to the collar. Standing there shivering he looked a pitiful sight.

"Oh, my God," she exclaimed. "Oh, my dear God."

Tears welled in her eyes and burst over her face. "Oh! Percy, what have I done? What have I done?" she cried. "Oh! Please forgive me, I had no idea any of this would happen."

She hugged him to her and cried as if her heart were broken. Percy's crying, however, was less audible as his voice had gone momentarily through the strain he had been under.

"Yer bruvver's gonna go mad when he sees 'is suit," he groaned. "I'll 'ave ta get 'im annuver."

"Oh bugger the suit, you silly young devil," was the reply.

"'E'd come an' finish me orf if 'e could see what I've done to it," Percy continued.

"No, he wouldn't, it wasn't your fault, those two swines back there did it, not you, besides, I shouldn't think it fits him now anyway," said Cathy reassuringly She was glad his anxiety had strayed away from her regrettable action, for the moment anyway. She burst out in a renewed fit of crying over his consideration for the property of another, when by the look of him, he had almost been beaten to death.

He said he felt tired and wanted to go home. Limping so badly with his first few steps, Cathy was forced to put her arm around his waist to assist him. Chuckling over his disability he said the last time he had dead legs was from larking about at school. However inconvenient, through her involvement, that he should attend a hospital casualty department, she urged him to do so, but being aware of the compromising effect this might have on her, he refused. Instead he went and cleaned himself up in the washroom beneath the clock tower, so as not to give his mother such a shock. As he would be arriving home that much earlier, through not attending any evening dance, she would not yet be in bed.

Because of his condition he became an object of concern amongst some of the other customers using the washing facilities in preparation for their evening jollity. At first glance, more than one considered an ambulance and a report to the police to be necessary. Then on helping him to wash away the dried blood and taking stock of his adequate constitution, those concerned decided he would be all right. But not before he had had a ten shilling note thrust in his hand for a taxi home and been assisted up the steps by two stalwart young men.

On reaching the street Percy found Cathy clutching at the railings that partly surrounded the edifice. Without doubt she was in considerable pain and greatly relieved to hear that there was money for taxi fare home. Rachel had taken all she had and she still owed a further two pounds, which unbeknown to her would have been cancelled out had the woman's two sons been allowed a few minutes each to relieve their lust. Not that being aware of this would have made any difference, for she would have been utterly repulsed by the condition anyway.

In the taxi they clung to each other in mutual sympathy. In spite of his clean up he still looked as if he had been in the path of the Light Brigade's famous charge, and she told him so. He left the vehicle with a promise from her of making it up to him. He was glad at the darkness of the evening for this made it less likely that the neighbours would see him impersonating Quasimodo, as he limped and shuffled, first across the pavement to the gate and then along the path to the house.

Fortunately he was able to reach his bedroom unobserved, where he changed from the ragged suit that gave such emphasis to his physical damage, before presenting himself, along with the best explanation he could manage, to his mother.

Over and above the sensation he aroused at the bakery the following day, which was quite considerable, the two homosexuals delayed him in the rest room when the tea break was ended and the others gone. As friendly and diplomatic as their attitude was, it was as intent on determining the truth of Percy's injuries as would the interrogation by any resolute policeman.

"Just a moment, young Percival," said Patrick Feeney as he sat down and gently restricted Percy from leaving the form upon which they both sat.

"Wacha want?" he asked, nervously aware of their strange compulsion.

"Tis alroight, young lad, don't you be frettin' now," Patrick said calmly, "'tis just that him and oi are somewhat baffled as to how a nice young fella as yerself came by such uncivil treatment."

"Fightin' o' course," he mumbled through swollen lips, placing his elbows on the table and cupping his head in his hands.

"And sure don't we know that me boyo, and a credit you were to yerself no doubt," said Patrick, giving Percy an understanding nudge. "But the thing is yer see, me young beauty, Danny there, and meself t'inks dat you've been used far beyond the realms of necessity, do yer follow me,lad?"

"Wot?" said Percy, moving his hands from his face and giving Patrick a puzzled look.

"Someone's gone too far wicha is what we mean," chipped in Danny. "And we'd loike to know what sort o' bloke would do a t'ing loike dat to yers."

"He must've been a big 'un roight enough, and a vicious sod as well," went on Patrick, who became exceedingly more angered the longer he looked at the battered youth.

"I 'ad 'im beat at first," explained Percy, with a hint of pride.

"What went wrong then, me young boyo?" asked Danny, somewhat perplexed.

"I'd practic'lly got 'is bruvver an' all," continued Percy.

At this the two men looked at each other in surprise.

"Ah,, two of 'em, eh?" asked Danny.

"Oi know, let me guess," said Patrick, "Yer took yer lovely young eyes off the first devil and he jumped on yer from behind."

"Tha's right," said Percy, sadly. "An' I couldn't get up after that."

"Yer must've give 'em hell fer a while though me bucko, by the state of yer knuckles," said Danny, cheerfully remarking on the lad's raw hands.

"No, tha's only fru covering me balls up when they was tryin' to kick 'em, tha's 'ow they got like that," explained Percy.

Hearing this made the slight smile leave Danny's face as he met the gaze of mutual disgust from Patrick.

"'Er just how old would these lados be? Nineteen or twenty, maybe?"

"'bout twenty-four," said Percy.

"Bot' of 'em? They were twins?" asked Patrick with feigned surprise.

"No, one was a bit younger, I s'pose, anyway, wocha wanna know all this for? It's all over, an' too late for anyone to 'elp now," said Percy wearily.

"Ah, but a little justice must be administered to round it off, so to speak. "Wouldn't ya say so, Percival?" Patrick's voice was gentle and assuring.

"Just loike it seeks us all out in time," added Danny.

"Tell the pleece, ya mean?" asked Percy suspiciously.

"Be Jasus, no, not at all young fella, t'ings need a bit o' rectifyin', not confusin'. Next t'ing yer know, they'd have you on the Moor and the others 'ud be decorated or sump'n. No, we had t'ings of a more personal nature in moind, yer moight say," went on Patrick.

Percy was in somewhat of a quandary as to what they thought they could accomplish. He was misled by their modesty. For as strong as he knew them to be, as they once picked him up and tossed him back and forth to each other with ease, he thought they lacked the tenacity necessary if a good hiding was what they had in mind for the brothers.

"They're wicked buggers yer know," Percy warned.

"Ah! And can't we jist see that now by jist looking upon the wanton brutality done to yer lovely self, me lad," agreed Danny.

"Why should you go after 'um, I aint a relative o' yorn or nuffin' ?" Percy was suspicious and the pair felt it.

"Calm yerself young fella, there's no strings attached where you're concerned. You're a nice little lad who, from what we know of yer, don't deserve to get treated loike dat, and we takes it poisonal, isn't dat so, Danny?"

"Undoubtedly," Danny confirmed, nodding briskly. "And we'd loike ta show dem de error of dere ways, so ta speak," he went on.

"Wocha gonna do, smack their bottoms ?" asked Percy sarcastically.

"Ah, well now, lad," Patrick chuckled, "you're in the roight area, roight enough."

"But we had sump'n udder dan smacking in moind," said Danny, whereupon they both laughed.

Thinking they took it all as a joke Percy began to get up from the table until restrained once again by Patrick, who apologized for their behaviour.

"I'm sorry, young fella, we shouldn't be laughing at these toimes of your misfortune. The joke's between him and Oi, and not on you, Percival, believe me," he said sincerely. "P'raps Oi'd better explain." Wondering how to begin, he was silent for some moments.

"Yer see, lad, it's loike dis, de last toime we saw someone in your condition was at Akaba in nointeen seventeen. He was a young Arab who used ta come inta da garrison to earn what money and food he could for odd jobs among da troops. Not British troops moind yer, I must correct dat. Dey was Turks. Oi'd better start at the beginnin'."

He pointed to Danny. "Him and Oi was in good King George's Navy, rest his soul. We was cooks on a cruiser which fancied it could stand off Akaba and shell it. Tree broadsides was all we got away before we was takin' to de boats. And when we see the size o' the fookin' big guns dat sunk us, we'd 'ave all kicked de captain in the goolies if he hadn't gone down wid de ship."

Patrick was interrupted by the foreman coming to investigate the non-appearance of the three back at their posts.

"You lot going to run the tea break into dinner time?" he asked, inoffensively. "Not at all, Alf, but we've got a few details to sort out and we'd be obloiged wit a few more minutes if yer don't moind, it's a bit important loike."

"Don't be long then," said Alf goodnaturedly, and knowing better than to insist on immediate resumption of work.

After he had left the room, Patrick turned his attention back to Percy.

"Where was Oi now, me bucko? Ah! yes, well, we was taken prisoner by the Turks ya see, an' as him and Oi was cooks, they let us bugger about in da cook'ouse, did they not. An' we noo more what went on dan de boys in de compound." He leaned forward to confide in Percy. "Most o' them Turks is a queer lot. Fook anything dey will, man, boy, or goat, and when dey sees us, an we was hansome boyos in them days right enough, even though I says it m'seself, eh Danny? dey thought we was lambs for da slaughter. But dey didn't know dat we was from Conemara, where da chastity belts are strapped back ta front on da boys an da rest of da country wonder'd 'ow we still got yung uns. We was forced inta contests wid dese Turks at foist. All we 'ad ta do was fight da bastards off. Big wagers used ta be made, and dem dat bet agin us lost every toime. Den one day we found dis poor little Arab. Fooked and beaten nearly ta death so he was, laying among da rubbish bins." Percy was in awe at the tale.

"'Tis the gospel I'm tellin' mind, is it not Danny?"

"It is roight enough, sad ta say," agreed Danny.

Patrick continued quietly.

"When da poor little bugger was able to tell us what 'appened we wanted ta strangle every bloody Turk in da fort. But if we'd as much as punched one on the nose we'd 'ave been bayonetted."

"Wot did yer do then?" said Percy eagerly. "Did ya get 'em?"

"A captain an' a sergeant was da ones who half killed the little fella, an' when we next did battle wid 'em to keep deir pricks out of us, we not only beat 'em, we fooked 'em good an' proper as well."

"We expected ta die on da spot," said Danny. "It emasculated 'em ya see. Dey couldn't hold deir heads up to da men. Dey was squealing like pigs when we let 'em go."

"God knows we had a hate fer dose bastards," said Patrick. "Dey put up a big reward loike for anyone who could deflower us, but all dem dat troied was made unfit fer dooty fer a few days. Interest became at fever pitch, we was respected an' treated loike champions. Dere was some talk of importing fresh talent from Turkey to regain deir pride. But it would've made no difference, dey'd never 'ave beat da hate we had fer dem."

"'Ow ja get free?" asked Percy, his mouth sagging open with amazement.

"Lawrence came across da desert an' took Akaba," said Danny.

Percy whistled with genuine admiration as the two Irishmen sat in silence while their words sank in.

"Now you puts us very much in moind o' dat poor little Arab by da looks of yer, and we'll be put out if yer don't let us avenge yer, so we'll be obliged wid a few details," said Danny.

"And don't you go worryin' about us young Percival, cause we're Connemara men, we survived Akaba, an' we knows what we're about," said Patrick as he gave Percy a smile and a wink.

FIVE
It's A Small World

Understandably, Cathy did not come to work and for the first half of the week it was straight home and early to bed for Percy, as a token of convalescence. His fellow workers proposed a whip round so that he might stay away from work until he felt better. Thanking them, he refused their offer with the excuse of being bored if he stayed at home, yet it was the desire to see Cathy, should she turn up, that drew him painfully to the bakery each day.

Lucy made an an excellent job of repairing and cleaning his jacket, and towards the end of the week he felt bright enough to don the suit he had thought past repair and take himself off to the cinema for the evening. As the main film was Top Hat, starring Fred Astaire and Ginger Rogers, the house was packed. Sitting next to him on one side was a man with his leg in plaster, which Percy had tripped over on the way to his seat, causing the man to cry out in pain, which in turn sent a titter through the audience. On the other side of him was an attractive well built woman of forty, who by the rustling of her clothes as she removed her coat, and the beautiful fragrance of her perfume wafting in his nostrils, commanded more of his attention than the film. Her nearness not only gave him a sense of well-being, but engulfed him in a mood of silent intimacy. She represented all the glamour and romance associated with the plush extravagance of the picture palace, and he fell under the spell of immediate infatuation.

Passions that had been pushed aside by Cathy's absence and the beating he had received, were now being revived at a ravenous pace. His leg and the woman's were barely touching, as was his arm with hers on the rest, but the contact was sufficient to enthuse him with desire. Wondering how he could affiliate himself to her in a more positive way, he clutched the box of matches in his pocket so as to be able to offer her a light the moment she put a cigarette to her lips. But she did not smoke and so the opportunity never arose. During the interval, however, she made the introduction by asking him to keep her seat for her and he watched her walk gracefully down the aisle to the ice-cream girl at the foot of the gangway. The lights were on, music came from the organ as it rose from its hide-out in preparation for the local talent show. There was a low chattering as people moved about the building for one reason or another before settling down for the on stage entertainment. How he wished he were the woman's companion.

When she returned it was as if she really was in company with Percy for amidst the thanks for minding her seat she thrust a choc-ice into his hand. Then she began enquiring sympathetically how he came by his still quite prominent cuts and bruises, and was more than favourably impressed to hear that it was in pursuance of rescuing a damsel in distress. So engrossed were they in their conversation that they saw very little of the acts, even though they looked up quite often and applauded with the rest of the audience. Percy began to feel happy again. For some weeks he had been in the doldrums with anxiety. Now in the conducive atmosphere of the cinema and a new female acquaintance however fleeting, as ships that pass in the night, the evening was proving to be therapeutic.

As the organ descended back to the pit and the lights went down in resumption of the film show, the pair held hands and their legs touched in mutual affection. By the end of the Movietone News, Percy's hand had wandered to her lap and was stroking the tops of her thighs through her dress.

After discreet glances in the immediate vicinity the woman spread her coat over his hand and he gathered her dress up inch by inch with his fingers. Feeling the suspenders and the silk undergarment at the top of her stockings was sheer heaven to him. It seemed ages since he had experienced such a thrill and as the woman's hand slid across to his groin, he already had an erection. Clutching at it through his trousers she moved down in her seat and slightly parted her legs to enable him to slip his hand between them. He longed to kiss her lovely face but the position they were both in made it impossible, and he certainly did not want a change in location of their respective hands in order to accomplish it.

As they both were sitting straight in their seats and not lolling towards each other, no one surrounding them was remotely aware of the intimate fondling being exchanged between the pair. Suddenly the woman held her breath, closed her eyes and began to manipulate herself rhythmically against Percy's hand. After a few moments she took a deep breath, then with a sigh that was barely audible, sat up in her seat, pushed his hand away and pulled her dress back over her knees.

So abruptly had his passions been rejected that he found himself looking around to see what had caused the mischief. He would not have been surprised, owing to his previous maulings to find he had been trying to perform in a crowded restaurant. He was being ignored, he felt dejected, and ridiculous to the point that he could not continue to sit next to her as if nothing had taken place. Thanking her for the choc ice, he made his way to the aisle, but could not resist giving her breast a squeeze as she stood up to let him pass. He could have been mistaken, but he thought he saw a look of puzzlement on her face.

There were quite a number of seats now vacant in the back row, so instead of leaving the cinema, which would have been sacrilege when he had not seen all of the film, he sat down to watch the remainder. How like old times, he thought. The independence and sense of freedom that he had all but forgotten about for almost a year, came crowding back on him as he made himself comfortable by cocking a leg over the adjoining empty seat. He had to admit that one way or another, life had become complicated since he had begun to indulge in the compulsions usually restricted to adults. Women could be hateful at times, he thought. But his mother was not like that, only his father had been. He found it too confusing to unravel at that moment, or at all for that matter.

Concentrating on the film, he took little or no notice of the sound of the seats springing back as people here and there got up and dawdled to the exit. Presently one of them came and sat next to him. Glancing to see who it was that had, as he felt, nearly flopped on top of him, he was more than surprised to find it to be the woman who not half an hour previously had caused his ego to plummet. After staring inquiringly at him for some seconds, she asked him why he had left her. And when he replied that it was because she pushed him away, her excuse was that she was merely having a rest. How unpredictable women are, he thought, as she suggested they move to the darkened corner at the end of the row. Once there a new thrill surged through him as they hugged and kissed passionately. With the flour loft in mind, he mentioned that he knew a place where they could be alone, but, was humoured with a promise of some other time. With the stealth of a pickpocket her hand retrieved his penis without him even being conscious of his flies being unbuttoned.

To avoid the substance that would be forthcoming going on to her hand or his trousers he reached into his inside pocket for a sheath, and felt a slight sense of shame when realizing his mother must have seen them when repairing his jacket.

Once sheathed he felt prepared for anything but was exuberantly surprised when she rose to her feet, lifted the back of her dress and settled on his lap as if she were gracing a toilet seat. Then with the minimum of wriggling and adjustment to her underwear she slipped onto his member.

Taken aback by the woman's audacity he peered cautiously in the direction of the aisle. He put on a look of feigned disgust and disapproval for the benefit of any observers. But had there been any, nothing looked out of place, other than what seemed to be a large woman sitting somewhat awkwardly in her seat. Her arms covered Percy's as he clutched her waist whilst peering around the side of her in pretence of watching the film. It was as if the subject upon which his attention seemed drawn, eliminated him from any guilt concerning the activity occuring under her dress. By another concept seen through dim eyes he could have been mistaken for a child hugging an oversized doll.

Being quite close to a climax he centred his concentration on the woman. But as disinterested as he was in the film upon which his misleading and inattentive stare was still directed, he hoped that at the moment of ejaculation any close-ups on the screen would be of Ginger Rogers and not Fred Astaire. The overwhelming pleasure came upon them both simultaneously and neither could deny the compulsion of thrusting at each other uncontrollably. The activity caused the seat to squeak in a tempo that the initiated usually associate with sexual indulgence in one form or another, and the backs of people's heads turned into faces as half the occupants of three or four rows swung round momentarily to see who dared commit such an act so blatantly. In order to dispose of the sheath and clean himself up in general, for the woman had left quite a deposit around his flies, he went to the men's toilet before the film had ended.

When he came out the programme was over, and he mingled with people in the foyer on his way to the exit. He noticed his workmate Ken standing on the steps outside, and before he could push his way through the people to speak to him he saw his very recent intimate acquaintance take his friend's arm.

In spite of his passions being well and truly spent, a slight pang of jealousy overcame him even though Ken's stature complemented her better than his.

By their attitude they were well acquainted and he could not understand how there had been no mention from Ken of such a beauty. Perhaps he kept it secret because of the age gap, thought Percy. It could not be that she was married, or the meeting would not be so open. She stopped for a moment to put on her gloves and what Percy heard as he got closer rocked him to his foundations, for in asking her if she enjoyed the film, Ken referred to her as *Mum!*

Percy began tremble on his journey home.

"Christ, 'e'll bloody kill me if 'e finds out," he said to himself.

"Frow me out the bloody flour loft e will, or shut me in the poxy fridge."

"Oh Christ, oh Christ," he kept repeating to himself as each new thing that Ken might do to him came to mind. Would he pick him up and ram his balls in the mincer, he wondered? Just what sort of retribution would a bloke demand from a friend who had got at his Mum?

Suddenly he saw the funny side of the incident and began to chuckle.

He no longer considered leaving the bakery, on the contrary, he could hardly wait for the following day to come when he would greet Ken with a "Allo my son", for after all, he had become his common-law step-dad incognito, so to speak. His mind even began seeking a connivance at getting Ken to invite him home for some reason or other. Then after his mother had recovered from the shock of seeing her back stall's lover, he could perhaps creep back on another occasion when Ken and his dad were out, with the pretext of changing comics which, like him, Ken still read.

The incident gave him a whole new outlook on the subject of male and female relationship. He found it reassuring that allowing for their unpredictable quaintness, women were every bit as accommodating as men when the fancy and opportunity presented themselves in the right circumstance. And apart from being incarcerated, their position in life made very little difference.

As he sat at his supper of corned beef sandwiches and cocoa, his mother wondered what was prompting his little outbursts of giggling. He had certainly returned home far happier than when he left, and it gave joy to her heart to see it. Had she known the cause of his humour, like most mothers she would have reprimanded him and very likely boxed his ears had his recent beating not been sufficient to pay for half a lifetime of mischief. She bent down and cuddled him in thankfulness of his recovery to the boy he used to be.

As he lay in bed he was still amused at coming to know Ken's mother in a manner that Ken himself was hardly likely to.

Blimey, he thought as he dropped off to sleep, *fancy 'er being Ken's mum. Would never 'ave guessed in a million years. Ken's mum as a girl-friend, engaged and on the 'oneymoon all in a couple of hours! 'Ad it off wiv Ken's mum, an' I can't even tell 'im 'ow luvly she was.*

Falling into the innocence of sleep did not neutralise his influence upon the world, for at that moment forces, in the form of Patrick and Danny, were being brought to bear on his behalf at the house of the abortionist Rachel. After barging their way in as she answered the door to their knock, they bound her to a chair and waited for Eddie and Jimmy to return from the Chalet Club where the two Irishmen had also been drinking that evening as guests, while they took the measure of their intended victims.

"Don't dey remoind yer o' dem fookin' Turks?" Patrick said as they observed the brothers directing unchecked arrogance upon two young women.

"Remoind me of 'em? Deir fooking Turks in da flesh, dats plain enough," Danny replied with conviction.

A little rhumba band began to play the Continental, and Danny remarked how like Charlie Chaplin the leader looked. The two brothers started dancing with the girls they had picked up and Danny tried to trip them as they went by, until stopped by Patrick.

"Well jist look at da pricks tryin' ta imitate George Raft," complained Danny.

"Leave 'em be fa now will yers. Jist let 'em jump about a bit longer, 'cause it'll be a fooking long toime 'for dey feels loike it agin," counselled Patrick. "Yer don't want ta fook tings up fer later do yers?"

The pair left sharp on closing time and hurried off to prepare a welcome for the brothers as they dawdled drunkenly home at their leisure.

It would have been awkward if the girls returned with them but fortunately for the plan they were cautious enough to say their adieus outside the club.

Rachel Pope was almost choking as the shrieks and screams she attempted to emit were imprisoned in her throat by the sanitary towel that had been rammed in her mouth to silence her. Before her eyes her sons were stripped and raped as if they were ripe young defenceless damsels in the hands of Amazons. They gave up shouting when a pillow was rammed in their faces at any sound louder than a groan or squeal.

After being taken from the back they were forced to look upon their seducers as they were made to double their legs up and subject themselves to a frontal assault. When, by being dismounted, they thought their degrading ordeal was over, and their mother closed her eyes in thankful relief, Patrick and Danny were no more than changing partners to renew the terror upon the trio. Rachel was sure that nothing could add to the nausea she already felt until she saw her sons expressing sperm liberally from their fully erect organs. After trussing the brothers together with strips of bed sheet, in a position where each faced the other's wet anus, the avengers calmly picked up their clothes and went off in search of the bathroom. After washing and dressing they returned and Patrick removed Rachel's gag long enough for her to direct him to some hidden money to compensate Percy for his injuries and damaged suit. Turning his attention to the undignified couple on the floor he gave each of the heads a mild jerk into the other's backside.

"Yous two jist wanna tank yer fookin' stars dat dis is England or yer'd bot' be buried up to yer fookin' necks in de garden wid yer bollocks in yer cheeks an' yer pricks sowd in yer mout's loike some Turks we know got from de Arabs when dey caught 'em. An' if yous two creepin' turds ever lay yer evil hands on our little lad agin, even if he wipes 'is shitty boots on yer tableclot' an' pisses in yers tea, me an' him'll be back to feed yer fookin' balls on a skewer.

"Der yer t'ink dey moight be Turks, Patrick?" asked Danny quietly.

"Would ya be of Turkish origin now me boyo?" Patrick asked Jimmy. "What moight yer name be?"

"Jimmy Pope," was the barely audible answer, which Patrick took for "Give me the Pope."

"What's dat he said?" asked Danny.

"He wants da Pope," said Patrick, to which Danny showed surprise.

"Christ, we never clouted dem anytin' loike dat hard for dem ta need him, be Jesus. Soides, he'd never come anyhow."

"We'll send ya a fooking priest if yer loike, but he'll only take his trousers down to yas when he see ya loike dat."

Patrick turned his attention to Rachel and she closed

her eyes in fear at his approach.

"And as fer you, you fookin' old pod o' maggots, if I hears one more toime of you stabbin' a young 'un ta deat' in it's mother's belly, oi'll bring it back an' make yer fookin' eat it."

Her eyes protruded and a gurgle of terror came from her as Patrick opened a large flick knife. But in spite of his menacing gestures he did no more than slash the bonds from her chest before they took their departure.

Almost the whole of a working week had passed since Percy had reluctantly given Patrick and Danny the information they wanted concerning his cuts and bruises. The memory of their vow to avenge him had worn thin. And had it not, he certainly did not expect the handful of notes that were discreetly passed to him by Patrick when he and Danny delayed Percy again at the end of the morning tea-break.

"Now you get yersell down ta the fifty-bob tailors and get rigged out wit' a couple a suits me beauty," said Patrick, wagging a finger at the lad.

Not ever having so much money in his hand before, Percy was flabbergasted.

"Christ, where the? Oo the? Where ja get all this from?" he gasped.

"Ah, well, we stated yer case for ya, do yer see, Percy, and on behalf of yer good self we accepted deir generous offer," said Danny. "Dey was most repentant for deir brutality to ya, is dat not roight, Patrick?"

"Roight enough," confirmed Patrick. "Oi've never seen none sorrier."

Unaccustomed to anything like such a gift Percy was embarrassed and tried to give it back but did no more than provoke well meant anger. Even the suggestion of sharing the money three ways brought a sharp reprimand.

"We won't bore ya wid de details of da settlement, but Oi'll tell ya dis much me boyo, who ever brings ya trouble an' misfortune in dis loife, dose fookers won't be among 'em," said Patrick as he gave Percy's shoulder a few reassuring pats.

SIX
Fresh Fields and Broader Horizons

Through a combination of low pay and a lack of desire to become a baker, pastry-cook or confectioner, Percy decided to seek a livelihood in some endeavour other than the bakery. Cathy never returned to work and there was somewhat of an anti-climax about the place as far as he was concerned. After collecting her insurance card from the office she made no attempt at even a curt farewell to any of her old colleagues. Percy took it as a personal snub and his previous doubts as to whether she was still interested in associating with him became confirmed. He had a sense of guilt about his age and the inability, through lack of money, to conduct a courtship in which she could have felt secure. Had his prospects been more advantageous he might have been inclined to try and rekindle the relationship. But in that circumstance the unfortunate situation would never have arisen.

His feeling of dejection did not minimise the deep sorrow he bore Cathy over the drastic measures she sought as a solution to end their romance. And even though he realised their relationship was destroyed on the Sunday she visited Rachel Pope, he still had pangs of remorse over the incident at the cinema with Ken's "Mum". In fact he often wondered whether his misconduct had, through intuition or gossip, become known to Cathy and been the deciding factor against her taking up with him again.

On his last day at the bakery he tried to take in as much of the surroundings that had been his stepping-stone into the world of toil. More than once his bottom was gently kicked to stir him from his day dreams. It seemed mere days ago that the foreman was showing him around the premises and explaining his duties. He had come to like everyone in the place and now that he was leaving it was like cutting himself off from his family. As he finished the last session of washing up he looked at the now still machinery and dwelt for a few moments on the silence of the place that never again would he see in a bustle of the contented little work force. His meditation was broken by Freddie, the cleaner, as he placed his pail clangorously in the sink. Percy spent more time talking to him that last day as if trying to hang on to the last human contact as long as possible and it was Freddie who broke up the conversation to get on with his cleaning, As he walked slowly up the stairs to the mess room Percy would have given anything to find Cathy waiting there for him.

Drawn to the flour loft where they had spent so many happy hours, he fancied he could still smell her perfume about the place. However, all the sacks they had ever lain on had long since gone, therefore it was only imagination and wishful thinking that prompted him to glance around for her as if she had been playfully hiding from him. In spite of the warmth a chill went through him as the winter wind howled through the intake flaps. Without her the place held a strangeness, and with a sigh depicting the sadness in his heart, he descended the stairs and left the premises.

His next job on the treadmill of survival was that of a

lorry driver's mate with a firm in the business of transporting sand, cement and bricks to building sites. The depot was situated on the Kingston wharf and ran eight lorries.

Scottie Andrews, a dapper young man in the dancing fraternity was one of the drivers and as he got Percy the job it was to his vehicle that the lad thought he would be immediately assigned, but this was not to be. Instead he had to assist mean, monkey-faced Ernie as he came to be known, who left Percy sitting out in the lorry in the freezing weather while he went into his house for a meal.

Being used to the warmth of the bakery and not having sufficient clothing to combat the cold, Percy shivered and shook for most of the day, and all but laid across the engine cover in the cab, to keep from freezing to death.

When railway trucks of bricks had to be unloaded on to the lorry they were thrown at him six at a time as if he were an old hand at catching them.

On these days he dragged himself home tired and hungry, with torn and bleeding hands, and wondered what possessed him to leave a comfortable job that supplied warmth, food and threw in the odd romance to boot. But with the transport firm he not only received more than double the pay the bakery paid him, the travel appealed to him as well. Some days it would be five tons of cement from Beeding to Portsmouth or Southampton. These were trips of sightseeing pleasure, apart from the unloading, but carrying hundredweights a few yards from the lorry did not come hard after the sacks of flour hehad fought with previously.

When he was not watching the passing scenery or waving and calling to young women as they passed, he was studying Ernie's hands and feet as up hill and down dale, he put the three ton Bedford through its paces.

After a month of observation Percy knew enough to enable him to control the vehicle, even to the extent of double declutching on a change down, without having driven a foot.

In spite of clips around the ear he still could not resist pushing the gear stick back to neutral as Ernie's attention was extended to watching for a break in the traffic before he pulled away from the kerb. He would stick an arm out let the clutch in and then think a half shaft had gone when the engine roared and they never budged an inch. As Percy was usually looking innocently out of his window, Ernie used to assume that he had forgotten to put the stick in gear.

But came the moment when Percy just had to see the look on his driver's face when he thought he had been absent minded again, and his sniggering gave him away.

"Pack that up yer young sod," Ernie would say as he took swipes at Percy's ear and missed more times than he connected. Joking aside, Percy had rather more in mind for the Bedford than merely moving the gear stick. Ernie came out from an office one day, where he had just picked up a loading ticket, and both the lorry and Percy were gone. He found them under the ballast hopper where Percy was loading the vehicle as efficiently as he had driven it to that position. Ernie was furious, he climbed up the side of the lorry and struck Percy hard across the face causing the lad to fall over.

However, he still had hold of the chain that released the ballast, consequently Ernie was buried in sand and small stones, and Percy dug away frantically with his hands to uncover his spluttering head. How much like a monkey coming out of hibernation, thought the youngster, as Ernie's face came in view. Or a vampire leaving his grave.

Percy Longprong

"You've done it this time," said Ernie as he swallowed his fright and fury, and proceeded to reprimand Percy on all the petty little faults he could lay his mean mind to. He was going to tell the manager for sure, and his manner was so determined that it looked like being Percy's last day with the firm. Pointing out to the disgruntled man that all the work would be his once his report went in, had its effect. For being aware of what a willing worker his mate was, caused Ernie to conjure up an element of forgiveness and no more was said on the matter.

Percy was undeterred by the incident and jumped into the driving seat at every opportunity, while Ernie suffered in silence. But most of the other mates were doing the same with their lorries, although they were not all as safe at the wheel as Percy. One drove off the quayside into the harbour, and only the mooring cable from the dredger stopped the vehicle and its terrified saboteur from going to the bottom. The drivers had to look upon it as fledglings trying their wings and accepted the annoyances as an occupational hazard, remembering that they began their driving career in exactly the same way.

Being less generous in understanding, Ernie cranked in silent protest every time he came out of a site office and was forced to sit in the passenger seat while Percy drove to the unloading point. The time came however when the youngster's daring and lively initiative became of tremendous benefit to the self centred man.

It happened on a day they delivered a load of cement to a farm at the foot of Fort Nelson at Portsmouth. After unloading, the farmer gave Ernie two jars of plums, one of which was meant for Percy. But as he was preoccupied with sweeping residue from the lorry, he never saw a jar being hidden away behind the seat.

Hardly were they six miles into the journey home when Ernie had emptied the jar he had not hidden. Only once did he offer his assistant a plum, which was refused because of the way Percy had seen the fingers he wiped the drips off his nose with wallowing in the juice.

Thirty miles ahead in a sandpit at Washington, Jack, the man in charge, was preparing for their arrival, or more precisely Ernie's. For they were to detour there to pick up a load of sand on their way home. Some days previously, Ernie had used the privy at the pit and had been specifically asked by Jack to avoid fouling his prize marrow which was growing at the bottom of the grave-like hole. Nevertheless, in spite of there being enough room for four to sit shoulder to shoulder and still leave the marrow untarnished, Ernie on his own, covered it in excretion. Jack had not been too pleased with him to begin with through his sly ways of making out there was something wrong with the engine while his mate had to do all the shovelling. But now his fury demanded satisfaction, which was the reason he replaced the firm sitting bar in the privy for one he had partially sawn through. This he hoped would hold Percy's weight if the need took him, but not Ernie's.

As if eager to act his part in a play, obligingly Ernie brought the lorry roaring into the sandpit and leapt from it while still in motion leaving it to come to a halt in a pile of sand.

As Percy jumped behind the wheel to position the vehicle for loading, his driver was tripping over his trousers as he prepared himself for action simultaneously with reaching the privy. Through his gluttony over the plums he had been in excruciating agony for the last ten miles to the extent that it was doubtful whether he would have made it the few yards to the bushes had he stopped along the road.

The front wheels of the transport had plunged up to the axles in the sand and the full throttle the engine needed to pull them free, blotted out the cry that Ernie emitted as he landed with a squelch, shoulder deep in excrement. Had he been there to see his contrivance work so well, Jack's heart would have jumped for joy. But as there was no gate to lock, he had straddled his bike and was away at the end of his hours.

Percy had shovelled half the load on when he decided to go and find Ernie, who he assumed was dodging the column as usual. Discovering his whereabouts brought a stream of abuse for not showing up sooner. Ernie seemed to have hurt his back and Percy had to throw the tow rope down to get him up. The sight and stench of him was sickening. He was plastered from the back of his head to his waist. His legs and buttocks were untouched as they had been lying against the side of the hole, and it was over his feet that Percy had dropped the loop to hoist him clear. With his trousers around his ankles he hobbled to a pile of sand and ran handfuls across the back of his head before rolling on his back over the mound, and swearing at Percy continually for not cleaning him off. But like everyone else, the lad had a natural aversion for the matter involved, and reserved such service, should they suffer the same misfortune, for family and friends only, neither of which categories fitted Ernie.

Water had not been laid on at the pit and while the wretched man did his best to clean himself off with sand, Percy finished loading the lorry. Throwing the shovel on top of the load, he sat on the cab step for a rest. Even though many would have shouted a thousand hurrahs at Ernie's plight, he thought the man looked pitiful and was sorry he could not have helped him get rid of the filth. Such sentiments however were pure waste where Ernie was involved, for as the lad went to his aid when he said he could not rise, muck was wiped onto his shirt sleeve.

"There's some for you as well you little bastard. Share and share alike's my motto," he said with an evil smirk. He stood up but as he bent over to pull his trousers up he could not straighten out and fell back in the sand with a groan as if, for his malicious act, he had been struck by the arm of justice. Whatever light Percy had accepted the man in before, in ways of tolerance for his mean attitude towards his fellows, was replaced with disgust. Somewhat enraged, he tore Ernie's trousers from around his ankles and wiped most of the foul matter from his sleeve with one of the legs, then dipping the other into the top of the engine radiator he washed off the remainder. Ernie's threats of violence meant nothing to him. He had knuckled under to his abuse simply because of his upbringing to respect adults and those in authority over him. Now the arrangement as far as this man's due merited was nil and void and should he show a hint of vindictive violence when he had recovered, Percy was confident of discouraging him. After throwing his trousers at him then having to assist him in putting them on, it became plain that he was incapable of driving the vehicle back to the depot.

Not mentioning his own capability behind the wheel, Percy suggested that he should make his way to the nearest house to telephone for an ambulance. Ernie, however, judging others by himself, saw him thumbing a lift home and leaving his poor crippled driver in the pit all night.

"You get me on board and get yer arse in that drivin' seat, yer cocky bugger," were his words. "Always braggin' you could drive to Scotland and back wivout kipp now let's see yer get the bloody thing back to Portslade," he challenged.

Without even testing what the state of the air would be inside the cab, Percy insisted that Ernie sat on the load of sand at the back for the journey home. Not being able to have stood the smell of himself in such a confined space anyway, he made little protest as he crawled up the two planks that Percy had placed at the side for him.

As the eager youngster engaged the clutch with the screaming engine the vehicle lurched as if it would snap in two under the load. Fearing the axle would break and they would be stranded, Ernie hammered on the cab with his fist and swore at his dubious protege through the rear window. But they were gaining momentum and the lad's interest was taken with the way ahead, not with the baboon pulling faces behind the glass at his back. Once on the road he went through the motions like a specialist, and very reluctantly, Ernie had to admit to himself that the lad was a natural driver.

On arriving at Ernie's house, his wife, who had been watching out of the window because he was late, came running out to see why he was on the back of the lorry and not at the controls. She was as attractive as her husband was ugly and Percy found himself staring at her wondering whether she had varicose veins or wooden legs or was perhaps affected with idiocy. His suspicions of a defect were well founded but it was a blessing to the man, for when she began to communicate, it was with the slurred speech of the partially muted.

How lucky Ernie was, he thought. He envied him her loyalty, for plainly she would never leave him. They were the ideal match. He looked like a monkey and she sounded like one. She gave Percy a puzzled look as she wondered why he did not assist her husband as he manoeuvred his way painfully down the side of the lorry to the pavement. Then, hit by the pungent odour, her look changed to utter bewilderment. Shuffling bent over through the front door was the last Percy saw of Ernie. The fall had dislocated his back and so made the heavy work involved in lorry driving impossible. The price he paid for fouling the marrow was heavy, far more in fact than Jack had perhaps intended. Nothing could have been read in his face however, when he was informed of the mishap by Percy when next he visited the pit as mate to his friend Scotty.

"Oi noticed it were gettin' a bit weak an' meant ta change it over. Then when I seed the bar layin' in the bottom, I said Good Lord, I do 'ope no one's come a mischief o'er that," said Jack convincingly, as his gaze turned searchingly skyward as if expecting a personal cloudburst or thunderbolt.

"Well, well," he continued lamentably. "Poor old Ernie. All over 'is 'ead n' back eh? Still, good job it was there ta break 'is fall weren't it?" he said, tongue in cheek. But looking Percy in the eye he was far more truthful when he confessed to being pleased it had not been he who had fallen in.

Through their mutual interest in dancing and being similarly acquainted with various people in their circle, Percy and Scottie were ideally suited as workmates. The lad's outlook towards the job was totally changed for the better now that he was not chained to Ernie's company. On the long journeys he did most of the driving while Scotty caught up on the sleep he had missed through the previous night's lechery.

As the fine weather came along he took to being dropped off in a country lane a couple of afternoons a week where a girl would be waiting for a romp behind a hedge. Percy would drive on to deliver or take on a load, then pick up the exhausted Scottie afterwards.

"You can 'ave a turn if yer like, Longprong," Scottie said quite amiably one day. "She don't mind. She's an oggy cow an' fancies you a bit."

Alas, she always turned up for these frolics with bare legs, and when it came to a choice between a girl without stockings and driving the lorry, the latter had the advantage.

"No fanks, it'll only sap me strengf at this time of the day an' make me shovelling hand go weak," was his excuse.

"It's a bunk-up I'm talking about, not sawing a bloody tree down," Scottie said. "What's a'matter with yer? You was tryin' ta chat her up at the Regent the other night," he argued.

"She should a' snapped me up then, shouldn't she?" said Percy.

If she had been the girl with the black stockings and suede shoes, and the hugging dress that showed off the ridges of her underwear, she had certainly changed, and he told Scottie so.

"Oh! you like 'em with all that gear on do yer, Longprong? Well, I like getting it off," he said, pondering, then saying he would see what he could do, which Percy paid little heed to. Lo and behold, two days later, Bella, as was her name, was waiting in the usual country lane, dressed for all the world as if she were off to a royal garden party. A carriage and pair would have been more fitting than the Bedford, but she jumped up into the cab and sat on Percy's lap as if it were the practice of a lifetime.

Not having a high opinion of himself he felt embarrassed that the girl had gone to so much trouble to seduce him and he felt pity for her. Seeing her close up in daylight she looked weary from an abuse which was more self inflicted than imposed by others. Behind the friendly smile he thought she looked hell bent on a gay but short existence. And in spite of her attractive adornment, which would have made him wild with desire in the atmosphere of a softly lit dance hall, in the cold light of day, a sexual encounter would, he felt, be like contributing to her suicide.

Nevertheless after the grinning Soottie dropped both of them off at the entrance to a meadow, Percy followed her over the gate and became frustrated by more than a glimpse of underwear and suspenders as Bella pulled up her dress to manoeuvre. Tempted by the sight, he wondered if perhaps he was being too fickle in his assumptions. His aroused interest led him to question his right to decide what was or was not beneficial for another. And by the nature of his present dilemma it seemed convenient to look upon it in the light that if sex made Bella happy, who was he to deny her that pleasure.

As enthusiastic as he was to cooperate with her, when they found a place to lie down, her performance was so direct and calculating, that as much as she worked on him with the pursuit of a lifesaver on a drowned man, he could not acquire the condition necessary for the occasion.

Exasperated, she gave up trying and they both sat and smoked in silence until they heard Scottie sound the lorry's hooter to announce his return. Percy felt at a loss for words over the disappointment he had been to her. He could not understand himself why he had not been able to rise to the influence, especially when prompted by such an experienced goader.

Bella climbed back over the gate, showing rather less of her tantalizing apparel than before. Back in the lorry, instead of sitting on Percy's lap she sat astride the engine cover with the result that as Scottie changed to top, the gear stick vanished up her skirt. Puzzled by her sullenness the mischievous grin contained in his glances vanished, to be replaced by an inquisitive frown. No answer came from either as Percy gazed dispassionately through the side window and Bella stared ahead.

In an attempt to break the silence Scottie remarked that a good time was had by all. But Bella only spoke when through a gap in the hedge she spied a handsome rustic in command of two horses dragging an implement across a field.

"Drop me off here," she demanded, as she clambered over Percy and began opening the door before Scottie had even begun to apply the brakes. Whether or not she would have thrown herself out Percy did not know but he grabbed her around the waist. He was forced to push his feet hard against the angled floor to save them both from falling out. This caused him to raise his torso and push hard against her, and as her legs were astride him she took the opportunity to interpret it as a sexual gesture. "Let me go, you've had your chance, you swine," she shrieked, slapping him around the ear.

After dismounting none too elegantly she stood and brushed her hand down her dress before making her way back up the lane to the spot where she could enter the field. "Christ! What was all that about?" asked the baffled Scottie as he and Percy watched her until she passed out of sight through the bushes.

"Search me, I dunno," said Percy innocently.

It was obvious to them both that Bella had made a beeline for the country lad.

"She must lave gone short with you, mate, to be forced to approach a stranger to make it up to 'er," reasoned Scottie.

"Must 'ave," agreed Percy. "Very likely take on 'is 'orses as well from wot I made of 'er. An' if 'e gives 'er a lift home on that bleedin' contraption, they won't 'arf bugger up the roads."

Percy forgot where he had heard the phrase, beware of another man's leavings. It could have been from his father who did little to practise it. However, the saying seemed to be proved beyond doubt when Scottie began scratching his crotch and testicles far more frequently than was normal. The condition needed very little diagnosing to confirm that he was in possession of "crabs". In fact they were more in possession of him. Percy could not remember seeing anyone scratch so much, especially when the parasites were in the throes of death through the application of the world renowned "blue unction" as it was popularly known.

Quite often the lorry slowed down on the road as Scottie was forced to take his foot off the accelerator in order to lift his leg to scratch. Sometimes he would swerve to a halt at the roadside, jump out and claw at himself as if demented. At times like this Percy was in agony trying to keep a straight sympathetic face. All it wanted was for him to be seen giggling and he felt a fight would ensue, in which case he thought some of the creatures would transfer to him. Scottie confessed that apart from his known condition he was somewhat concerned as to whether something of a far more serious nature was incubating in his prize possession. And Percy was doubly thankful that his constancy had been inoperative on that afternoon with Bella.

To take Scottie's mind off things Percy suggested they should keep an eye on the ploughman whenever they were in his vicinity. And it was agreed to be an interesting idea.

"We can spend a few minutes wochin' 'im ev'ry time we're round that way, an' when we sees 'im 'aving a scratch we can jump about an' yar boo at 'im," said Percy excitedly.

The trend of the conversation allowed him to laugh at the situation without Scottie thinking it was directed at him.

"'Ere, an' p'raps we'll see is orses doin' a bunk all over the field as well, draggin' their cobblers fru da brambles an' nettles. Then we'll know that naughty Bella 'ad a go at them an' all," he chuckled excitedly.

After two days of unscheduled detours to the area, which involved a five minute observation morning and afternoon, their token surveillance was rewarded.

The man and his team were not in their usual field but were furrowing in the next, and Percy and Co. would not have known had they not heard him swearing at the animals. The commotion was brought about through him being unable to scratch himself and steady the plough at the same time. Plainly he was at the stage where the irritation could not be put down to perspiration, but was something that demanded attention. The state of the furrows looked like the first day attempts of an apprentice.

Suddenly the plough overturned and the man was nearly strangled by the reins around his neck. Pulling the animals to a halt he fumed and swore as he frantically raked at his crotch with one hand and tried to right the contraption with the other.

Percy and Scottie burst out laughing and he turned angrily upon them.

"You be wantin' somat? cause if you don't, take yersels art o' it 'fore yer gets me boot."

He was a good looking young man of around twenty-two and Percy thought how successful with the women he would be in the town dance halls.

"Oh, that's a nice fing to say ta someone oo's come all this way to apologise," said Scottie. The sarcasm escaped the man and, still scratching, he asked him what he meant. They watched him turn white as Scottie went on to describe the wicked town girl who, in spite of her numerous incurable diseases, went about willy nilly infecting unsuspecting men. The yarn was hardly finished when the man unhitched the plough, threw himself over the back of one horse, and leading the other at a gallop, rode off towards the road that led to the nearby village of Storrington.

"I think you was wrong about the 'orses, though," said Scottie as they watched them out of sight.

"I know," replied Percy. "They was both mares."

A short while later while driving through the village, they saw the two animals tethered outside the chemist's shop.

"Betcha 'e's in there gettin' some blue jollop," chuckled Scottie as he pulled up.

"Well, 'e aint rushed orf like that ta buy himself a jar of 'air cream 'as 'e?" gloated Percy.

As the young man came from the shop clutching the precious carton he came face to face with Scottie leering out of the cab window.

"Got the magic mixture, then, mate?" he asked, grinning.

"What bloody business o'yorn be it?" he shouted angrily. "Take yersell off, less yer wants trouble."

"Calm down now, mate," said Scottie quietly. "I just wanted to tell ya anuvver way to get rid o' them little rascals wivout all that messy treacle."

Misled by the seemingly good intent, the man grunted

an apology and waited for the advice. He began nodding obediently when told to get a cup full of petrol and pour it over the affected parts. But then when told to put a match to it he realized he was being taken for an object of amusement. He struck out at Scottie, who, anticipating the outcome of his taunt, wound his window up in time for it to take the blow and not him.

As the man had obviously put himself out of action through at least two cracked knuckles, Scottie felt it safe to wind the window down again.

"Buggered 'is scratchin' 'and up that 'as," said Percy dryly.

"Don't fink you got all the 'ard luck mate," Scottie said to the man, now wringing his hand with pain. "On top of everyfing else, that poor cow's got foul pest an' swine fever after goin' wiv you."

Rallying himself, the man grabbed at the door handle but the door was kicked open in his face by Scottie who then leapt from the cab in a murderous mood and stood over him as he sat stunned on the pavement.

"Come on mate if ya fancies ya chances," he challenged, pushing the man with his foot. "Ya bloody turnip muncher, take pokes at me will ya? Well, get up an' I'll show ya wot a town bloke can do wiv a bumpkin."

Suddenly Percy was struck with how stupidly out of hand the whole affair had become, and he leapt out of the cab to restrain Scottie.

"Come on Scottie, leave 'im alone, 'e aint done us any 'arm, 'as 'e?"

"You shut ya mouth or you'll cop out an all," he warned, glaring at Percy menacingly.

But 'e aint done nuffing to us 'as 'e?" insisted Percy. "Come on, let's go 'fore we gets inta trouble."

"'E aint freatnin' me wiv a couple o' boots up the arse an' gettin away wiv it," spat Scottie.

"We was annoyin' 'im wasn't we? You'd do the bloody same wouldn't ya," continued the lad as he took Scottie by the arm and attempted to pull him back to the lorry. All he got for his trouble was a punch in the eye that sent him reeling on the pavement.

"There, that'll teach ya ta take 'is bloody side," specially when it was your idea ta start wiv," said Scottie furiously.

Anger welled inside Percy to the extent that it was touch and go whether Scottie's testicles would suffer from far more than irritation.

"You fuckin' bastard, if I was on 'is side you'd be down there rolling about like a barrel in a boat," he shouted. "'e's in the same state you are aint 'e from that scraggy cow that you picked up.   'E should be 'avin' a go at you."

"Let 'im start 'avin' a go at me then. Come on my son, let's see if ya muscle matches ya mouf," he said giving the young man another dig with his foot.

"I'm warnin' you Scottie," said Percy, "If you don't leave 'im alone an' stop makin' bloody fools of us bof" you won't be drivin' that lorry 'ome."

Scottie was flabbergasted and enraged. He had never considered the likes of Percy as being able to threaten him.

"Do wot, yer bastard? You'll wot?" he spluttered. "I tell yer wot, you might be walkin' 'ome or more likely crawlin' after the bloody 'idin' I'm gonna give yer." He stepped away from the fallen man and turned to face Percy.

"I've survived a battering that you won't come close to

givin' me. An' you'll be fucked for a long time after you try," warned Percy as he prepared to put his defences to work.

Scottie checked his hostile manner, for at that moment he saw in his assistant an element of danger that called for the utmost caution. From his knowledge of him he knew that his self assurance must be based on something other than bluff. A split second premonition of wracking pain and numbness passed through him and he darted to the lorry and drove off, leaving Percy with the young man on the pavement.

"Aw right, George?" Percy asked smiling, as he sat down beside him.

"Alright, kid, thanks ta you," he replied, looking curiously at the lad as if wondering how so much courage and sense of fair play could be exercised by one so young.

"'E don't play the white man, do 'e? that mate o' yorn."

"Tha's where you're wrong, George, 'e plays 'em very well. A lot o' the bastards I've met any 'ow," corrected Percy. "I'm surprised at 'im though, I must admit."

"My name's Ned, not George. Ned Patchin' that's me," he said, holding his hand out which Percy took an he told him his name also.

"It was good of ya ta take my part against yer mate like that," he went on.

"When they turns mean an' nasty, they aint mates o' mine any more. A joke's one fing, but when they starts wantin' ta bash people about fer nuffin', well, I just gets the needle to 'em, I can't 'elp it." Percy's explanation was almost apologetic.

"Well I won't ferget it, I can tell yer, lad," said Ned, getting to his feet.

Percy chuckled as he did likewise.

"'Ere, yer know wot we gotta watch out for now don't yer?"

"No, what?" asked Ned, with concern.

"'E'll try and put a couple of old birds on us wots got shagger's weep or crotch corrosion, just ta get 'is own back," laughed Percy.

"And we'll send 'em back wiv 'ard pad and foot an' mouf," laughed Ned as he scratched himself fiercely.

"I'd 'ave 'ad a dose of them if I'd 'ave got the 'orn," said Percy. "I dunno wot was wrong wiv me that day. Never fancied 'er properly I s'pose."

"I wish ta Christ I hadn't," said Ned, sadly.

As Percy was stranded, Ned helped him up on one of the mares, then after mounting the other himself they rode to the bus stop at the far end of the village.

It was the first time he had ridden a horse, and he felt like a soldier taking the animals to a place of safety after the guns had been positioned.

Looking at Ned he imagined how handsome he would look in uniform and what a fine comrade he would make in such a circumstance.

"I s'pose the army takes horses like these when a war comes along," he said.

"Not any more, they're mechanised now. It'll be tractors and lorries pullin' the equipment for the next lot," Ned said calmly. "Nelly and Queeny here will be safe any road."

After Percy dismounted at the bus stop, Ned told him that any time he needed a favour he knew where to come. "Just ask anyone round 'ere for Ned Patchin" an' they'll put yer right," he said.

Sitting on the bus, Percy was still smiling to himself thinking of how furiously Ned had been scratching as he rode back into the village. A few miles along the road Scottie overtook the bus, then brought it to a halt by pulling the lorry up in front of it.

"Come on, Longprong, yer silly sod, get off," he shouted along the bus after he jumped on the boarding platform.

Back in the lorry Percy listened to what passed for an apology from Scottie. He was on edge over his condition, but as much as he tried to excuse his behaviour as being natural under the circumstances, Percy could not agree with him.

Scottie got rid of his parasites and nothing more unpleasant followed. The experience never deterred him from having the odd girl turn up in a country lane once or twice a week. But he now carried a magnifying glass with him and when the females thought he was about to kiss the furry cup, he was doing no more than intently examining the hair with the fervour of a naturalist looking for signs of life. Whether it could be taken as trick or treat, he never again attempted to entice Percy to participate in the pranks. For the way he had put newspapers on the driving seat before he took over the wheel, when he feared being contaminated, the lad would have shied away from a girl as pure as a sincere nun if Scottie introduced her to him.

Nevertheless, the working relationship was as good as ever. Percy's interest was in driving the lorry as much as possible, and no word of criticism or complaint did he utter over the extra work it involved.

They were not altogether settled times. There was an uneasiness in the air due to the expectation of war. When the uncertainty was ended by Mr. Chamberlain's announcement that a state of war existed, the air raid sirens began and before the wailing had ceased, Percy saw that nearly everyone in the road had put on their gas masks in anticipation of the first air raid.

When the initial excitement subsided, everyone went about their business safe in the knowledge that the army would be marching through the enemy capital by Christmas. Morrison table shelters were erected in all the front rooms of people who wanted them on the estate. Each street had a roster for firewatching, and when the farce fell to Percy and his mother, she was so steadfast in her duty as to patrol the street all night. But it was doubtful whether her neighbours even stayed alert an extra half hour before bed when it was their turn.

It became a time of movement. Everywhere, men were either flocking to one branch or another of the Forces, or making for the big cities where they hoped to sit out the war as insignificantly in crime as possible. Being only a year away from the time when the military machine could claim him, Percy wondered whether he would submit or run when that day came. He certainly did not feel he could participate in the abominable ferocity he had heard described so many times by his father. Evidently he had gone ignorantly, perhaps eagerly, to an adventure in foreign parts, partly because his own father had experienced nothing more exceptional than the countrywide fight for survival in the land of his birth. But once he was aware of the carnage, who other than the deranged would answer the bugle's call a second time?

Hopefully, Percy thought the war could be over before he had to make a decision. After all, the Germans would not hold out for long, when like the last time it was inevitable that they would be beaten.

Due to a manpower shortage, Percy became a fully-fledged driver overnight. He was put in charge of the vehicle he considered to be the pride of the fleet, a three ton short wheel base tipper. Such was his elation when he left the depot, he would have driven without wages had it been possible financially. His manner was almost arrogant when parking the lorry along with the other vehicles outside the transport cafes before strutting to the counter to order. His greatest pride however came from pulling up outside his house for dinner and hearing his mother tell him that she could hardly believe that her son was capable of driving such a huge mechanical monster about, and how Sylvia would never believe it when she wrote and told her.

As the lorry was a tipper, no mate came with it and Lucy took to accompanying her son on some of the journeys when her own charring duties allowed. It became a whole new way of life, for never before had she travelled so far or seen so many people and places.

Although totally unaware of it herself, Lucy was still attractive, and collected quite a few admirers on the travels. At times she blushed like a young maiden at even the most innocent of compliments or remarks she received at building sites and supply depots. After being married to Horace, she had little or no confidence in the possibility that, apart from cleaning floors and polishing furniture, she had retained any desirable attributes.

However, a forty year old widower named Bill Matherson, who also drove on the same transport firm, had his interest aroused in her when he was sent to tow Percy's lorry in through a breakdown. For safety, Lucy travelled back with Bill and a friendship ensued. Percy knew him to be a respectable man who never exchanged or even listened to the coarse talk that was bandied about in the yard. He was a man the lad would have liked to fashion himself on.

It took quite a few weeks for Lucy to come to terms with the fact that a man was trying to court her. But once she accepted it, the red velvet costume bought for her by Percy with the money his well meaning friends had claimed for him, no longer remained unworn in the cupboard. Furthermore, despite her protests, Bill bought her another of emerald green, a blue dress, and two pairs of shoes that were the height of fashion.

Lucy truly felt her cup was overflowing. Never before in her life could she remember feeling so vital and alive. It was as if the clock were turned back and she was once more a young girl about to cross the threshold to womanhood. Overwhelemed by the considerate attention shown to her by Bill, she realised fully what a nightmare life with Horace had been. Furthermore, she wondered how she managed to survive those hideous years with her sanity still intact. Since he had left school Percy had come to understand somewhat the extent of his mother's unhappiness when his father had been alive. This influenced his answer of approval when Bill asked the lad whether he would mind if he married his mother, to include as a matter of a friendly warning, that she had better be kept happy.

Knowing enough of Lucy's previous hardships, Bill accepted the caution in the spirit in which it was uttered. He had no doubts about meeting Percy's condition, for Lucy's happiness was his erstwhile wish also.

The wedding took place at the registrar's office two days before Christmas, which made it possible for Sylvia's husband Frank to get seasonal leave and attend with her.

Bill did the day proud. He hired the Co-op hall and a three piece band for the reception. Everyone on the firm had an invitation to bring their wives or in the case of the bachelors, a friend. This left Percy wondering what sort of itchy-coo Clara Scottie would arrive with. He was relieved that it turned out to be Joy Clancy, the office girl who every man on the firm was secretly in love with. Not that Percy's feelings for her came anything close to hidden by the way he used to grab her arm as she passed him his worksheet through the office hatch. Although she would reprimand him most severely for trying to pull her through the opening, then upon failing, kiss as much of her arm as he could reach, she had fits of laughter afterwards.

What with the friends and neighbours from the street, Bill's personal acquaintances, relatives and workmates, there was as goodly a crowd as on any Saturday dance at the place. And with ample to drink and eat laid on trestles at the back of the hall, there was not a bored face amongst them.

Percy could hardly take his eyes from Lucy. He found it difficult to believe that the lovely woman dancing around so happily, even if at times awkwardly, was his mother. For a moment or two tears welled in his eyes and he could have cried for the stupidity of his father in almost laying waste the life of such a dear creature.

Noticing her son in somewhat of a pensive mood she stopped dancing and leading Bill by the hand she went to Percy and hugged him.

"I've never been so happy, and I owe it all to you. If you hadn't taken me out in your beautiful lorry, I'd never have met Bill. Thank you, thank you," she said, wiping a tear from her eye and hugging him again.

"Same here, lad," said Bill, putting his hand out which Percy shook for about the fifth time that day.

"Only it's me that's got the bargain all the way round,

'cause I've got you for a son as well." Then taking him by the shoulders and looking solemnly into his face he assured the lad that not only had he not lost a mother but he had gained a father as well. Then giving him a man to man hug he led Lucy, now shedding tears of joy, back onto the dance floor.

Shaking off his sentimentality, Percy threw himself back into the spirit of the party by making a bee-line for Miss Clancy. She was sitting cross-legged while waiting for Scottie to get her another drink, and was showing far more of her legs than was good for Percy's sensual temperature. Pulling her to her feet he led her amongst the dancers and held her tight enough to feel her form from her cheek to her knees.

Her over all loveliness, her perfume and her silk clad thighs moving against him sent his passion soaring, and he wanted her desperately. The attraction was not only in one direction. She had until now only seen him in his working clothes and had no idea how different he could look on social occasions. Now that she had seen the measure of his taste in clothes, she was pleasantly impressed. He had on a light grey double breasted suit, with light blue shirt and white tie. On his feet were smart tan suede shoes, which she all too frequently trod upon as they clung to each other and shuffled around out of step with the music, in the pretext of dancing.

Seeing the pair so obviously engrossed with each other, Scottie thought twice about claiming back the partner he came with. Therefore, in the true manner of a randy devotee to danceland, he recognised the night as still being young and full of promise. But like numerous times before, he underestimated how many of what he considered to be available and tolerable prospects were already spoken for.

Two or three times he had, after intimate cheek to cheek

dancing and neck kissing, thought he was at the point where he could safely speak of his carnal desire, only to feel a stronger hand than his, grabbing his collar as the process of partner changing. The brisk, melodious little band went through their repertoire of Deep Purple, The Ferry Boat Song, Begin the Beguine, and a host of waltzes. When tangoes such as Jealousy, and La Composita were played, the female's threw themselves heart and soul into what they believed to be an identity with Dolores Del Rio. Halfway through the tune most of them had tripped over their unsteady partners and left the floor, while those remaining gave an impressive floor show. At the turn, after the sharp, snappy steps, the women were lying back more in resemblance of dead ducks than dying swans. Two of their partners could not hold the weight and dropped them to the floor with a thud, to the amusement of everyone watching.

Scottie had thrown all caution to the winds and was cuddling up to all the women he could before he was checked. No female was eliminated from his amorous slobbering. Even Sylvia braved two dances with him and Frank broke in on them at the beginning of the third. Pretending he thought he was the one Sylvia's husband wanted to dance with, Scottie good naturedly took hold of him and whirled him around for a few steps. Nothing being sacred he then tried his antics on Lucy, and almost got a thick ear when Bill returned from the toilet in time to cut short his cheeky routine. But everyone made allowances for him. He was a big fish in the dancing world trying to operate in a small pool.

The trio played Henry Hall's signature tune, "Here's To The Next Time", then "Goodnight, My Love", and then the National Anthem, with everyone standing to attention as best they could. Amidst the final best wishes and congratulations to the happy pair, Percy slipped away with the inebriated Miss Clancy. Making their way up the yard in the direction of the bakery, which adjoined the hall, he noticed Scottie coaxing Beaty Grayer, the local wallflower, into the stables, evidently implementing the first rule on the emergency page of the lecher's handbook, which advised any old port in a storm.

Percy had fancied her quite often at other times, but never had the pluck to dance with her. Then when he had looked for her at the end of the evening, someone else had always pipped him to the post.

Climbing the stairs to the flour loft brought memories flooding back, and he would not have been surprised to discover that the girl staggering up at his side turned out to be Cathy. The smell of Evening in Paris was too overpowering to be imagination, and he lit his cigarette lighter to substantiate who was accompanying him. After a minute or two's preliminary display of chastity from Miss Clancy, Percy began to fulfil a desire he had nurtured for over a year. Although she was not a virgin, the gasp she emitted as he entered her proved she had not been making a habit of donating her favours. As the wonder of her engulfed him, his mind strayed alternately between her and Cathy and he truly could not remember a more lustful experience.

As they relaxed afterwards in silent tribute to each other, Percy thought he heard whispering and movement coming from the far corner of the loft. This served to give substance to the fragrant perfume that he had come to associate solely with Cathy. Tempted as he was to climb through the gaps in the sacks of flour that led to the corner, he declined, for to have found her there with someone else would have been unbearable.

Springing to his feet he hurried the surprised Miss

Clancy out of the building as if it were ablaze, never once looking back for fear of whom he might see making an exit after them. On the strength of that night Percy tried desperately to seriously court Miss Clancy. But as much as she was attracted to him, she rejected all his attempts to take her out, and in a few weeks she left the firm, supposedly to join a branch of the women's services.

SEVEN
What's It All About?"

Bill had a nice little house overlooking the golf links, and after Percy had helped him redecorate the rooms needed for immediate use, they all moved in. It all seemed luxurious to him as it did to Lucy. His bedroom peered out on to a panoramic view of the little Norman church on the distant slope, the farm manor house nestling in the surrounding oaks and elms, and the whole lush green of that section of the course where so often he played in earlier years and caddied in later.

It all seemed serenely middle class and both Percy and his mother loved the house intensely, while Bill was overjoyed at the happiness they had found with him. How proud Lucy felt as she kissed them both and waved from the gate until they were out of sight, as stepfather and son set off to work together. And how eagerly she looked forward to seeing them again in the evening or perhaps at lunchtime if one or the other was in the vicinity.

Apart from the news bulletins on the wireless, the war was far away and not particularly menacing. But it did not remain that way. The episode of Dunkirk came and went without many being aware at the time of its jeopardising significance. Dorniers took to flying in unchallenged along the coast at almost tree top level to strafe and bomb the gas and electricity stations, the railways, and anything else that took their fancy as they banked inland for a return run. When Percy first saw them he thought fireworks were being let off from the aircraft's tail until the tracers ripped open the top of the cab and filled his tailboard full of holes. After his lucky escape he became the hero of the yard.

"They're tryin' ta get yer now, Perce, 'cause they know what's comin' to 'em later when ya joins up," one of the other drivers jokingly commented, to which all the rest agreed, adding that they thought he should be given something to shoot back with.

The news of his encounter with the enemy spread far and wide and none of the cafe owners on his run would take a penny from him for his meals. Consequently he began stuffing himself in some, and giving it away to his mates in others, until the excess food started to affect their shovelling. They were exciting days on the road. In all the drivers' retreats the juke boxes were resounding to either Vera Lyn rallying the nation with "We'll meet again", or Bing Crosby still dreaming of a "White Christmas", even though that season had long since passed.

Nothing being perfect, the happy contentment of the trio became marred when Bill, being in the Naval Reserves was ordered to report to Ayrshire in Scotland, and Percy was left once more to look after his mother. For a while she began travelling with him again, but after a Spitfire nearly hit them on take-off as they were making a delivery at Shoreham airfield, she decided to stay at home. Also, overtaking the thirty foot long fusilage transporters used to be considered quite a hazard.

Gradually the dance halls were becoming populated by an ever-increasing number of Servicemen, who were being concentrated in the South for the purpose of staving off the expected onslaught. All the beaches and most of the promenades became restricted areas fenced off with barbed wire, and an assortment of guns were mounted at strategic positions. Such was the overflexed state of nerves in the area that courting couples had a job to find places of privacy. Lovers could hardly relax when at any moment the very bushes they lay amongst might begin falling about with laughter, or if the male felt a bayonet prodding his rump simultaneously with an order of "Who goes there?" which was very likely to happen on the slopes of the Downs, now riddled with bunkers and gun emplacements.

From what his father had told him of the Germans, Percy could not see how such meagre fortifications would keep them at bay for long.

"Come at yer in thousands they do," Horace used to say, "An' don't care 'ow many of 'em yer blows up. It was heart-breaking watchin' 'em fall, even though they was remorseless in their attacks."

To console himself, Percy thought the generals must be well aware of the true situation and no doubt had something quite impressive that would be brought to bear when needed. Nevertheless, if there had been a chance of moving inland, he would have gone and taken Lucy with him.

All about him friends and acquaintances who were obviously older than he, were being called for their medicals and drafted to one or another of the services soon afterwards. None of whom, it must be added, went willingly or without quaking in their shoes. The long weeks of tension until Percy's company was requested at the examination centre, seemed endless. Then when the papers arrived simultaneously with an eighteenth birthday card from Sylvia which was two days late, his tenseness vanished, for right there and then he decided not to go.

His affairs at home and at work were soon put in order. He drove with a heavy heart on that last day at work, and when he slammed the lorry door that evening, knowing that never again would he go roaring around country lanes or on to construction sites with it, he felt he was deserting an old friend.

Lucy made no comment on his decision to "go on the trot," which was the phrase the caper became known by. She just cried for the rest of the day after he set out to seek a dubious refuge and existence in London.

Sylvia was living in Camden Town and Percy went to stay with her for a few days until he could find lodgings of his own. Knowing only too well what war could do to people, with their late father as an excellent example, she condoned wholeheartedly Percy's intention to absent himself from the present conflict, and wished to God that Frank would do likewise. He was in a bomb disposal unit and so was at risk nearly all his waking hours with the deluge of unexploded devices being dropped nightly on and around London.

During Percy's first evening in the capital the sirens went at the same hour they had wailed at home, but the explosions that began soon after were a great deal louder and closer at hand. He wondered what had possessed him to seek asylum in London at the height of the blitz. The house shook, the windows rattled, and debris played tunes as it fell in numerous fragments upon dustbins, railings and rooftops.

Sylvia said it was time to take shelter. As they hurried down the road Percy glanced back over his shoulder at the flashes from the ack ack battery just inside the South-East entrance to Regents Park. It sounded as if he were in the centre of the worst thunderstom he could ever imagine.

Down in the Underground station the platforms were swarming with people. Some were laughing and chattering while others were tucked up as if in their beds. Children played hide and seek amongst the throng and Percy shuddered at the thought that one might fall under one of the incoming trains that came in so unconcerned and insensitive to that possibility.

Due to the excitement of the moment, coupled to the sounds of young children crying, and the coughs, snuffles and general fidgeting of the rest of his fellow shelterers, Percy got no more than a cat nap of sleep. Emerging bleary eyed from the Underground simultaneously with the wail of the All Clear, he was surprised at the lack of damage in the immediate vicinity. He had expected to find the streets littered with the rubble of blasted buildings. But on that occasion the only signs of war on that chilly, grey dawn, were in the wretched expressions of others who had suffered a sleepless haven, and now hurried home for a soothing cup of tea. Then, if daytime raids allowed, an hour or two's sleep.

There was no relaxing for Percy. He had to find other accommodation. He knew that after being missing from home the authorities would extend their search for him amongst his other relatives. He took a small room at the top of a house behind Cricklewood Broadway for six shillings a week. Having no clock he had no idea of the time and the first night at his new abode saw him standing at the bus stop at midnight believing it to be a dark dawn.

Exhausted, he had gone to bed around ten o'clock, slept for a couple of hours, then been awakened by the shunting from the goods yard behind the house. Not wanting to be late in starting his new job with the little general delivery firm in St. Johns Wood, he dressed and rushed out. On being told by a passer-by that the buses did not start until six a.m., he wandered down to an all night cafe in Kilburn. There, amongst an assembly of disreputables he dozed off with an assurance of being aroused at seven a.m. by a dubious looking young man who introduced himself as Liverpool Loui.

Actually he was ahead of time for it was only five in the morning when Percy awoke as the result of Loui attempting to go through his pockets while he slept. Due to the angle, a punch would have been ineffective, so Percy slammed his elbow into the pickpoket's face and he fell to the floor. His nose was spurting blood, and he lay wailing that he was a victim of an unwarranted assault. The tubby proprietor shuffled from behind the counter and with no more ceremony than ejecting a dog that had just fouled his floor, he picked Loui up by the collar and tossed him on to the pavement. Percy thought he was next when the man stopped in the gangway and looked seriously at him. But he merely winked understandingly and retraced his steps behind his barricade, strewn with an array of unwashed crockery.

Percy spent the next couple of hours swapping yarns with two damsels of the night named Monica and Jessie. In between tall stories of their distinguished clientele they propositioned him to pimp for them with offers of oodles of money and a daily intimacy with each included. He was asked to consider how much he could earn from the fees of high-ranking Army and Naval officers who frequented the vicinity of Paddington Station. As pretty as they both undoubtedly were, their appearance and deportment lacked that necessary to excite such clients. And Percy told them that Popeye the sailor would probably run back to Olive if they approached him in their present slovenly state.

"Wocha 'spect us ta wear leanin' against the bleedin' wall fer ten bob a time, bleedin' beaver lamb coats?" said Monica peevishly.

"Yeah, or gettin' rolled in the dust of 'yde Park," laughed Jessie, "an' the odd dog comin' up an' pissin' over yer, then sittin' there watchin".'

"Probably waitin' for a turn," said Percy, laughing as he got up from the table and made his way to the door.

"An' there's been times we'd 'ave took 'em on as well if they'd 'ad 'alf a crown in their mouf," Jessie shouted as Percy left the cafe.

He had barely let go of the door handle when two figures rushed at him, one being the aggrieved Loui, the other a sturdy Scotsman who put Percy in mind of a Mexican bandit.

"Ye bastard," spat Loui as he punched Percy in the forehead simultaneously with the Scot delivering a blow to his cheek. Loui's second punch however, missed its target and hit the door post with force causing him to forget all else except leaning against the window and closing his eyes in agony. As Percy had started to fight back the Scot was forced to break off his attack momentarily. They both stood back taking the measure of each other with fists raised in true pugilistic fashion. As Percy had not been felled to the ground by the initial assault, and so become a candidate for the boot, the Scot felt apprehensive over the situation now that his companion had disabled himself. To him, one against one was an unfair contest and he was never at his best unless he had at least two more aiding him in such a situation. Percy was trying to remember what his father had said about the way Jocks fought. "If they've got nothing in their hand, watch their heads." Just as it came to mind, the Scot rushed at Percy, grabbed his lapels and attempted to butt him in the face. More out of surprise than strategy Percy quickly bowed his head as he saw his assailant draw his back to give force to the blow. Although unintended, the timing was perfect. The Scot smashed his face heavily on the top of Percy's lowered head and his nose and mouth gushed with blood.

Unaware or not that the event had put paid to what was left of the cowardly Scot's will to fight, Percy slammed his knee twice in his testicles, then punched him with considerable force in his blood spattered face.

Monica and Jessie came out of the cafe just in time to stop Loui from attacking Percy with an empty beer bottle he had grabbed from a side doorway. As his recent adversary lay moaning on the ground and no longer a threat, Percy turned his full attention on Loui. Now deprived of the weapon, he stood as if transfixed between the two girls until he received a fist in his eye and another in his mouth.

"Dat's enough mate, I've 'ad enough, it was my fault, I shouldn't 'ave tried it on wiv' yer, honest, I'm sorry," he cried as he clutched at Jessie for protection. But calling him a creep she pushed him away and told him she had no time for the likes of him or his mate.

"Serves yer right yer fuckin' pig. 'That's wot blokes like you an' 'im want is for some one ta give yer a fuckin' good 'idin'. P'raps yer won't be so bloody keen then ta 'ave a go at young blokes on their todd."

"Come on, love," she said to Percy, grabbing his arm, "let's get away from 'ere in case any coppers come, or worse, some of 'is shitpot mates turn up ta count out their night's proceeds from thievin'."

Hearing the last part of the conversation directed at Percy, misled Loui into thinking he could still intimidate him.

"Dat's good advice dat is mate," he said arrogantly. "Yer'd better piss off 'fore Billy Acker an' Stutterin' Wilf gets back from down West. An' if Spotty Pelgrave's wiv 'em, they'll be sweepin' you up from the bleedin' gutter."

Percy stopped walking with his new found female friends and looked back at Loui who still thought it safe to utter threats.

"We'll find yer, mate," he shouted confidently. "If yer twenty miles of 'ere by ta-morrer yer wana be shakin' in yer shoes, don't you worry, kiddo."

As much as Percy felt like sprinting at top speed to pummel his tormentor into the ground, he approached him casually so as not to cause him to bolt. Both Loui and the Scot bore more than a vague resemblance to the couple who had beaten him and his father years before. One had gone down, and because of his mouth his mate was about to join him. Then they would be left aching and bleeding as had Percy and his parent been after the attentions of just such a couple.

For a few seconds he waved his arms playfully in front of Loui who ducked and weaved quite impressively. He even felt confident to throw a token punch, but as he moved one leg away from the other to do it, Percy struck. A look of agonised dismay took over the Liverpudlian's expression as he became wracked with pain from his damaged testicles. The blood drained from his face, his mouth sagged open and his eyes all but popped from their sockets. His hands went unchallenged to Percy's shoulders for support but as he applied a feeble grip to steady himself he took two butts in the face and fell to the pavement. Leaning over him Percy issued a warning.

"Don't you start freatnin' me wiv all your fuckin' cronies unless you got 'em round yer night an' day."

Loui began losing consciousness and Percy shook him and shouted. "Are yer lis'nin'? If you an' your mates come lookin' fer me you'll be fuckin' sorry if yer finds me."

Looking up, he saw most of the people who had been in the cafe had now come out to watch the entertainment. Jessie and Monica each took one of his arms and pulled him away.

"Come on," said Jessie frantically. "Leave the Scouse bastard and that Scotch git alone now an' come away, 'ness ya wanna get nicked or sunnink. You've done 'em both a fair treat."

"An' I've never seen any one ask for it more," added Monica as all three set a good pace towards Maida Vale.

Percy thanked them for their help and mentioned that he thought they were too nice to be getting a living the way they did.

"Taint so bad really, bit of excitement aint it Jess? 'Er mum wanted 'er ta be a secretary. Sent 'er to typin' classes an' all," said Monica dryly. "But she never liked it, did yer Jess? She turned it in."

"Yer should 'ave kept it up, typin's a fair ol' job," Percy said.

"I'd 'ave been dead by now if I 'ad," said Jessie quietly. "The very evenin' I stopped goin' the bleedin' place was bombed wannit, an' everyone killed."

"The pleece even went round 'er 'ouse an' told 'er poor ol' Mum there was no survivors, didn't they Jess?" said Monica, adding to the irony. "If that weren't an omen against bein' a bleedin' typist I'd like ta know what is."

"My mum aint stopped cuddlin' me since, poor ol' cow. Still it's lovely though," said Jessie.

Before taking his leave, Percy thanked them again and told them that should they have any bother from Loui he would do his best to avenge them when next he was in the area. As reluctant as he was to return to what might prove to be a nest of vipers, if the girls suffered through helping him he would find some way of making someone pay for it.

However, it seemed they had protection enough.

"Dontchu worry about us, love, my bruvver Terry could do that fucking lot an' read the 'Otspur at the same time. 'You see as yer look after yerself."

So saying, Monica gave Percy a friendly slap on the back and they went their different ways.

EIGHT
The Inevitable

Percy was happy with his new job. One of the brothers who employed him, a shabby little man who wore a Homburg hat and tortoiseshell framed glasses, took him around for a day to give him some idea of the routine. There were pickups to be made from the cold stores at Cannon Street, Billingsgate and sometimes Covent Garden. Deliveries were made to Amersham and Great Missenden to the North of London, and as far as Reigate and Croydon to the South. He was awed with the size of the capital and the colossal heartbeat of pride within its boundaries, which many on the outskirts claimed reached almost to Brighton.

The Albion lorry Percy was given was so ancient he wondered why it did not have solid tyres, yet it handled beautifully. It was as if, like the London taxis, it was designed for nipping in and out of tight spots, for it could turn almost in its own length. And the thrust of speed was enough to warrant two fines of seven shillings and sixpence each. These were paid by his kindly employers, Billy and John Pargeter, who, along with hundreds of other small business owners, were the heart and soul of the London scene.

Percy was impressed by the Londoner's spirit and sense of belonging, and, even in such hazardous times as the blitz, they felt an inexplicable security. Despite the Cockney friendliness he still had to have extra wits about him when backing up with open doors to an unloading dock. For if he did not leap onto the bay within two seconds of the van coming to a halt, a couple of lamb's carcases or half a pig would be removed before the count began. And when in cafes he had to leave the Albion where he could observe while eating, any attempts to syphon out the petrol.

Inevitably events caught up. After repeated requests to no avail for his employment cards, it became apparent that he was on the run. With all the understanding in the world the Pargeters could not become a party to harbouring someone wanted by the authorities, and he was reluctantly discharged with two weeks' wages to help him on his way.

Applying for a job as barman at the Chippenham Hotel, Paddington, he was welcomed with open arms. Their staff problem being so acute they would have employed Hitler youth had any applied. It was a living-in position, which suited Percy ideally, as lately he had suffered the shortage of both food and warmth in his austere accommodation. In contrast, his new job was a cosy shelter. The tit-bits he frequently found irresistible on the hors d'ouvre counter in the lounge bar were sufficient for his needs even without the worthy fare supplied to the staff. And the patrons, although at times unsavoury, he found interesting and on the whole educational. Further, it gave him respite from the rigours of driving.

The pub had the reputation for being London's busiest. Understandably there were many other landlords claiming the same for their premises, but by the volume of the crowd patronising the Chippenham, Percy knew there were none busier.

Although another evening out besides the one he had with his day off would not have gone amiss, he did not find the hours unsociable. On most afternoons he was off in a flash as soon as the tidying up had been done. He would make for one of the tea dance establishments, usually the Astoria in Charing Cross Road. For a couple of hours he would find ecstasy in the tangos, foxtrots and waltzes with intemittent tête-à-têtes in a secluded corner with one damsel or another who appealed to him. He was fully captivated by the beauty and generous disposition of London girls, and he knew there could be none like them anywhere else in the world.

Necessary to the hour, and befitting his pocket, he would take a taxi back to the pub and usually be standing outside the door just as the bolts were being drawn for the evening drinking session.

The pulse of life quickened to a pace he could barely contain. Every night after closing time he was in the local churchyard making love to some female or other he had plied with free drinks during the evening.

On one occasion when climbing back in over the side gate he was taken for a burglar and nearly arrested. Fortunately not all the staff were asleep. Someone answered the bell and verified Percy's right to enter the premises, and the policeman released the grip on his collar.

Once a week he received a phone call at the pub from Sylvia. She gave him news of their mother and of the numerous visits made by the police in the dead of night, hoping to catch him sleeping there. One weekend when Lucy made a rare visit to Sylvia, Frank brought them both to the Chippenham on the Sunday evening. Percy slid over the bar and embraced his mother and both were hard put holding back the tears. He found the little get together rather upsetting. The anxiety of Frank's daily gamble with death was marked clearly on his and Sylvia's countenances, while Lucy suffered the pangs of loneliness and worried about them all. Like many others they had all known happier times and the situation being none of their making, was neither in their power to remedy.

Whatever kindred spirit Percy liked to think he shared with his fellows, it was quickly being eroded as his education to big city life advanced. As randy as he considered himself to be, his appetite never came anywhere near the antics that others took as a way of life. The age of the footpad was by no means past. Each park and heath in London had a quota of villains preying upon unwary courting couples. As they lay fully occupied with their natural desires a walking stick would silently hook the girl's handbag away. Her shoes would also vanish along with the man's jacket should they happen to be off.

On Hampstead Heath Percy caught just such a thief making off with the belongings of another couple. He gave him a hiding, unaware that the man was part of a gang of six who, like the legendary bandits of Sherwood Forest, came bursting from the thickets to take revenge.

The couple Percy had helped quietly left the scene as the man he had beaten came charging at him with a thick tree branch raised to strike. Before he reached his goal Percy's bold companion threw herself in his path and brought him to the ground. As she lay with her dress up around her waist, the gang stopped the advance on their intended victim to stare like hungry wolves at her desirable form.

This gave Percy precious seconds to draw the razor he had lately taken to carrying. However, he thought they backed away and dispersed rather too readily on seeing it. Against one or two it was a formidable weapon, but it would not have worried six determined injurers for long. Relieved at their retreat, when he picked up his standard apparel for young men with loving natures, that being his mac, he found out the reason. His girl friend's handbag, which had been beneath it, was gone.

Unneedful of his warning, Gillian, as was her name, hurried off in a fury in the direction the gang had taken. Percy, not wanting to tempt providence after his lucky escape, made his way back to the road where he told her he would wait. Dusk had fallen, and half an hour passed without her appearance. Then three of the men arrived to keep a watch on him from over the road as he sat on one of the seats opposite the pond.

The atmosphere was charged with menace, and fully aware of the danger, he moved off in the direction of the Underground station a mile down the road. They followed him, and to elude them he walked casually into a side street then bolted frantically to the bottom where another led him at speed back to the main road. Panting breathlessly he hid behind the wooden gate of a small forecourt for a rest and to urinate.

Unfortunately the liquid did not run to the drain in the centre of the yard as expected, but trickled unobstructed across the pavement just as the hunters were passing. But through the side of the gate Percy saw them. One placed a finger to his lips in a sign for silence from the others as all three crept stealthily towards the entrance.

When they were in range Percy slammed the half open gate at them. One groaned in agony over a shattered knee-cap. Another was caught in the face as he stooped for low profile and the third backed away in terror as Percy came out of the gate brandishing the razor. So incensed was he with rage he would have slashed him to ribbons if he had not fled. Even so a swipe as he turned to run almost severed his ear and cut his cheek to the bone.

Further to his deliverance from a maiming, a car containing Gillian and two men pulled up and advised him to get in as a reception committee awaited him at the Underground. On the jourey home he learned that Gillian had been raped by five of the thieves including the three he had just had a tussle with and she was still without her handbag. By the reckoning of her two rescuers Percy was lucky to be still in one piece, as only a fortnight before, even a policeman had nearly been kicked to death on the heath. But having a good instinct for a dangerous situation Percy was very conscious of how fortunate he had been to escape from the district uninjured.

Another act of rape perpetrated against a girl in his company came from a totally unexpected source and brought about an end to his dubious freedom in Civvy Street. That particular day began much the same as many others for P.C. Charley McGrath as he stood with his colleagues at West End Central listening to the daily orders from the inspector. Apart from the list of newly wanted men, he, along with the others, knew the speech word for word, and every spot the orator halted at to emphasise a point.

"We live in hazardous times, very hazardous indeed, and big cities are not only a haven for top notch criminals but all the smaller nasties are finding the pickings plentiful as well." The inspector spoke as if he missed not haveing a share in the spoils.

"Catch enough of the little 'uns and they'll lead us to a few big 'uns," he continued. "Don't be compromised or intimidated. Stand up for the unifom and it will stand by you. Don't tolerate back chat or contempt. Feel their collars first, and we'll sort it out later. Keep the peace on the King's highway. Right, off you go, left, right, left, right."

Around four o'clock in the afternoon of the same day, Charley McGrath's sexual desire was at a peak. All through the day misdemeanours in the form of petrol being syphoned from lorries, fist fights, shoplifting, and vehicles being driven in the wrong direction on one way streets had gone on under his nose. But he was far too engrossed in looking at the legs of young women to have noticed.

Nearing the end of his stint of duty he came through the back streets behind Tottenham Court Road on his way to report in. Seeing a young couple enter a bomb damaged building and guessing their purpose, drew him to them like a thirsty man to an oasis. His lust craved satisfaction without a thought for the consequences. For a while the P.C. watched the pair through a broken partition and had to adjust the swelling penis in his trousers for comfort. Percy would have been shocked to know he was being observed, and doubly shocked to find it was by a policeman. The fact however came to light when Charley stepped on some glass which cracked loudly and so gave him away. Stepping into view he made all the noises his uniform sanctioned. He accused them of trespass, lewd behaviour and breaking and entering. He told Percy to get outside as he wished to question the young lady about whom he claimed to know all. Being on the run and thinking no harm could come to a girl with a policeman anyway, he obeyed. But within minutes he was grappling with Charley after hearing the girl cry out for help. As if in a trance Charley held himself between her legs with a vice like grip and carried on rocking at her oblivious of Percy pulling at him.

Percy never considered striking him even though he no longer looked upon him as a policemaan. He was at his mercy and wide open for the special coup-de-grace, had the lad wished to administer it. Thinking his understanding to be something of a curse he could identify to a point with the way Charley felt. After all, he had not hurt anyone, and short of throttling him or clubbing him senseless with a chunk of the ample wood that was strewn around, he could do nothing but watch.

It merely left him feeling like a cheetah being robbed of its prey by a jackal. And he always said that girls who went with him would go with anyone.

The girl stopped yelling and settled back in wise acceptance, but not soon enough for her noise to have gone unnoticed on the street. Hardly had Charley rolled off to lay panting with ashamed relief when three more uniformed police and two C.I.D. men charged in and took them all to the station.

Percy found himself sharing a large police cell with four other young men who had also been dodging the call-up. Confronted in court the following day with prison or an army medical, he chose the latter, and by six p.m. he had been taken in handcuffs to an army training depot at Blandford in Dorset.

Not being a stranger to hard work the training came easily. But the ingredient of sarcasm in the discipline provoked him to anger, and he became a frequent visitor to the guard house. By and large he was eager to take in all the information the weapons instructors issued and was somewhat disappointed at the meagre arms issued to the infantryman.

"Wocha want, a bloody 'owitzer strapped to yer back?" joked a big sergeant on hearing the lad complain about the lack of effective weapons.

All too soon the six week period of training was over, and Percy's capabilities were as dependable as any young soldier expecting action could hope for. With the whisper of embarkation leave came speculation through the camp as to the destination. Everyone hoped for a peaceful posting to a tropical paradise. At least a hundred different outposts were guessed at as possibilities. But never once was the place for which they were bound mentioned for not a man among them had heard of Crete.

Percy spent some of his leave in London. His mother went with him to make more of a family get-together with Sylvia and Frank but two nights of air raids sent them hurrying back to Brighton. As Dorset was so quiet, Percy had lost the tolerance he had for sleepless nights. And being in uniform gave him the feeling of being leashed, and smothered his zest for the town. He was pleased to have his clothes back home. Sylvia had collected them from Chippenham when she had been informed of his arrest.

For the rest of his leave he hardly left his mother's side. They walked the hills, decorated parts of the house, and tended the garden to combat the strain of the events. It was with great relief that he sat back in his train seat after waving farewell to her until she was out of sight.

Going into Crete, the landing craft Percy was in was put out of action by a Stuka before it got to the beach and its occupants had to struggle through the surf to get ashore. Two or three asked with justified anger where the R.A.F. was. Then someone stumbled over the body of an airman floating in the shallows, then another shouted, "That's where they are."

Percy soon fell in with the routine of things. First the

dive bombers, then the Junkers troop carriers. The defenders reckoned to wipe out sixty per cent of the paratroops at each drop. Waiting in his slit trench for the Germans to float down within range he saw a mystifying sight. One of the enemy with a flame thrower turned it on and burnt two of his comrades' chutes, thus sending them hurtling to the ground. Others of the descending troops near the culprit shot him, and his equipment burst further into flames as it hit the ground only feet away from Percy. The burning fluid ran into the trench, causing those nearest to scurry away until it burnt itself out.

After as many of the enemy as possible were despatched before they hit the ground, there were those to be dealt with who took shelter in the nearby buildings. These had purposely been left vacant for the survivors of the drops to take cover in. Charges lay waiting for them and after the plungers had been pushed, Percy's Company was required to rush in and finish off any survivors. Then more explosives would be laid before going back to their positions.

Each dash into the narrow streets was like a recurring nightmare. The chances of survival diminished with each attack. Percy ran in weighed down with grenades and tossed them with both hands through the familiar bottom and upstairs windows. Many times there were practically hand to hand encounters where his rifle would have been useless and his life forfeit had he not had a pair of Lugers which he had taken from dead German officers. The situation of excitement and death hardly seemed real. He blazed away with the pistols as if he were Johnny MacBrown, one of his cowboy heroes, except that the enemy came at him steel helmeted instead of feathered, and fought back with schmizers and spandaus, not bows and arrows.

The sight of so many young men on both sides being mutilated sickened him and he felt burdened with guilt at his own contribution to the massacre. He found little consolation in his sergeant's quotation of "Ours is not to reason why," nor did "There but for the grace of God go I" calm the mounting terror of one day falling from grace.

Studying their reference maps the Germans concluded they were suffering a hundred per cent annihilation to the drops in that sector. Even though it was a key coastal position their losses could not be tolerably looked upon as a calculated risk, and that particular target was abandoned.

During the respite, attempts were made to repair the buildings and so lure the enemy back to a false refuge. But as the many explosions had hardly left one brick upon another, it would have taken more building talent and time than was anywhere near available, and so the idea was discarded. Instead, the detachment restocked with ammunition and caught up on well needed sleep. When they were awakened it was not "Once more into the breach dear friends," but with orders to evacuate. Each one was given a choice. They could either be taken to the mountains to join the resistance to carry on the fighting or take a chance of a boat picking them up from the beach. Another alternative, that of running to the enemy with their hands above their heads, was greeted with the same sinistrous manner in which the suggestion was made.

It was rumoured that life with the freedom fighters was unashamedly licentious. Most of the island's women, in their flight from the Germans, had joined them in the mountains. Their only justification for the ample supplies flown in was to fire a few rounds at observation aircraft and lob the odd mortar shell into obscure ravines where game had been spotted.

Although this band of revellers never caused them the slightest ruffle, the Germans had no intention of letting any British personnel organise them into a force to be reckoned with. A heavy cordon was set up blocking the mountains off from Percy and his comrades, giving them the option of a dubious escape by sea, or surrender.

The scene on the beach was that of a miniature Dunkirk. As the odd boat pulled in, exhausted men ran up and down the shore like anglers trying to cast into a constantly moving shoal of mackerel. Percy heard a captain reminding his men of military dignity as he tried to use his rank as priority for a place in one of the boats. But throwing him overboard he was told there was nothing military or dignified in a rout.

Defeats being difficult if not impossible to plan for, the evacuation from Crete was chaos.

"Put up the bloody transport an' know 'ow to get yer 'ere don't they? But when it turns sour yer gotta drag yer bollocks out by yer own steam," complained a corporal.

"They won't be sendin' my old lady a telegram and stampin' my name on their bleedin' remembrance plaques, I'll see ta that," answered Percy. But the speech was bravado, for by the look of things he knew he would be hard pressed to survive. Seeing very little chance of fighting his way onto a boat, he made his way to the headland where he had spotted a naval launch rounding the point. Discarding most of his equipment as he went he arrived panting just as a dinghy containing naval officers was approaching the craft. His heart beat wildly as he ran towards it through the shallows, for he knew that being alone they would not turn him away. He felt further relief when he saw someone he knew on the foredeck.

"Ned," he yelled, "Ned Patchin."

Ned looked hard in Percy's direction, wondering who it was that had called his name.

"It's me, Ned — Percy, you know," he shouted, as he started to scratch himself to jog Ned's memory.

On recognising Percy, Ned almost threw himself in the water to get him, but the depth would have made it pointless. Instead he waved him to a small jetty where he said he would pick him up.

At that moment a German crew arrived to dismantle the charges the British officers had just laid in the barrels of the huge naval guns they were forced to leave behind.

Four of them chased Percy into deep water and he killed two with a pair of grenades. The remaining couple however, pounced on him and held him under. Even though he knew his struggles were useless he still writhed about in an attempt to kick a vital spot. How near he had been to rescue he thought as he tried to hold his breath yet knowing he must face the pain of that awful gush of water to his lungs.

Ned had watched in near panic as he raced in with the launch to a spot where he could not miss the mark. Leaping to the foredeck he opened up with the heavy calibre machine gun on the two who were drowning Percy. Chunks of flesh and bone flew from them as if it were no more than pastry. Then both sagged over as their spines were shattered by the gun that had brought Stukas down.

Percy came to the surface covered in their blood. He was barely conscious, but on being brought aboard by willing hands and given artificial respiration, he rallied and burst into tears.

NINE
Brave New Terrors

Percy returned to England somewhat of a hero though he could never understand why. All he had done was to survive through a campaign of slaughter that he had unwillingly been a party to. He had done no more than defend himself against those who came to kill or capture him and prompted his instinct for staying alive to the best of his ability.

He was made up to sergeant and posted to a commando training camp in Kent to give them the benefit of his hand to hand experiences with the enemy. Hands however came into it very little for it was mostly about boots to crotch.

"Can't you suggest anything other than kicking them in the bollocks, sergeant?" asked the captain, with an over-ripe Oxford accent.

"Never see nothing work as well, sir," explained Percy. "'Cept at night when they 'ad their greatcoats on. Ya can't kick through a greatcoat or parachute harness."

"Jove, what did you do then?" asked the captain, all agog.

"We used ta creep around with a mouthful of whisky, an' spit it in their faces when we came across 'em unexpected sir."

"My God, what a waste," went on the captain sadly. "What did you do then

"Knifed 'em, sir."

"Do you think the War Office would sanction whisky on their manifest of approved ammunitions, sergeant ?" laughed the officer.

"Keep the troops 'appy sir."

"They'd be too pissed to fight though, sergeant," said the captain.

"Wouldn't need to," said Percy. The enemy would join 'em just like they did with the resistance in Crete. We 'eard the Germans go an spend their leave with 'em rather than go 'ome, sir."

"Good lord," said the amazed officer, as he wandered off shaking his head.

"Whatever are wars coming to?"

Percy's posting gave him the opportunity of getting home quite often. It was convenient also for trips to London to see Sylvia and visit old haunts and acquaintances.

The war had settled to a pace of acceptable excitement in the capital now that the bombing had been checked. American servicemen took up residence in their thousands, bringing glamour and romance to an atmosphere of drabness. Their spectacular uniforms, their music, mannerisms and money, to say nothing of their presence as comrades, boosted the British morale to an assurance of victory.

Most weekends in hundreds of homes identical scenes were enacted. "This is Hank, Lee, Gary, Spike, Chuck," some young starry-eyed girl would be saying as the ex-colonial was introduced to her fanciful mother and justifiably suspicious father.

It became a time of quick maturity and delayed senility, stimulated by the fact that the bewitching period would be the one and only of many lifetimes, and so should be embraced at every opportunity. In the dance-halls to which they thronged, the Americans attracted an ever increasing crowd of females. All were hell-bent on going back to live on the ranch or enjoy the riches of the oil-wells or real estate businesses that they had heard all G.I's were heirs to.

Percy never got upset over the competition, for there were always many more girls in the dance-halls than the Americans could deal with. Further, the versatility of his dancing always secured him partners for both the melodies inside the hall and intimacies outside.

One evening at Brighton's Regent ballroom, he saw Honey Dowset, who, not surprisingly, was in the company of a handsome American air force officer. They looked the most glamourous couple Percy had ever seen as they danced cheek to cheek to the tune of Perfidia, played in the Glen Miller style. She had matured more beautifully than he had ever thought possible, and in his mind she was well out of his reach. Yet he felt her eyes upon him many times during the evening.

Later on she waylaid him as he came out of the cloakroom, and asked with a captivating smile, if he were not the audacious boy she knew years ago. Her inquiry was genuine, for Percy's physique had attained handsome proportions of manhood since they last met and she could have been mistaken. After telling him her boy friend had returned to his base to prepare for an early flying operation the next day, very little was said as they clung to each other during a tango. Percy could hardly believe that he had taken the enviable place of her previous partner. For the remainder of the evening they danced together in mutual fascination for the moment both recognised as being a tailor-made preliminary to a renewed coition.

Over supper in a small restaurant they unfolded their experiences to each other, those, that is, which were favourable to the occasion. Afterwards, they took a taxi to where Honey lived. It was a large three storey house in the Drive. Her mother and father were away at Epsom and her married sister was staying in Bournemouth for a few days.

As they entered, a bull terrier, growling viciously, came bounding at Percy.

Honey called him off and he obeyed.

"He's harmless really, but a good house dog," she explained in an attempt to pacify Percy's momentary fright.

"He belongs to Bo-Bo, and his name's Croc, short for Crocodile."

"'E belongs to who?" Percy asked, screwing his face up curiously.

"'Bo-Bo Johnson, the flyer I was with earlier. Actually he's Beauregard Gifford Johnson of Florida. His father owns umpteen mines and an R.T. factory. R.T. means radio transmitter."

"I'm well aware what it means," interrupted Percy. Wouldn't you think 'e'd have picked a better looking animal than that ugly looking bastard, after all 'e's got good taste in women."

Smiling, and with an arm around each other they went, guided by Honey, into her bedroom and stood either side of the bed to undress. Percy stripped in a flash and turned to grab playfully at Honey's crotch just as she was pulling her dress off over her head. She gave a loud squeal of surprise and excitement which brought the snarling dog rushing in to sink his teeth in Percy's testicles.

Honey screamed and Percy swore but hardly dare move as he gripped the animal by the back of its head to stop it trying to rip away what it had in its mouth.

"What shall I do? What shall I do?" Honey cried frantically as she turned about as if looking for a weapon.

"'Old 'is back legs off the ground so's 'e's got nothing ta grip the floor with," shouted Percy desperately as the sweat ran off him. All the time the dog was trying to take a bigger bite but could not, with his bottom jaw being firmly held. For ten minutes Percy was in the grip of not only the dog, but terror. To him, genitals gave a purpose to living, but they could also prove to be an Achilles heel.

"Twist his balls," he shouted, but Honey could not bear to, and he could not reach them even if he dared let go of the creature's head. All the time vicious growling came from the dog's throat while its eyes glared with savage hatred.

"I don't 'ave to ask why 'e's called Crocodile," joked Percy, "wiv bleedin' fangs like that 'e could 'ardly be called Clarence."

In the struggle to free his back legs from Honey's grasp, Croc fell over, and Percy, with a groan, was forced to go with him to the floor. Putting a knee across the dog's neck he reached out for his jacket, and taking a box of matches from a pocket, he struck one and inserted it in the animal's nostril.

It leapt in the air with such a force that had it not opened its mouth to let out a hideous wail, Percy in that instant would have become lighter by some very important ounces.

"Croc," stood for a moment snuffling, whining, and rubbing his nose with a paw, until Honey grabbed his collar and dragged him from the room.

"You horrible naughty beast, how dare you behave in that way," she said. Percy noticed the lack of conviction in her tone as he sat on the bed examining his male equipment.

When she returned he was dressed and she inquired if he was alright, or was he on his way to a hospital.

"I'll be back in 'alf an hour, be good enough to wait," he said, which was more in the manner of an order than a request.

Feeling a portion of blame for the incident she willingly said she would. There was an element of curiosity too in her passive reply. Outside, Percy waved a taxi down and was taken home. After rummging in the garage for a while he returned to the waiting cab and was driven back to the Drive.

Back inside the house Percy gave Honey a cloth bag and asked her to put it over the dog's head before bringing him back to the bedroom. To allay the suspicion showing in her face he said he just wanted to make it right with the animal and show it that he meant its mistress no harm. Although not totally believing him she felt obliged to comply with his wish.

Returning with the hooded creature, she was asked to undress as far as her petticoat and stockings. Percy meanwhile, after slipping the

noose of a slender wire cable over the animal's head, climbed through the window leading to the garden and secured the end to a downpipe. Stripping off he displayed a healthy erection, the sight of which caused Honey to breathe deeply.

"Doesn't seem to be any the worse for wear," she said.

"That aint wear what that bastard tried to do, that's total war as far as 'e's concerned. What we're about ta do now yer can call wear."

Hardly giving him a glance he snatched the bag from Croc's head and leapt on top of Honey who let out a similar squeal to her previous one. The sound was not necessary to arouse the dog's displeasure. The sight of Percy pouncing on his mistress set him leaping with a snarl in that direction. But both the snarl and the leap were cut short as the creature was jerked to a halt at the end of the wire.

"Well, that works," Percy said, with little doubt that it would. "Now let's see if this does." He thrust his penis into Honey without any of the usual ceremony and began pounding away at her with the fervour of a rapist. Tantilisingly he went through the motions of clawing at her buttocks and made loud groans of pleasure to further incite the dog's fury.

An inkling of Percy's intentions came to Honey and she began to protest. But her thwarted attempts to push him off and take the dog out of danger only added to the overall excitement of both Percy and the animal. Her struggles brought a measure of realism to the scene and Percy was hard put to stay in her. Her unintended contribution to the proceedings sent the dog into a frenzy of renewed charges, of which a couple were above and beyond the designed stress of the cable.

But Percy had faith in the ex hand brake cable except for a moment when the animal decided to try pulling his head free of the noose instead of his endeavours to snap it.

The downpipe however could not stand the incessant pressure and one of Croc's determined charges ripped a small section away. The sound of it cracking caused the blood to drain from Percy's face as he prepared to receive a mauling in the fight for his life.

Thinking itself free the dog gave a blood-curdling wail as it shot towards its hated tormentor. But its charge was only extended by some three feet. The window dropped down and trapped the pipe attached to the wire, causing Croc to somersault with the force of the jerk. Encouraged by his partial success he made an all out effort to close the gap between himself and the pair whose organ scent incensed him with animal desire and ferocity. He was so close they could have reached out and touched him as he strained every fibre to effect another extension of his leash. "If 'e breaks free it's a toss up whether 'e tears my throat out or plants 'imself in you," Percy said.

Feeling that the episode was past the point of no return, and considering the damage to the dog to be irreversible, Honey stopped complaining and settled down to enjoy the intimacy. Locking her silk clad legs around Percy's waist they rocked methodically together oblivious of the animal throttling itself on the cable at their side.

"This is the way I've always remembered you," she sighed. "Bo-Bo's hopeless, it takes him ages to get the horn then as soon as he's got it in he turns into a Charley-Come-Quick and leaves me flat. Oh, God, the difference between him and you is astronomical."

After a climax that could not have been surpassed anywhere in the world, they noticed by Croc's silence that he was dead.

"Was that really necessary?" she asked quietly as Percy withdrew from her with a great deal more gentleness than when he mounted.

He took a cigarette from his jacket, lit it and lay back on the bed.

"Got a great respect for balls, I 'ave, especially mine. "There's been squaddies with terrible wounds that yer think would 'ave seen 'em off this earth. Arms an' legs off, an' guts 'angin' out. Or 'alf their faces blown away. But soon as the field surgeon told 'em their old John Thomas an' their goolies were intact, they found summink ta live for. An' I've known poor sods who've only lost their tackle but died for no other reason than that life would have been unbearably monotonous without it."

"Really? that's unbelievable, " said Honey.

"'Ark at 'oo's talkin'. 'Ow would you feel if your fanny was permanently sewn up?" asked Percy.

"Need you ask?" she replied.

"There you are then, if a bloke's got 'is pecker there's always the chance some bird'll come along an' take an interest, but wivout it the ugliest ol' cow in the world won't come near 'im," reasoned Percy. "An' 'e feels useless to everyone includin' 'imself. 'E can't 'ave kids so 'e's shackled to a life of loneliness."

"Oh! It's terrible, don't go on," begged Honey with a hint of sarcasm.

"One thing more," he said. "I 'ad a bastard exactly the same as that go for me when I was a kid, an' now I feel I've got even."

"Bo-Bo's going to be furious, Croc was a sort of mascot to him," she said.

"So are my dumplin's to me," Percy said.

"He always carries his picture when he goes on ops," Honey went on.

"I takes grenades, guns an' a knife when I go playin' silly buggers, they do more damage," he taunted.

"God, he will be angry. If he ever finds out what happened I'd hate to think what he'll do," she said anxiously.

"If 'e fights anything like 'e fucks I've got nothin' ta

worry about," said Percy, getting off the bed. "Where's the bathroom?"

"The door opposite," Honey said curtly.

Percy stopped and looked down at the dog.

"You nearly done what 'alf the German army never could. Better for you if you'd gone for me throat."

TEN
Some Things Take Priority

Percy was out on the range giving instructions, amidst the mock-up of ruined buildings, on the art of 'Booby trapping' when he was summoned to the telephone.

In the sergeants' Mess where he took the call he heard that Sylvia had been assaulted and was in hospital. With a forty-eight hour compassionate pass in his pocket he went to visit her at London's Middlesex Hospital, where Lucy and Frank were already at her bedside.

Percy was furious at the sight of her bruised and battered face. He learned that her attacker had continued to hit her long after her resistance had been overcome. Her main injury however, was brought about by the miscarriage of a four month pregnancy.

Not that he pressed for the information, but he was told by the ward sister that the child would have been a boy. Memories of Cathy and the action she took that deprived him of what would have been a most welcome young relative came vividly to Percy's mind. He began to wonder if fate decreed otherwise than that he should become an uncle or father. He left the hospital with rage and sadness tearing at his heart and barely spoke a word to Frank and his mother on their way back to Sylvia's home. He looked for the reward in Frank's face for all the jeopardy he still submitted himself to daily, but saw only bewilderment and despondency.

Sylvia's description of her attacker was that he was a giant of a man who smelt of beer and rotting meats which conjured up visions in Percy's imagination of a creature devouring his victims as he raped them. Lucy told her son he should leave the matter of catching the man to the police when he made it known he intended absenting himself to search for him. He told her the police were fully occupied with those who they considered were impeding the war effort. He spurned also his brother-in-law's offer to assist him.

This is gonna be old hat ta me, Frank," he said, putting an arm around his shoulders, "and I wouldn't let you soil yer hands on the bastard."

The stature of the man not being all that commmon, Percy located him in two days. After dozens of enquiries the landlord of a pub in Kings Cross pointed the way.

"Sounds like Tiny Mafyews to me, son," the publican told Percy. "What? Like 'is oats? 'E'd shag a dead dog till it barked would Tiny." He went on, "You'll find 'im up the slaughterhouse in Caledonian Road. Only watch yerself mate, 'e's partial to young fellas as well," he chuckled.

As he walked through the slaughterhouse the stench reminded him of Crete and the bodies that were left unburied and so putrified progressively with each day. After being directed by two or three men, Percy saw his quarry.

Even from a distance the man looked massive and indestructible as Percy sauntered towards him. The description was correct, for a giant he undoubtedly was. It was never Percy's intention to go charging in on sight and kick and punch the living daylights out of him. The punishment had to be far more sophisticated than that. Besides it would have needed a kick from a mule to penetrate the thick rubber apron Tiny wore as he worked with gusto inside the killing enclosure.

Percy was horrified by the way cattle were put to death, for like countless thousands of other people he never gave a thought to the unpleasantness connected to the Sunday joint. He saw a cow chained by the feet pulled to the ground where it lay writhing as blood gushed from its severed jugular. Another was placed into a metal cylinder where clamps then held it firm as it was turned upside down, placing it's head in a position where it too could have its throat cut. Meanwhile, another was despatched by what was known as a humane killer. An implement not unlike an electric drill, that by a cartridge shot a spike into the animal's skull, where a stick was then inserted to destroy the brain of the twitching beast.

Such was the haste to fulfil the quota, some of the creatures were being hoisted by hooks and partially skinned and disembowelled before they were dead. A sight equally saddening to Percy was that of the gallons of life-giving milk that swam around the floor with the blood and urine of the poor beasts. Noting Percy's obvious interest, Tiny called to him.

"Fascinatin', wouldn't yer say ?" he said sardonically.

"Er, what?" said Percy, taken by surprise.

"The power o' life and deaf, cock. Fascinatin' I sez," Tiny went on. Percy made no comment and Tiny looked at him with a mild suspicion. His presence made the big man ill at ease and prompted him to put on a demonstration as a form of sabre rattling.

"Sometimes I gives 'em a fightin' chance," he said, pushing aside a colleague who was about to chain another of the condemned to the wall. "I lets some of 'em fink they're bulls in the arena."

He locked one of his huge arms around the neck of the cow that had been momentarily reprieved. For a while the animal charged around tossing its head and bellowing in an attempt to shake off the stranglehold on its neck. Then, to heighten the tenseness of the scene, Tiny began growling loudly as he increased the pressure on the creature's windpipe, causing its bellows to become barely audible wheezes. Soon, through lack of air and the weight of the abnormal man bearing on its neck, the animal just stood and allowed itself to be strangled. Tiny still held his grip even as the beast fell lifeless to the floor. Had he brought his Luger along Percy would have shot him as he partially lay across his victim, for quite logically he could identify what he had just witnessed with the attack on Sylvia. Undoubtedly, Tiny had established himself as a dangerous psychopath, and Percy went away to arrange for his downfall.

As the result of a telephone call, Percy and a fellow sergeant had a discussion in the cafeteria on Victoria Station. Before he departed on a train back to Kent, he passed Percy a grenade and asked for reassurance that neither by accident or intent would there be a killing. Two days later the sergeant, accompanied by another six commandos, arrived back in London in a Humber staff car. That evening after Tiny had had one of the best drinking sessions in his life he was abducted by the very soldiers he had found so generous and companionable earlier on.

Believing at first that he was being taken to an all night drinking party, he climbed clumsily but willingly into the back of the Humber. But after a short stop in Camden Town where

Sylvia was brought out to make a positive identification, he became a problem even with a service revolver pressed against each ear. As drunk as he was he knew they would not shoot him and he said as much to that effect.

"Shoot me at this range and you'll shoot yer fuckin' selves," he said to the men brandishing the guns on either side of him.

"This suit yer better?" said Percy, placing an open razor so firmly against Tiny's throat that a swallow would have taken a slice from his Adam's apple.

"That's it, you sit still or you'll be breathin' through a fuckin' gash in yer throat instead of yer nose, and you'll know how those poor fuckers feel that you take such a delight in slaughterin'".

Hampstead Heath was the destination and Percy directed the route as Tiny's arms were bound to his sides.

"Don't stand on ceremony by parking at the kerb, drive straight in an' keep goin' till yer find a reasonable thicket," Percy advised.

After a couple of minutes of bumps and jolts they came to a halt, and Tiny, after being tied above the knees to restrict any violent moves, was dragged out of the car and thrown to the ground. Each of his arms was released separately, then pinioned down with barrage balloon stakes. His legs were treated likewise. When he had been gagged and lay spreadeagled looking every bit like Gulliver, Percy tore open the man's flies and laid bare his genitals.

By torchlight he connected wire and fishing hooks, none too gently, to Tiny's testicles, then, while the others lit cigarettes and sat around, he quickly put together a large box kite that he had brought along in a holdall.

Soon the kite was soaring up into the darkness above the trees. When Percy was satisfied with its flight he tethered it to the trace attached to Tiny and inserted in sequence the grenade given to him by his colleague two days before.

Tiny's eyes bulged at the sight of the grenade. He made muffled sounds and rolled his head from side to side in an attempt to speak. His face was bathed in sweat as he brought such pressure to bear on the hoops and stakes holding him that Percy felt the ground tremble. Indeed, he would not have been surprised to see Tiny rise in the air with a ton or so of heath fixed to his back.

"Let's evacuate then, lads." Percy held the tension of the line from the pin of the grenade while his friends got back into the car. He then spoke to Tiny in such a sympathetic and pacifying tone it could have been directed to a wounded comrade on the battlefield.

"There, there, don't you fret yerself nowt fella, yer worries will soon be over. Yer know that 'ampton's givin' yer more trouble than a rotten tooth. Never mind, we'll soon yank it free for yer." So saying he joined the others in the car.

On the way back to Sylvia's place where supper was awaiting them, the sergeant, somewhat agitated, spoke to Percy. "I thought I had yer word that it wouldn't be a killing," he said with stifled anger.

"Nor will it," answered Percy, calmly.

"So blowin' 'im in 'alf an' sendin' 'is cobblers 'igh enough to bring down a barrage balloon won't kill 'im?" said the sergeant, flabbergasted. "Since when?"

Reaching in his pocket Percy brought out a paper bag and tipped the explosive and detonator from the grenade into the hand of the sergeant.

"Yer better pop this back in the armoury and 'ope they don't miss the bit that goes round the outside," said Percy drily.

Back on the heath the night was becoming the terror of Tiny Mathews life. All he could do was stare up at the distant blob that was instrumental to his excrutiation. What sort of sophisticated kite was that? he wondered, that barely deviated a yard in any direction. Yet it strained to go forward with each fresh surge of the wind. The high gusts seemed endless, and at any moment Tiny expected his lot to be torn from him. He could not understand how the force that had already stretched his flesh some three inches or so, did not snap the line. But it was fishing line with a forty pound breaking strain, so any chance of a reprieve was only possible by a lull in the wind. As the grenade had not exploded he assumed it had been placed to go off when his flesh was ripped away and so finish him off.

For a few moments he thought his prayers had been answered when the line slackened and the kite came topsy turvy towards him like a crippled pheasant. But the wind had not abated it had merely changed direction, and before the contraption came to earth it was plucked hungrily by a renewed blast and whisked off to a different course. As it became checked by the line Tiny felt himself ripped by the jolt, and the kite's new position drew his penis straight up in front of him. The slight weaving and bobbing made it look like a mute Buddhist at prayer. Tiny closed his eyes, for it could only be a matter of time before his prize possession became detached from him and was trailed across the heath by the escaping kite.

The new position was anything but stable for the aeronautics of the kite, and it came down on the far side of a line of trees. The first indication came to Tiny, not by the relief from his now feelingless member, but by the line falling across his face. By a mixture of fatigue, alcohol, and alleviation of fear, he fell asleep, consoled with thoughts of vengeance.

Just after seven a.m., while Tiny was still snoring as blissfully as if he were in his bed, a worker from an aircraft factory was taking a short cut across the heath after finishing the night shift. Spotting the kite hanging within easy reach from a tree and knowing how delighted his young son would be with it, he reached up and began tugging it free.

Thinking it to be caught in the foliage on the other side of the trees, the man tugged until the line cut into his hands. When at last his efforts were rewarded and he gathered it all in, he could hardly believe what he saw dangling from the end.

After Tiny's injuries had been treated he was tranquillized enough to give the police a rational statement. As the truth would have brought to light at least one of the half a dozen cases of rape he had committed, he told them the I.R.A were responsible.

"I bin shoutin' me mouf off abart them disloyal bastards yer see," he explained. "Even beat a few of the fuckers up. An' then 'fore I knows what's 'appenin, they jumped me an' done that."

ELEVEN
Now Once More Into The Breach, Etc....

Percy first became acquainted with Harry Staglan when he was journeying to the West country where he had been transferred to a new regiment. When Harry boarded the train at Dorchester his wife came along to see him off and Percy heard every word of the farewell conversation that for the remainder of the war stamped Harry as Hubby.

"Now don't forget to write, Hubby, as soon as you get to your posting. 'An' do keep your feet dry Hubby. Oh Hubby, whose going to wake me when I have a nightmare? I am going to miss you so, Hubby. Oh Hubby, do look after yourself. I do wish you hadn't got to go, Hubby. Remember, I love you, Hubby."

Aware that Percy had heard it all, Harry looked decidedly embarrassed as he took a seat opposite him.

"What a treasure," said Percy sincerely, and with a smile that put Harry at his ease as he modestly agreed.

Both were bound for the Royal Tank Regiment at Salisbury Plain, where they were destined to be welded in comraderie to see the war to its conclusion. Like Percy, Harry was a survivor of a rout, for he had come through the ordeal of Dunkirk.

Percy had not particularly volunteered for tanks.

Thinking he would be transferred to the Service Corps where he had heard the fiddles were, he had placed his name forward when drivers were asked for. Having little or no knowledge of tanks he was totally unaware of the devastating attention they received from the enemy, but was merely impressed by the armour and the big gun which he humorously considered he should have been issued with originally. And after being subjected to ferocious onslaughts from heavy equipment at Crete, with very little of anything impressive to hit back with, a tank seemed like an avenging haven.

Percy had lost his stripes back in Kent when after an evening of revelling in Sevenoaks, he had a set to with an exceptionally obnoxious Military policeman. He turned out to be none other than one of Percy's childhood bullies, Arthur Potter, who along with two of his fellow despicables received a considerable battering before they overcame their would-be charge at gunpoint.

Percy considered the thirty days he spent in the glasshouse well worth the week the M.P's were in sick bay. He did not mind losing his rank for not being sergeant material, he had found it cumbersome and isolating.

The new regiment bore little resemblance to the previous infantry one, except that the name of Longprong was used so liberally by officers and non-coms alike, it might have been Percy's official name. Indeed, so familiar had he become to answering to it, a nudge would have been required for him to acknowledge his real one.

The tank training was intense but interesting. As soon as he had grasped the basic fundamentals he could hardly wait to let in the clutch of the big V8 engine and hear the crack of the massive seventy-five millimetre belching a shell at a

German emplacement or tank.

Each of the five man crew was trained as both gunner and driver so as to keep the vehicle functional to the last trooper. "Hubby" became the official gunner of the seventy-five, while Percy was the tank driver. Next to him on the front machine gun was a fellow Brightonian, Johnny Morton, who had rubbed shoulders with Percy in the dance halls many times, and shared the benevolence of the same damsels on different occasions. He was good natured and had a mischievous twinkle in his eye that was tailor made for his sense of humour. Like Percy he was hell bent on survival to return to the bewitching magic of the dance halls and all they entailed. He was an ideal comrade. Billy Perkins, nicknamed "Diesel", was the gun loader for "Hubby", and Corporal Neville Bentley was tank commander and wireless

Adding to the tank's specification a small hole an inch in diameter was cut, at Percy's insistence, in the floor immediately below the front machine gun. The modification was without official permission and brought feigned protest from the rest of the crew, except Johnny Morton, who were all puzzled as to its purpose. They made mild complaints that all sorts of small creatures would invade their steel monster, particularly snakes and scorpions should they be sent out East.

They were not kept in suspense for long as the hole was simply a means of connecting a thin cable to the machine gun trigger to enable its manipulation from beneath the tank.

"Add to its capabilities," Percy announced to the others. "There might be times when it would be fatal to go climbin' in the top."

The idea seemed logical and the others never argued with it. Nor was there any protest at the name of The Rattler being given to their iron charger.

When the rigours of training were over, the exactness of repeated practice was applied to the squadron, but with more time for relaxation. During these periods Percy busied himself in one of the workshops designing by forge and anvil, trial and error, a metal testicle protector. Every day for a week he was trying out the contraption while on duty, then making the necessary adjustments to it in the early evening. No-one else knew of his invention but many of his acquaintances were puzzled by the somewhat awkward gait with which he walked before he perfected it. The appliance gave him an immense sense of security and he felt he could drive into Hell and back with impunity.

Soon it seemed as if they were en route for this destination as they clanked through Italy on the heels of the Germans, who although retreating, were digging their toes in periodically and making every mile taken costly both to the advancing armies and civilians alike.

By the time what remained of the squadron of Shermans had reached the outskirts of Salerno, most of the crews had learned to distinguish the array of weaponry they were coming up against. Spandaus and heavy calibre machine guns gave no more sound than peas dropping in a bucket, and unless an antitank shell hit a track or the fuel tank they were impregnable to all except the dreaded, versatile eighty-eights and Tigers.

When at the cost of three tanks and their crews they had overrun their first enemy stronghold, the sight of the captured eighty-eight's huge shells almost sent Percy and his comrades running for the German latrines.

Rumours circulated that it was better to be hit at close range by such a weapon for then the missile would speed its way out of the tank a split second after it penetrated. Otherwise, at a distance it would enter, whizz round and take everyone's head off.

Johnny Morton voiced the opinion held by the rest of the crew in that the daft bastard who put that story about must have thought the eighty-eights fired solid cannon balls instead of impact explosives.

The Germans used the ploy of luring tanks to what seemed an easy target, then these devastating weapons would open up on the flanks and take a terrible toll. Each day the tank commanders would draw lots to determine who would lead the column, and as yet Percy had been lucky enough to take the perimiter where they took many an opportunity to nail the big guns before they could traverse round to line up a shot at the Rattler.

As valuable as the capture of such guns was at first thought to be they still served one more purpose for the Germans. In anticipation that such a formidable weapon might fall into enemy hands and so be turned against them, a booby trap in the form of an automatic barrel block slid irretrievably into place unless it was periodically locked back. Consequently, the first shell fired by its captors exploded in the barrel, killing everyone in the immediate vicinity.

After many abortive attempts to take a German crew alive, two were captured and tied to the gun while preparations were made to fire it from a safe distance. Only then was it learned that the regimental emblem on the side of the barrel was the key to the mystery. Hinged at one end, it had to be lifted and turned every hour and was the foremost and most rigorous instruction connected to the weapon's maintenance while in action. When in transit or while the crew rested, a special ram kept the barrel clear.

Through having to run from two outgunning Tiger tanks, Corporal Bently had not been able to lock on to the new radio frequency given out daily, and so they were lost and without contact with the rest of the column. They halted at the top of a ridge and studied, through binoculars, the villa nestling in the valley below. Then with all guns at the ready they tore down the slope at a speed that caused one of the tracks to slip a cog and jam. As they slid round it was all Percy could do to keep the vehicle from turning over, which, after a brief period of taking stock of their surroundings, brought congratulations from the rest of the crew on his handling of the situation.

After manoeuvring the Rattler by means of tacking back and forth on the functioning track to more or less level ground at the foot of the slope, they hurried cautiously towards the wall surrounding the estate. Each carried a captured German machine pistol which were now as commonplace among the Allied tank crews as if they were WD issues. Keeping close to the pillars they slipped through the ornately sculptured archway and ducked behind the well kept evergreens that bordered the driveway.

"This place hasn't been evacuated long," said Hubby as they surveyed the neat layout of gardens.

"If at all," chipped in Morton as he tried to take in every direction at once through the binoculars.

"I smell Jerries," said Diesel with a degree of nervousness.

"You've got them on the brain, they'd have smashed this place up just for the hell of it if they were around," said the corporal.

"Yeah, you even thought you smelled 'em back on the

plain when we were training," went on Hubby.

"I was right though, weren't I?" claimed Diesel, eagerly. "'Member when we had to pull up and let that convoy go by? What was in them trucks then, eh? Jerry prisoners."

"That's right, you were on the mark there Diesel, mate, but I only hope they're a bit further away and not so many of 'em this time", said Percy.

Diesel's intuition, already proved reliable once, put everyone on edge. It was bad enough that they were cut off from brigade and had to leave the haven of their Sherman without the threat of Germans being close at hand as well. With the exception of Percy and Hubby, both of whom were more or less veterans on infantry capers, the rest of the crew felt an element of nakedness outside the tank.

Without undue stealth, after deciding to split into two groups and meet at the back of the villa, each party scurried away in their designated direction. Hubby led Diesel and the corporal around the East side while Johnny Morton and Percy took the West. As they made their way past the proud colonnades bolstering the building's frontage, no one saw the figure hiding behind them.

Each side of the house had identical garden layouts of terraced lawns and flora edged by patiently shaped, exotic shrubbery, and Johnny remarked on what an unusually tranquil place it was to have to anticipate danger.

"That's war for yer. Danger's a commodity not a location especially," answered Percy. "It all depends on whether anyone's around to shower you with it."

Even with such wisdom it was impossible not to be pacified by the beauty of the place and try as did both parties reconnoitring each side of the house, to remain fully alert to the possible dangers, they were wide open to any ambush that might have been laid. Nevertheless they rejoined without incident at the rear of the villa where they came upon what could only be described as a miniature colosseum, with its main feature being a vast pool that was on closer inspections cluttered with the putrid carcases of lion and shark.

After the civilized splendour of the gardens it was something of a shock to come upon not only an arena, but one where such ancient cruelties were so recently practised. Being totally out of character the area was a blight on the whole estate and revived the air of menace to the seeming innocence of the surroundings.

A colloquy of speculation brought forth theories that prisoners were thrown in and wagers made on whether the sharks would beat the lions to the meal, or that it had been used for interrogations by the Gestapo.

The excitement subsided leaving everyone baffled over the lion-shark remains, and attentions were turned towards the villa, for second to their survival by winkling out any hostility, and despite the orders that Italians were now to be treated as allies, the crew of the Rattler had booty in mind.

In a seeming attempt to isolate the paganized area, a high stone wall with an unimpressive gate separated it from the rear of the house, and between were dotted half a dozen or more small outbuildings that no doubt held maintenance equipment and perhaps a generator for the dwelling.

Quite obviously as they had not run up against any hostility in the grounds; the only place left that could harbour a threat was the villa, and they approached it with every caution. In search of snipers, eyes darted alternately between windows and outhouses, but no shots or grenades were forthcoming.

Lying horizontal to the building and parallel to the pathway leading to the porched doorway was a wire mesh enclosure. It drew very little interest until they passed a covered section that was at the end farthest away from the house, then they came in view of the three Dobermanns that threw themselves at the stout wire in a terrifying rage.

Two exclamations of "Christ!" and one each of "Bloody Hell!", "Sod me!" and "Well, I'll be buggered!" came from the startled crew as they ducked for cover back behind the kennel and strained their eyes to the limit of the now fading daylight for the sight of a movement at the windows that the commotion might have attracted.

After some two minutes when no volley of shots or mortars came their way, they crept once again past the kennelled section to where the dogs had returned.

Once more there was a crescendo of blood-curdling noises from the animals as the trespassers came into their view.

As their presence had been heralded, Percy saw nothing untoward in shooting the dogs, which apart from his abhorrence of their obvious savagery was distracting to the concentration needed for survival.

Hubby was nearest the enclosure and Percy, pulling the loading catch back on his machine pistol, told him to move out of the way. Hubby, however, being somewhat of an animal lover and lacking the unpleasant and terrifying experiences suffered by Percy, pleaded for their lives. "It's not their fault, it's only what man's made 'em, we'll be away from their sight in a minute and they'll calm down," he said.

Respecting Hubby's wishes before his own, Percy gave way. After all, the wire mesh did encircle the enclosure and apart from a slight distraction they posed no threat. On the contrary their commotion had proved that no Germans were around or the Rattler's complement would have been annihilated where they stood.

As they passed along the enclosure the vicious animals kept pace with them until they came to the end where upon standing on a prepared spot a secret catch sprung open a gap in the wire, and with exalted wails the creatures leapt upon Hubby.

Their attack upon him was hideous, fangs ripped furrows in his forehead, shoulder and leg sinultaneously, as the training of the three Dobermans passed into practice. Being far keener on their destruction than the rest, Percy was more alert to their behaviour and had riddled all three before they could take second bites.

Just as the shots had stopped echoing amongst the buildings, a tall distinguished looking Italian came running from the doorway of the house.

His distress was obvious as he wrung his hands and cried "Mama mia", over and over.

Hubby looked as if he were bleeding from every pore as Percy dragged the Dobermans off him and threw them aside. Fortunately most of the blood was theirs, and although Hubby was very distraught, his jugular vein was intact and he was in no danger of bleeding to death even though he was open to infection. Looking down at him trembling with shock, Percy thought what a turmoil his young wife would be in if she could see him now.

He was jogged from his unpleasant day dream by a hard shove on the shoulder from the newcomer whose priorities of the situation were to disregard the injured Hubby and drop sobbing to his knees beside the lifeless dogs.

"Your government will hear of this outrage," he cried.

"We have been promised immunity and I will see that this terrible indignity to my status is brought to the attention of your highest superiors. You will give me your names, numbers and rank. I've watched you ever since your tank came down the hill. You are meant to be our liberators, not our killers." He turned his attention once more to the dogs.

"Ah! my poor Bella, Tony and dear Mitsi, " he wailed as he rocked back and forth over them.

Anger mounted in Percy and walking sharply to the Italian he booted him across the dogs and drew back the firing lever on his pistol. Expecting instant death the man cried out and covered his face with his hands.

"You blustering greasy bastard, we 'aven't come all this fuckin' way through eighty-eights and diarrohea to become snacks for your bleeding mongrels," spat Percy.

"That's enough, Longprong," ordered the corporal.

"Is it," shouted Percy, giving the man another kick. "You 'eard what 'e said, he watched us all the way in. 'E could 'ave stopped all this. Look at Hubby."

"You know our orders are to give them every protection," went on the corporal.

"Yeah ! and that should work both ways, but 'e's only interested one way.

"'E's a bloody sadist, don't forget the sharks and other bits back there. 'An now 'e was goin' to gloat, watchin' us get mauled by his hounds," Percy shouted, as he fired a few more rounds into the already lifeless dogs. "'ow many prisoners did yer throw in the shark pit down there eh? Come on, tell us, 'ow many yer bloody turncoat."

"None, none, I swear it," he shrieked. I lost a son to lions when he fought in the Abyssinian war. And then my younger son was killed by a shark off the coast of Sidi Barrani, and so I have an insatiable hatred of the creatures, that is why I have built the arena, to watch these brutish cowards torment each other. But men, no, I swear to you," he wailed pleadingly.

Percy stooped down beside him. "Do yer think your sons looked anything like our mate there?" he said quietly, and jerking his head towards the bloodstained Hubby. The man looked away guiltily.

"And you could 'ave prevented that couldn't yer? You're a bloody fine ally aren't yer?"

Percy's anger cooled slightly through both the man's diminished dignity, and his explanation concernng the animal carcases. Pulling the frightened man roughly to his feet he spoke to him as if he were a waiter with a large capacity for familiarity.

"Now listen, Spaghetti George, first we want to clean up our mate and patch 'im up with a bit of first aid, then while we are bathing, you can get some food ready for us an' don't forget a few bottles of wine from the cellar."

Percy then changed his tone to a confidential manner. "And don't insult our intelligence by telling us you're short of food and bevvy, 'cause you're the sort 'ood 'ave nicked the grub from the disciples at the Last Supper."

In an attempt to assert the authority of his stripe and protect the respect due to the Italian's position, Corporal Bently tried to discipline Percy.

"Leave him alone, that's an order," he shouted. "You know we are instructed to treat them as allies now."

"I don't want 'im as a bloody ally, not even when I'm safely back in England. I'm treating 'im as a bloody enemy an' keeping my eye on 'im, an' you better do the same," warned Percy.

"It's a government order," yelled the corporal.

"Would that be the same goverment that told my old man he'd fought the war to end all wars?" Percy asked, pushing the Italian towards the doorway of the house. "They're back there in safety, but we've got to play it by ear."

Morton and Diesel helped Hubby to his feet and followed Percy and his captive to the doorway but all were confronted by corporal Bently who ran before them and brandished his gun. "No one's going in and you're going to let him go," he ordered, pulling the lever back on his pistol.

Morton sprang to one side and did likewise with his weapon, but it was not aimed at Percy but at the corporal. Percy also made his gun ready for firing.

"'Ark at us, we sound like a lot of tarts from the typing pool pushing back the carriages on our typewriters," Percy said.

"You joke as much as you want, but I mean what I say," said the corporal.

"You won't put that slimy bastard before our mate there and live to talk about it," said Morton.

"'E's right an' all, corporal. This Wop 'ere was gorging himself silly while the likes of you and me was wallowing in shit, cabbage stalks an' corn beef scraps. Don't try an' win their favour, 'cause the ponces 'll never accept yer."

"Do you think that's all things boil down to? Winnin' favours," demanded the corporal.

"'Course it is yer bloody idiot, yer don't think the ruling classes got there by brains do yer? Some of 'em can't even tuck their cocks away unless it's up some frightened little chambermaid's fanny. You'll go out an' fight some foreigner once in a lifetime an' the rest of your natural you'll be fighting the same sort of bastard as him for a livin' back 'ome. Now make yer choice which side yer gonna die for," said Percy impatiently. "You're playin' the game they always set for us.

Divide and conquer," he added in an attempt to disarm the explosive situation. "Survival's the trick, corporal, at any time of life," he said, giving a reassuring wink.

Plainly, Percy's words struck home, for to everyone's relief, the corporal lowered his gun, turned casually around, then kicked the door open, upon which act everyone hurried inside.

In keeping with the splendour of the outside, the interior was lavish in rococo furniture and ornamentation. Busts and small statues stood in recesses all over the house, while the walls were richly adorned with tapestry and paintings. As the crew relaxed in the large kitchen over a stew of some unidentifiable meat heavily seasoned with garlic, Hubby, with neatly bandaged forehead, thanked Percy for his alertness in saving him from a far greater mauling. The reply was that if he had let the dogs be shot sooner, he would not have suffered what he had.

Count Celano, as was the Italian's title, was more than liberal with some very fine old port and magnums of champagne which he said he had been keeping for just such an occasion. Under the circumstances his generosity was highly suspect and Percy grabbed a few unopened bottles which he said would refresh them later when they resumed their advance. To the mild complaints of the others he gave good reason for his action.

"'Ow would yer like to come to in the morning all nicely trussed up with a few revengeful Germans standing over yer, eh?" he asked quietly.

"Tony here is not like that," defended Hubby. "He knows when he's beat."

"'E's always been beat right from the start, but it don't stop 'im from jumpin' which ever way he thinks victory's going. If enough Germans come by 'e'll side with them," said Percy.

"And shut your face for once, Hubby, I'm getting a bit sick of your bad judgments," he added angrily. "Yer should know better, what does it bleedin' well take to keep you on yer toes."

Feeling Percy's anger to be justified, Hubby said no more, and after the duty watches had been allotted, and Percy had shackled the Count to the arm of a heavy chair with handcuffs that he had taken from a dead German and had no key for, they settled down for the night, each in a different part of the house. Having the dawn watch, Percy was awakened by Diesel at six a.m. which by the state of things was a sensible hour to rise, duty or not. He had spent the night in an alcove within earshot of any attempts of the Count to break free from his fetters. Not being in the habit of consciousness at that hour the captive still snored heavily in the chair while Percy warmed up left-over coffee on the oil stove.

In due course while patrolling the front of the house, he was startled by a figure waving him back to cover from the distant gate. Grabbing at his binoculars for a clearer view he could see no one, yet when he looked again with the naked eye there stood the man still frantically waving and crying a warning that was soundless. As if magnetically drawn he broke into a trot and with shivers running up his spine he went through the archway expecting to see,the figure behind one side or another of the walls, but was not overwhelmingly surprised when he did not.

Even at a distance he recognised the face as being the same as the youth who pulled the Potter boys from him, saved him from drowning in the harbour, and was spying on him and Cathy when they were about to make love under the cliffs. Realising what it was that he had been seeing occasionally over the years he looked back at the house, wondering what the others would think if he told them.

A series of bangs brought his attention to the far end of the valley. They were not the sounds of a weapon being discharged but the back-firing of a Tiger coming down the far slope, for its engine was prone to this when pressure was put on to it before it was properly warmed.

Percy shuddered at the thought of the Panzer being parked only a mile away while he and most of the others slept soundly. Obviously it had tracked them until dark and then given up until the following day.

As the enemy passed out of sight momentarily behind a clump of trees Percy raced hell for leather to the Rattler and began frantically trying to line up the gun in their direction, but because of the awkward angle the tank lay at on the hill he could not elevate the barrel sufficiently. Popping out of the hatch he hurriedly untied a dustbin lid from the rear. Taking it back inside he poured a mixture of oil and petrol into its hollow from an old Tizer bottle, set fire to it and held it up to the opening.

To the approaching Tiger's crew it looked for all the world like a Sherman ablaze, yet they were puzzled how it had come about as they had heard no sounds of battle. As they came closer Percy wondered whether they would put a couple of practice shots into him but mercifully they were low on ammunition and would only fire out of simple necessity.

Coming to a halt a mere twenty yards or so from the Rattler two Germans came out to investigate. One placed a hand on the side of the Sherman and thought it strange that he could feel no heat, and told his comrade so. Walking all the way round they saw evidence in plenty of the tank's prowess and involvement in battle, but none of a blow that would have caused it to catch fire. Percy became aware of someone climbing onto the tank and was somewhat mystified at the lack of the spirit of self preservation being exercised. The impracticability of approaching any burning vehicle was bad enough but regulations of tank forces of every country strictly forbade approach to burning tanks for any reason whatsoever, and yet here was a soldier of the best trained army in the world climbing onto one.

Catching a glimpse of the German directly outside the hatch, Percy hurled the blazing contents of the dustbin lid over the man's head causing him to throw himself screaming off the side of the Rattler. In the action some of the burning fluid dropped onto Percy, consequently his right sleeve and leg of his trousers were on fire. Nevertheless he still took time to peer through the periscope to see how the enemy tank was reacting, and saw that it had stopped right in line with the Rattler's gun. Without hesitation, he fired, blowing the-side of the track and its cover into a twisted mass. Immediately the Tiger's huge gun tried to traverse in Percy's direction but jammed on the wreckage before it came anywhere close.

Scrambling out of the hatch Percy leapt upon the German who was preoccupied in putting a coat over his comrade's head to extinguish the flames. As they rolled over and over Percy's flames were put out also, and it was not long before he was getting the better of his adversary who had nowhere near the experience of rough housing he had. Suddenly he was struck on the side of the head and the barrel of a Luger was pressed against his temple as a voice in broken English said, "Get up Englander."

As he rose, somewhat dazed, to his feet, the newcomer slammed his foot in a death dealing blow at Percy's crotch, sending him reeling under the front of the Sherman. The

German he had fought got to his feet and was about to shoot him with his machine pistol but was stopped by Percy's assailant, who he guessed was the Tiger's commander.

"No, Horst, as he likes to fight with fire so much, he shall die by it. Fetch the flame thrower," he ordered, to which Horst ran over to the immobilised Tiger and gathered the weapon from one of its compartments.

As the officer stood ready to burn him to a cinder Percy pulled the cable hanging beneath the Rattler and unleashed another of its surprises. The Beza machine gun jerked into action exploding the flame thrower and piercing the commander and Horst with the same bullets. The fourth member of the Tiger's crew however came at Percy from an angle that the Beza could not cover and just as he thought he was about to run out of luck the German fell dead with shots from Hubby's machine pistol as he came racing through the archway followed by the others.

The dying officer's face wore a look of sheer amazement at the sight of Percy approaching him on foot after the kick he had received.

Made of iron we are, mate," said Percy as reading his thoughts he crouched down beside the German. "Come up with a few tricks an' all we can when we're up against it. Bloody devious lot we are."

As he stood up and undid the front of his trousers the commander thought he was about to be urinated upon but Percy merely displayed with pride the steel testicle protector.

"'Ow about that then, Fritz," he said, tapping the appliance with his knuckles. "Better bit of metal than that fucking ol' junk there," he said, nodding towards the Tiger. "'Ave ta keep me bollocks well greased though in case they turns rusty." He began buttoning up his trousers in case, as he put it, someone pinched his copyright. On doing up his belt and looking down at the German, he realised that his last joke had fallen upon deaf ears, for although smiling, the man was dead.

"I 'ope I can go out with a smile on my face too, mate, when my time's up," Percy said quietly.

No one had given a thought to the German who had been burned until a shot rang out and he was discovered with a Luger in his hand and a bullet hole in his head.

Diesel began running to everyone reminding them of his super awareness to the presence of Germans.

"Didn't I say I could smell 'em eh? Go on admit it, didn't I?"

Now at a peak of nausea over his mounting disgust for the slaughter, Percy told him in no uncertain terms to shut up. And when the question of the Rattler's repair came up he suggested they left it as it was and sat out the rest of the war as unpaying guests of the Count.

Needing little reminding of the perils they had come through virtually unscathed, when they had seen so many of their compatriots and many hundreds of the enemy crippled or killed, they all agreed that it would be tempting fate to go on.

The Count was freed from the chair by removing the rung he was shackled to, but alas he was destined to wear the manacles for some considerable time until a tool could be obtained that would cut through the specially hardened steel.

Through besting the Tiger, the Rattler's crew became famous for miles around, and they were inundated with food, wine and various other gifts in appreciation of their deliverance by visitors to the scene of the renowned and grossly exaggerated battle. For many months they lived the life of Caesars, indulging in the like of their excesses to the hilt. By and by their lives became a round of boring repetition and lacking in all sense of challenge except that of enduring the nightly revelry which for them had long since lost its magic appeal. The war had been over for some weeks and they longed to be back in England with their families and friends, who by now must have been notified of their disappearance or death.

In a week of working fervidly on the Rattler, they had it tuned up to practically mint condition, then after draining what remained of the once proud Tiger's fuel, which to each resembled drinking the blood of a vanquished enemy, they took their departure amongst a multitude of grateful well wishers.

For the remainder of the journey to the coast they were kept well supplied with food and fuel by the Americans who had taken up the 'luxury of occupation', in that sector.

Although their intention however foolhardy, was to somehow get the Rattler back to England, they were forced to abandon it at the port of Sorrento. Reporting back to headquarters it was touch and go whether the five would be court-martialled for absenteeism and derelection of duty, but their plausible story of being put out of action by a Panzer and having to hide from their pursuers, was accepted.

The excitement and celebrations of victory were over, but needless to say Lucy's joy at Percy's homecoming was stupendous, for he had been reported missing in action and she had feared the worst. Bad news awaited him however, for Bill had lost a leg through frostbite while on escort duties to Murmansk, and Frank had suffered a complete mental collapse and was now in a psychiatric home, so the family by no means came through the war unscathed.

TWELVE
Never In Heaven

In doing the rounds of the old haunts, Percy found they lacked all similarity to the atmosphere of the war years, for with servicemen being demobbed, there was an anti-climax everywhere, nowhere more so than the dance halls. It became a different age, for there were no fruits of victory to be enjoyed, but only wounds of mourning and austerity to be licked. Slowly the memory of the past punitive years became more tolerable, as over a decade went by without further incident.

Now at the age of thirty-four and after years of being a likely catch both physically and financially to quite a number of young women, many of whom would have dedicated their lives to pleasing him, he took up with, and married, a girl whose attitude to the relationship was non-contributory as far as moral support and initiative were concerned. Her sense of humour was non-existent, consequently her dubious wits were forever keen to find offence at the slightest opportunity. Indeed, Ena was the victim of such an inferiority complex that the remonstrations she applied to cover her failings, both real and imaginary, threw the marriage so far off balance as to make it a far more unhappy state for Percy than legend could ever impart.

Even though she was fourteen years younger her

temperament would not allow her to benefit from Percy's wide experience of life, and her ignorant and independent assessment of priorities, more often than not ended in violent rows. Percy stopped accepting invitations to parties and the like for Ena's possessive nature seethed with incessant jealousy over each and every female who spoke, however briefly, to her husband. In the street things were no different, even a curt "Hello" from a young woman, whether accompanied by a man or not, would denounce Percy of either having had an affair with her, having one going, or having one in mind.

Forever optimistic over life's setbacks he cut himself off from friends and acquaintances in the hope that his dedication to her would be appreciated, but the enmity remained.

Ena was a pretty girl with blonde hair and petite figure, and Percy was greatly saddened that a girl so fortunately endowed could be so ill natured and irrational. At the same time he was angered at the thought of all the crippled youth of her age he had seen who, with every reason for being unpleasant, could still smile even under cruel privation.

Having never experienced any dilution of life's necessities when living with her parents, both of whom were properly attentive to family obligations, survival to Ena was a God-given right that needed little effort to accomplish and she lacked the ability to contribute to its demands.

Lucy, being her exact opposite in temperament was soon aware of her incapability, but could not convey to Percy what he was saddling himself with, and he being amongst the world's worst judges of what constitutes a good wife, had rushed in with all the naivety of a seventeen year old. It seemed a compulsion that he married someone of that age group with whom he had associated in the carefree days before he was put in the army, perhaps in an attempt to relive his youth and eliminate the memories of some of his wartime experiences.

Ena was not a dancer, she had been to one or two of the dance halls on odd occasions, but had none of the devotion that Percy had been smitten with, and what they had in common was too little psychologically for the physical side of the marriage to be of any value. Nevertheless, the alliance bore three children, two girls and a boy, and the degree in the inspiration of each was at the minimum needed for conception. The girls came along first and were drooled over and treasured by Ena and Percy alike. There were two years between them, the older was named Gloria and the younger, Penny. Their son Oswald was born when Penny was six, and although they had wanted another girl they came to love him every bit as dearly as their daughters. While they were small toddlers Percy often pondered on how sad he would feel when he had them no longer as children to be cuddled and amused.

To her credit, Ena looked after them tirelessly, they were kept well fed, clean and snug, and both she and Percy were complimented by neighbours on their children's polite conduct.

Percy had left the army with a great deal more than his gratuity. He had found a thousand pounds in fivers while scavenging around inside the defeated Tiger, and although guessing the notes to be forgeries, he used them to buy a roadside cafe on the A23 which his mother and Bill were pleased to manage for him. Due to his previous occupations involving travel, he had purchased an ex-army Bedford and carried on a small builder's supply business for his own employment. Now and again he was greeted in cafes by a few of his old working acquaintances who through the damage of the years he could barely recognise as the spritely young men he had learned to drive with. Ena turned down every offer of keeping Percy company on his journeys and so,at around one year old, Oswald alone, strapped in his pushchair which in turn was secured to the passenger seat of the lorry, was to his great delight, taken out on pleasant afternoons to do the rounds of sand pits, brick yards and building sites.

As much as the infant enjoyed the outings Percy enjoyed his company and wondered how long it would be before his son would playfully push the stick out of gear as he himself had as a driver's mate.

With so much to occupy his mind, Ena's dissatisfaction of things took little toll of his cheerfulness, but the lack of loving encouragement did curtail his ambition and he stayed a one vehicle firm. Nevertheless, Ena's antagonism towards him was but the tip of the iceberg and he began to glimpse the hidden depths of her indifference to his feelings when he became injured. About to unload a consignment of rubble, the tailboard of his lorry dropped down unexpectedly and knocked him to the ground, whereupon he was struck heavily in the back by a sizable chunk of concrete that came tumbling off the rear. In his semi-conscious state it felt as if his ribs were crushed and his back broken, and for a few seconds he thought he was back in the war and had fallen prey to its tradition. He ceased to breathe for it seemed unnecessary as he lay ashen faced staring at the ground.

Suddenly the sound of little Oswald's chuckling revived him to the realisation that it was not the Rattler that he lay wounded beneath, but his beloved "Ivanhoe", as he had named his lorry. Also they were out on the Romney marshes, dusk was falling, and the child that had come to be the delight of his life could not be left to perish of exposure in that bleak desolate spot, for it was still only early March and very cold at night.

Still not breathing, he clawed his way towards the cab, caught sight of the lorry's foot pump strapped to the side of the chassis, and with fumbling ard trembling fingers released it and gripped the end firmly with teeth and lips. Frantically he pressed the pedal with both hands and only seconds away from oblivion he felt the lifegiving air surge into his empty lungs. With tears of relief rolling down his cheeks he dragged himself into the driving seat.

"Done it again, Ossy darling," he said, half laughing and half crying. "Luck's still with us, me little beauty, we aint gonna go down without a fight are we, little sweetheart," he cried, as he revved the engine to operate the hydraulic tip and shoot the load off as Oswald cooed and giggled.

Although racked with pain on the journey home Percy was filled with a sense of joy at their survival. As much as he had loved life before, he had recognised it as doubly precious since Oswald had come into existence, and the thought of being parted from him under any circumstances was inconceivable.

Surprisingly, X rays showed no bones to be broken but he was forced to lay up, and by doing so, as well as experiencing more discomfort than he had ever known in his life, he saw his wife in a light that was impossible to ignore or forgive. Her action cancelled out on her part the redeeming quality of pity from the marriage, for Percy, in his hour of desperate need, was denied succour by the one person from whom he had every right to expect it.

After three days of crawling and dragging himself in extreme pain around the house, he awoke one morning from a drugged sleep unable to move more than his ankles and toes, and arms from the elbow only, and his fingers. It was, he felt, as if all his other joints had been welded into immobility. Nevertheless, being aware that to all intents and purposes he was incapable of obtaining a cup of water for himself, Ena left the house with Oswald to spend the day at her mother's home, and only returned when Penny and Gloria were due back from school.

The day for Percy was yet another challenge which he took up with unashamed yells of agony as he wrenched his locked muscles free from their encumbrance.

That evening, like a dried out alcoholic going back to the bottle, Percy returned to the world of dancing and pushed himself to the brink of exhaustion as a token of the first giant step back into the familiar atmosphere of people expressing themselves to music.

On his return he was met with a flurry of abuse that continued until the small hours of the morning, and as he ploughed aching and tired through the day's tasks, for he would not have been able to rest at home, a chill premonition of being past the point of return ran through him. He realised he would be hard put, even living under the same roof with Ena, let alone carrying on any basic relationship, but he loved the children desperately, especially Oswald, and he was prepared to put up with a living hell to remain with them.

In true tradition of life's unrelenting tribulations, a foggy evening killed his stepfather Bill, and injured his mother when their car went over a bank on their way home from work.

Against the strongest medical advice Lucy discharged herself from hospital to attend her husband's funeral, and collapsed at the graveside, from where she was rushed back to intensive care. When she was allowed home to convalesce, Percy had already moved in with his family to look after her. As well meaning as of course his intentions were, the effort had precisely the opposite effect and Lucy died midst turmoil, after weeks of being subjected to angry bickering between her son and daughter-in-law.

On the fateful day, Percy arrived home late in the evening after doing repairs on his own house which was up for sale. Taking the covered plate containing his dinner from the oven, he sat down at the table with a sigh of relief. Before he could convey a forkful to his mouth, however, Ena pounced with heated indignation because he had not waited for her to put the plate before him. He had not intended to antagonise her; on the contrary he thought he was being helpful, after all, she would have been quick enough to accuse him of expecting to be waited on hand and foot had he just sat at the table as if he were in a restaurant.

It was merely another example of not being able to please her no matter what he did, but it came at a time when he was feeling the pressures of life a little stronger than usual, and grabbing her with great force, he bundled her through the house and threw the struggling woman, followed by her coat, out of the front door.

Lucy was no longer in the dining room when he returned, and Percy knew she had, as on similar occasions before, gone to her room to get away from the unpleasantness and he was further angered by Ena's insensitivity towards her frail condition. He had looked forward to chatting with his mother while he had his meal, now he had lost his appetite and everything, including Ena's cooking, seemed a wasted effort.

Looking in on his mother to say good-night, he found

she was not in her room, but the French windows, that led on to a small verandah, were open, and on rushing through them and looking down, he saw Lucy lying quite motionless in the garden below.

THIRTEEN
Enough Is Enough

Ena had remained as unaffected and aloof over her mother-in-law's death as she had over her infirmity, nor did she show any pity for Percy in his tragic loss. Ever since he had been aware that everyone at some time must die, the thought that his mother would not always be around horrified him, and he could not imagine being able to cope with the heartbreak of losing her forever. At that unbearable time he expected his hair to turn white overnight, but he paid little regard that there was no noticeable change.

Percy needed a reciprocation of comfort and soothing over the bereavement from someone other than his sister Sylvia, but it was not forthcoming. It was just one more painful example of his wife's lack of feeling for the situation, and summing up her attitude to their relationship as honestly as was humanly possible, he was of the opinion that she would be no different with anyone else, except that one of her frequent hateful outbursts would have most likely seen her killed or crippled long ago by someone less tolerant.

In spite of her indifference to his grief, Percy pitied her, and although this sentiment has been acknowledged as being kindred to love, it was insufficient on its own to revive a failed marriage, and he being favourably responsive only to love and goodwill, could not by their absence make any pretence of caring for her.

Getting over the shock of his mother's death, he began to come to terms with the situation. He stopped bursting into tears while driving along the road, then having to pull up to compose himself. On the last occasion he began to laugh as he thought of the times Scotty had stopped the lorry to relieve his irritation. How dearly he would have loved to return to those unhurried and secure days, except that to be back would cancel out the lives of his children, which brought to mind what he already knew about the problems of life having to be faced and surmounted as they come, and which cannot be sidestepped for happier times.

Although Ena looked after the physical welfare of the children, their psychological side was poisoned, as they were forced to witness not only her verbal abuse on their father but vicious physical attacks as well. Thinking it to be a game, little Oswald laughed and chuckled gleefully when his mother, fists swinging, piled into her husband with demonic fury. When he could understand the nature of the demonstrations however, he screamed out in terror.

Not all of Ena's attacks on Percy were so inconsiderate to the children by taking place in their view, although the girls were frequently awake listening to the commotion of Percy being kicked and pummelled in the back as he lay trying to sleep in the bed he had put together on the lounge floor. All appeals and pleading for consideration to the children were useless as she unleashed her hatred in as many hurtful ways as she could think of, and the hour of the night mattered little.

Percy would pull the blankets tightly around his head and back to cushion some of the blows while waiting for her to wear herself out, but when she stopped for a rest she would lean close to his ear and tell him that he was not the father of the children, and give details in some length of who was. He would give a sigh of relief when, slamming every door on her way, she would go back to bed, but then return to give another performance when she thought he was dropping off to sleep.

There was no doubt as far as Percy was concerned that he was married to a very unstable person who at times was on the verge of outright insanity. There had been occasions when he had retaliated with a few slaps, but this had worked Ena up into such a frenzy that he would have had to render her unconscious to restrain her had he not grabbed his coat and fled the house for a few hours, rather than have her injuries on his conscience.

He would drive aimlessly around the town or kill time at the cinema, and Ivanhoe could be seen parked outside so many obvious places of entertainment that inquiries were made, first by the police and then by officials of customs and excise, as to what a goods vehicle was doing being used for social occasions.

He bought a second hand car and was accused by Ena of having it to enhance his adulterous behaviour, and so he had to leave home in his working attire for any evenings out, then change into a suit he kept in the car, otherwise it would have been ripped from his back as he left the house. Before he returned home he would find a quiet side street to strip off and don his working gear again. How he wished he was back at the Italian villa with no encumbering misery like having to drag off a sweat soaked shirt and vest on very cold nights, or being pounced upon by the police, then kept two hours at the station explaining his singular state of near nudity in the back of his vehicle at one a.m. which consequently made a further ordeal to face when he got home.

Apart from Ena's strong complaints about his evenings out, which were understandable even though they were a matter of being self inflicted, Percy's ears were bombarded with a stream of insipient accusations and statements that were impossible to answer. Indeed, any attempt to justify himself over some point was frustrated by Ena either gabbling on and refusing to listen or walking away hurling insults behind her. He realised the futility of trying to communicate, and so took on the attributes of a deaf mute when she was on the rampage. The measure was never meant to cool her temper, on the contrary not being able to diminish whatever dignity he still clung to, unintentionally infuriated her further. He attempted to make the girls useful around the house, only to be baulked by Ena letting them off the light duties allotted to them as a token return for the generous pocket money they received. Percy felt it important that they should make some contribution towards the running of the household even if it was only in the form of picking up a piece of noticeable cotton off the carpet. But alas the only time they would have taken any notice of rubbish in the abode was if it stank or they tripped over it.

Over the years Ena's disrespect for her husband had registered on their minds and they too treated him with enmity. Any endeavour to correct them for some ill mannered act immediately brought Ena to their defence and they became unruly and against their father as she promised him many times she would bring about. With so much animosity directed at him, Oswald seemed the only reason, or so he believed, for remaining in the house, but as desperately unhappy as he was he could not bring himself to move out even though he had thought about it often enough, and had been urged in no uncertain terms to do so by his wife and daughters. It often struck him as comical that after Ena had likened him to every kind of unsavoury bastard on the face of the earth she would appeal to some gentlemanly quality hitherto denied as being in any part of his make up, and ask him to pack his belongings and leave. Whereby other wives, if in some way annoyed by their husbands, will bring them down to ground level and then lovingly pick them up, Ena would continue to stamp on Percy until he sank beneath the surface.

Since his fortieth birthday she had never ceased reminding him of how ancient he was and how his useful life was long past. Now at fifty-three he felt like agreeing with her as with great deliberation she made him feel like a hundred.

"You old bastard, old, old, old," she said with all the hatred she could muster, short of striking him.

In an attempt to turn back the ravages of time as far as his hair was concerned, which was as plentiful as ever but going grey, he bought a hair dye. But he did not take the necessary precautions and so came out in a rash and was foreed to have most of his hair cut away in order to treat it. Not blessed with the patience to wait for it to grow, and not being able to go dancing in a cap, he bought a wig, cut to the latest fashion as his own hair had been, and danced with as much confidence as he ever had. He did have to be careful however that no friends came along and ruffled his hair good naturedly, as one did, causing the wig to swivel back to front on his head.

Later it went through a greater hazard when Ena knocked it off his head into a saucepan of stew he was cooking. For the moment his imagination ran away with him for he could have sworn he heard the hairpiece cry out as it touched the hot gravy. Snatching it out he quickly put it under the cold tap to clean it before putting it back on, dripping wet.

Failing to get him riled over that Ena knocked the plate of stew from his hand but he did no more than scrape it unceremoniously back on the plate, then sat quietly down and ate it as if nothing untoward had occurred, even though despair and loneliness clutched at his heart as if they would crush it. He wished with every fibre of his body that Ena was different enough for him to want to stay in with her instead of gallivanting around. Yet plainly he had not been the right sort of husband for her from the start, and his mind boggled trying to imagine a man who would have been.

Stalwart though he was in controlling his temper, there were times when Ena's treatment of him was somewhat risky. On odd occasions he became very depressed when overtaken by an accumulation of pressures and sad memories. As much as others had seen far more hideous atrocities, for which he pitied them, Percy had observed enough results of savagery during the war for the visions to remain imprinted on his mind for life. He was thankful however, that in all the carnage he had never been confronted with a dead child. But like all veterans the ravages of war had left their mark and at times a great anger welled up in him at the greed and corruption of society when so many had died in an attempt to bring victory on the side of love and justice. Not that he had ever been deceived himself that anything other than unfeeling hypocrisy ruled the world, but the toll of innocence it continuously took, he knew, would remain until the world's end.

It was while he sat in the lounge one evening, lost in sorrowful reminiscence, that Ena pounced on him with one of her numerous trivial grievances. Shaken out of his thoughts he began concentrating on the previously ignored television programme, as his wife worked herself up for yet another row.

Percy knew the routine by heart; first she would shout and rave, then as he ignored her she would turn the television off and begin to slap and prod him before grabbing his legs and pulling him out of the armchair on to the floor where she would begin kicking and punching him. The episodes were nightmares to Percy, as he silently prayed for her to be blessed with enough sanity to realise what she was doing but found respite only when she was weary of raining blows upon him.

On this occasion his pent up tolerance exploded, and before she could reach anything like a peak performance, he had shot from the chair and, with open hands, slapped her to near unconsciousness. After she reported the attack to the police his arrest was a foregone conclusion. While he waited to be taken he wrote to Sylvia explaining how ashamed and demoralised he felt at not being able to maintain self control and therefore playing right into his wife's hands.

Down in the cells at the station, three policemen, only having heard about Ena's version of the incident, pummelled Percy about the body with truncheon and fist, then left him vomiting with his thoughts for the night.

Due to the nature of the offence, he was only allowed a brief supervised visit home to collect a few essentials, after which he found himself in a bed-sitter situated a mere stone's throw from the road he had been born in. At his age he had no illusions of starting again with anyone else and as a prelude to a life of loneliness he existed in a state of drunkeness for the best part of a month.

Divorce was automatic, and being a person of no identity so to speak, he became unwelcome in homes previously open to him, in all except one. Out of the Rattler's crew, Johnny Morton was the only one Percy had been able to keep in contact with. He had chatted with him in dance halls and later when having his own vehicle repair shop, Johnny had, by his skill in welding, kept the swiftly corroding "Ivanhoe" on the road for more years than its designer intended.

To Percy, Johnny's life was enviable. His wife, Jill, had his happiness at her fingertips and the evidence of this was in the endeavour that he applied in making their home as luxurious as he could for her and their three children. Percy used to marvel at the tranquil atmosphere of their home as he had over the dwellings of other happy couples. How nice he thought it was that they were not slanging and clawing at each other, but lived by a code of mutual respect with love as a bonus.

The difference in ages between Ena and Percy could in no way have doomed their marriage from the offset, for the same age gap existed between Johnny and Jill, yet their successful relationship made it look as if there were no other way to live. Percy could only assume that he had been denied such a heaven on earth existence through offending the gods by some flagrant act.

FOURTEEN
Time To Adjust

Legal costs of the divorce, and settlements, took a heavy toll of Percy's finances, and he was restricted to quite a menial mode of life which he found was reminiscent of his days as the Co-op bakehouse boy. The exceptions being that now, along with a multitude of others, he was disillusioned through the parting by the years, from almost everything he held dear. Besides the irreplaceable loss of dear ones from his life, "Ivanhoe" had gone to the scrapyard, the cafe he owned was sold for debt, and he was left with just a ten year old Citroen, and wits he considered dubious, to get a living with. Some acquaintances went out on the knocker, buying antiques and had money to burn through their cheatery, but considering that line to be too technical and needing the experience of many years, Percy went in for second hand household goods. It was mostly junk and he became an expert at bodging up articles he bought from houses for next to nothing.

Patriotism and conscience would not allow him to lumber his own countrymen with shoddy goods, and so any leaking spin dryers were sold to Indian restaurateurs, but without the information of their secondary function as garden sprinklers to boot. Also as their premises were always dimly lit, they could not notice the clouds of dust from the vacuum cleaners that blew out instead of sucking in, until Percy had long gone. He considered them fair game too for refrigerators that would not shut off. "'Ere, read about them Pakis freezing to death 'cause their fridge wouldn't turn off?" he would say to an acquaintance. "Well they did ask me if it was reliable an' I told 'em the truth, it'll keep going, I said, when all the others 'ave stopped."

Similarly, he would exaggerate with a story of another proprietor who, through his refrigerator having an adverse function, now bakes his jupatties in it. Percy had not the slightest qualms over such deals for he considered these customers would all buy corpses from the undertakers if they could get away with serving them up with the curry. Also, for the perfect article they thought they were buying they would knock him down to a ridiculously low price that would have put him in the poor-house had it not been useless junk.

There was of course another aspect besides sentimentality that would not allow him to sell this unworthy merchandise to his own countrymen. They might have recognised him later, somewhere, whereas as much as "Dagos and Asians" all look alike to the whites, then likewise the reverse is assumable.

Now and again he was able to chuckle over catching one or another of the antique barons who bought what they thought to be a four legged table until, when moved away from the wall where Percy had placed it, it toppled over, because a leg was missing. Or a faint signature on a picture of no consequence that turned out to be the marks of a modern Biro pen instead of an old master's.

By and large Percy managed pretty well for he was no stranger to washing shirts and cooking. He had come to terms also with the pangs of loneliness and no longer laid awake half the night pondering on his plight, but fell asleep with exhaustion within minutes of his head touching the pillow. Besides the absence of soul destroying rows, another consolation was that on returning to his dwelling at night, he could walk straight in instead of hesitating while his eyes became accustomed to the darkness, wherein Ena may have been lurking ready to strike with some implement or another, when he had been residing with her. Nor was it paranoia that prompted him to barricade the door before he slept.

Thinking of little Oswald's cherubic face and his hair of blonde ringlets was the only thing that brought tears to his eyes and tugged at his heart. But he had enjoyed four years of cuddling and fussing over him and no one could take that away. Now he was allowed access to him every other weekend even though Ena tried to spoil the arrangement time and again. Had it not been for Oswald, Percy would have gone to Australia with Sylvia and her husband Frank, who had relatives in Sydney.

The excited chatter in the car as Percy drove them to the airport was as if they were only going a stone's throw away for the weekend. And while the promises of letters and visits were reiterated at their farewell caresses, he knew it would be the last time he would see them. After watching their plane out of sight he turned for home, immersed in utter loneliness.

As unethical as his business dealings were, his social life took on an element of mild buffoonery. There were not many strict tempo ballroom dances being operated and when Percy came upon one unexpectedly he was refused entry through lack of a tie. In the car the only thing he could find that came close to the requirement was a strap from a lady's handbag that he had collected from a house clearance, so with this and a pair of Western styled boots from the same source, he went into the mirrored foyer to put them on. Only one of the boots would go on, and then he had to call on the aid of a young lady to help him get it off after he had nearly thrown a fit trying to do it himself. In the hall the strap kept curling back to its original shape, causing it to look as if it was either growing out of his partner's chin or her ear. Also, the tyre paint with which he had hurriedly touched up his grey sideboards ran down a girl's face that he had been dancing cheek to cheek with, causing her to think her eye mascara had slipped when a friend mentioned the black streaks.

Dressed for the occasions he became a frequent visitor to the hall which was supposedly a club for the divorced and separated, although the majority of the patrons went home to their husbands and wives afterwards. Compared with dancers in other halls they were a hard faced bunch, devoid of all the niceties usually associated with unattached merrymakers.

"The only time you'll get a smile out of these Dragon-tits is when it's pissing with rain an' they want you to put the spare wheel on their car for them," he told an acquaintance.

"Or if you're loading 'em up with booze all the evening, then give them their taxi fare home. Then like as not the taxi driver will finish up having what you've paid for."

One evening he dropped a pair of women's pants on the crowded floor, which caused shrieks of laughter when someone carried them to the bandstand where they were held up for recognition and collection, while another evening a brassiere went through the same routine. Percy chuckled at the thought of any amount of the males thinking they might be dancing with a woman who was minus her drawers or brassiere.

Another prank he played was to throw a provocative little nightdress to an attractive woman, adding as he did so that she forgot to take it with her that morning. One evening he danced for a while with a coat hanger still in his jacket and complained, to the great humour of a few companions, of a shocking pain across his shoulders. At another session a partner remonstrated against the weird antics he began inserting into a foxtrot, but he was doing no more than trying to relieve the pain from a hernia that had, as on previous occasions, started to strangulate.

Some nights, when leaving unaccompanied by any female companion, he would subsidise the evening's expenditure by doing a bit of piratical taxi work with his car. After dropping off his fare from the dance hall he would cruise around the town with a finger on the switch of his smart little "For Hire" sign in readiness to turn it off when any police cars or other taxis came in sight.

One night after an exceptionally uneventful evening at the dance, he accosted Terry Jones who was about to telephone for a taxi. He was a tall debonair looking man of thirty-five who had no love for Percy on account of the vexing competitor he proved to be as far as the right damsels were concerned. Too often had he been the purloiner of women who Terry considered were more his class than they ever were Percy's. And so as intoxicated as he and the companion with him both were, he jumped at the offer of immediate transport with the firm idea of belitting Percy in any way that presented itself.

At the beginning of the journey no hint of the animosity was discernible but as they neared their destination Terry sarcastically commented on how nice it was to be offered a free lift home. On pulling up at the address given, Percy ran around to the passenger side in order to be able to loom over Terry before he could leave the car, but his non-paying passenger was unimpressed by the menacing pose and threatened to report the matter of a car being used illegally as a taxi, to the authorities.

Angered by the affront Percy punched him in both eyes and began dragging the struggling man from the car by his legs, as his companion came to his aid thus ensuing a considerable brawl.

The odds were pretty well even for although Percy had been drinking it was nothing like the amount consumed by his adversaries, which made their movements as predictable as if they were on a film in slow motion.

Because of the commotion windows of some nearby houses were thrown open as the occupants called for the hullabaloo to cease or the police would be called, and knowing how appealing they would immediately consider the situation to be, Percy desired to remove himself and especially his motor, which was parked in the centre of the road, from the scene.

As tempted as he was to dip into the pockets of his new inactive fellow combatants, in order to find a couple of pounds to compensate his trouble, he thought better of it, and swallowing his losses, he leapt in his car and sped off down the road only seconds before a police car arrived on the scene.

In the brief skirmish Terry had snatched at the "For Hire" sign and stripped the wire that had been attached, none too professionally, to the battery; consequently, when Percy arrived home flames were coming through the sides of the bonnet. Fortunately only a few strands of wire and some oil soaked rag were alight which to his great relief he was able to extinguish by standing on the wing and urinating on the flames before the carburettor and fuel pump became ablaze.

Added to the discomfort of his bumps and bruises he lost the profit of half a day's trading by having to replace damaged wires which when tested, much to Percy's surprise and delight, did not see the windscreen wipers come on instead of the radio, nor the hooter sound when the direction lights were supposed to flash.

Understandably, Percy could be forgiven for his strong vindictiveness towards the bestower of his inconveniences, and he set forth to bring a measure of aggravation to the culprit.

A few brief enquiries into his affairs proved how vulnerable he was. At the same time Percy found it puzzling to understand where anyone stupid enough to make unnecessary enemies raised the money to owning as Terry did, a flourishing garage business complete with petrol pumps and car showrooms.

Percy felt inclined to flood the forecourt with petrol and throw a match on it as poetic justice for his own fire, but this measure was far too drastic and would involve the police far too extensively for it would be taken as an act of terrorism. As a compromise he settled for splashing half a dozen cars with acid, and tying bolts and fishing weights to the revolving mops in the car washing facility which resulted in the first car going through the following day emerging as if it had been fired upon by a company of riflemen.

The total cost to Terry in compensating the owner, not only for the damage to his car, but for the terrifying experience he suffered, added to that for the respraying of his own showroom stock amounted to over two thousand pounds. He was in little doubt as to who was responsible and dwelt on the thought for days of hiring a couple of brutes to pommel Percy to death. But not being sure which he feared most, the punishment from the law for their success, or the ultimate retribution from the intended victim if they failed, he cast the idea from his mind. He was only thankful in the successive weeks, that no further acts of revenge were taken against him, although he was unnerved when in the dance hall he would notice Percy staring at him in a non-committal way that was devoid even of a glimmer of satisfaction.

FIFTEEN
Tiny Mathews

Percy never suffered from a lack of variety in his life, indeed, there was so much to do that twenty-four hour days and seven day weeks were inadequate for him to capitalise on every opportunity, both business and social, that came his way. Even so he did not mind getting roped in on a game of football with some lads as he took a short cut through the park to a corner grocer.

"Gonna get a match started Percy?" someone would shout, and he could not resist another encounter with a second childhood. Once whilst running headlong with the ball towards the opposing goal, a voice yelled, "Don't chase 'im, yer won't catch 'im", and he was amused to think of the three youths behind toppling over him if he suddenly dropped with a heart attack, at the same time he was pleased with his fitness which he put down to the abandonment of smoking several years before. After the park keeper had locked up he would find himself bunking back over the gate and then running like a mischievous child with his companions when the keeper came back to give chase. Many a time he put a bag of eggs and tomatoes by the side of the goal only to find them unusefully crushed after the game. As his young friends dispersed to their homes he knew that not one could be anything like aware of the times of plenty they lived in compared to his own childhood, and had he the choice he would never inflict any part of those harsh years upon them merely for a moment's appreciation.

On one of his rare visits to London he and his lady companion, a young widow called Sheila, so named because of her father's association with Australians in a Japanese P.O.W. camp, spent an enjoyable evening dancing at the Hammersmith Palais. Then after a light meal they put up at a small hotel in Kensington for the night and before returning to the coast the following day, they paid a visit to the War Museum. The all too familiar equipment brought memories flooding back to Percy and all the voices he ever heard in the war flashed through his mind as he passed, tense and excited, by the deadly devices he had so often operated.

As they approached the tank section he almost broke into a trot in his haste to begin admiring a magnificent Churchill and Centurion, then passing on to the next exhibit a shiver went through him and he became rooted to the spot as he stared open mouthed and transfixed at the Sherman. Other visitors, Sheila included, wondered what he was doing when he went down on hands and knees beneath the front of this particular tank. But there sure enough, was the hole that saved his life so many years before. He rose slowly and his gaze roamed over the beloved Rattler as his hands caressed it as if it were a giant kitten.

Unable to control himself he leapt onto the track cover with almost the same agility he had possessed in the Rattler's time of glory, then clambering up the superstructure, he climbed into the turret. Unaware that the tank was, apart from ammunition, still operational, he automatically flicked switches and levers as routine tests had demanded in the days of its element. He was momentarily surprised that the electrical system was live, and smiling whimsically, he donned the helmet he found on the map shelf,then sat back in the pose of commander, with his arms resting on the turret sides, totally oblivious of his surroundings as the whir of the hydraulics traversed turret and gun in a continuing circle while the headphones crackled with static. Had he taken the driving seat, doubtless he would have driven the Sherman off its display stand and into the street via the wall, if the vehicle had fuel, so immersed was he in the fantasy.

Contributing powerfully to the mood, the background music changed from "Rule Britannia" to the tranquil "Prelude and Sunset", causing tears to roll down Percy's cheeks without a quiver from either eye or mouth as he sat deeply entranced in the revolving turret.

Two attendants came hurrying on the scene. They were members of the Corps of Commissionaires, ex-servicemen who merited special attention in civilian life but settled for humble reception posts in the establishment for which, ironically, they had to have suffered near mortal wounds to qualify.

Neither man attempted to come too close to the revolving gun, but just gazed at Percy in disbelief along with the rest of the audience as he sat as placid as a child in a fairground roundabout.

As the tune came to an end he allowed the gun to swing back to its original position before shutting off the hydraulics, and after a few more seconds of profound recollection he clambered out of the metal creature that to him had a soul as had all things mechanical.

The two attendants breathed a sigh of relief as he leapt to the ground.

"You seem to know all about tanks, sir," said one of the attendants respectfully.

"I know this one," answered Percy, still gazing adoringly at the now peaceful Sherman. "There were quite a few scrapes she pulled me and my mates through. I know every scar she's got even though she's had a few coats of paint to cover 'em up."

It was customary for such unusual behaviour to be brought to the attention of the curator, and perhaps, depending upon the offence, the police also.

However, as Percy had plainly shown a great reverence for the exhibits, it was all resolved over cups of tea in the attendants' restroom, where daring exploits were then eagerly unfolded by all three, even to the interest of Sheila. She inquired what the fascination was in reminiscing over such a hazardous occupation as fighting a war.

"You rarely have to think for yourself, Luv," said one of the men. "And when yer do, there's no comebacks if yer mess it up. There's no quotas to fill like there is in civvy street, ya do ya best, dodge what you can and marvel at the stupidity of it all."

On the way home the Citroen had a puncture and having still a considerable distance to go and not wanting to risk another one without a spare wheel, Percy pulled in at the first available garage. After parking in an out of the way spot on the forecourt he rolled the damaged wheel to the rear workshop. Entering through the partially open sliding doors and seeing no one, he called out, "Anyone about" a couple of times in case any of the staff were beneath one or other of the vehicles in for repair. There was no reply but as he walked to look behind the cars the silence was broken by a belch so loud, it reverberated around the building. Turning to see who had emitted it caused the blood to run cold in his veins, for there in the doorway, still adjusting his trousers on returning from emptying his bowels, stood Tiny Mathews.

Understandably, by his size, he was immediately recognisable and Percy's aim was to put as much distance between himself and the locality as soon as possible.

Sensing the fear in his visitor Tiny had but to study him for a few seconds to realise his years of search were at an end, and he calmly turned and closed the heavy doors before Percy was anywhere near them. Even without his path being barred he could never have reached the top bolts that had been thrown. Tiny stood for a few moments with his forehead against the door and his eyes closed as if giving thanks for the deliverance of such a hated one into his hands, and Percy knew he would be fighting for his life as never before.

"You can't imagine what my life's been like since that night," said Tiny, as he slowly turned to face Percy. He spoke with a calm satisfaction as if revenge was a foregone conclusion and afforded time to justify his intentions to a co-operative victim.

"I've been at my wits' end at times wondering where I'd most likely run into you again," he continued. "I must've worked nearly every place within a twenty mile radius of London, looking for ya. I even prayed you'd survive the war, do ya know that?"

"Your prayers were answered. I did," said Percy glibly.

"Not through Christian charity though, but dedicated hatred as I'm sure you'll appreciate," Tiny explained.

Percy, sick with fear, tried telling him that he had mates waiting for him outside, to which Tiny closed his eyes momentarily while he shook his head.

"One mate, and female at that. I spotted 'er when I left the bog. Good taste, I'll say that for yer. I hope yer last screw with 'er is fresh in yer mind 'cause you won't be having another, not with 'er or anyone else. Oh no, me ol' china, I aint gonna kill yer," explained Tiny, not wishing Percy to get the wrong idea.

"Just emasculate yer, as you did me, an' then you'll know what I've 'ad ta bear all these years."

As Tiny closed in on him Percy summoned up all the speed and energy he could muster and automatically slammed his foot into his crotch, with the swiftness of a striking serpent, the second that he came within range. Relief overwhelmed him as Tiny let out a hideous cry and doubled over, but as Percy tried to move towards the door he slowly straightened up and looked at him with an evil grin of self gratification for the convincing act that gave his intended victim false hope.

At the same time, giving a sharp whistle, his hand made a short slicing movement across his abdomen, indicating the absence of the parts that would have given the kick effect.

Never before could Percy remember feeling so helplessly trapped. Even the menacing situations he had been in during the war had offered some small option to seize upon, but prepared as he was to use the wartime necessity of no holds barred, without a weapon, he could see not the slightest chance of escaping by merely pitting his own strength in unarmed combat against Tiny.

However, he was not one to give up easily or at all, he thought, if it meant opening his trousers for the giant to hack off his balls and pecker with his boy scout safety knife. He remembered hearing somewhere that there existed a means of escape from every peril if it could be discovered in time, so he glanced around but with little hope of seeing anything that would begin to fit the bill. A can of petrol or a welding torch would have kept Tiny at bay, he was sure, but he remembered that since giving up smoking, he would not have had the means of igniting them anyway.

Then he spotted a familiar piece of equipment, a hydraulic jack with a sturdy detachable hadle. The glint of battle sparkled in his eyes as with the handle raised menacingly, he turned to face Tiny.

"Come on then, you big, ugly bastard, meet Jack the giant killer," goaded Percy. "I've dragged yer bollocks off, now I'll take yer fuckin' 'ead off."

Seeing the need for caution changed the expression of satisfaction to that of concern on Tiny's face.

"It's all right with me, mate, if yer want to prolong the inevitable and take a bashing as well," he said goodnaturedly, as if Percy's wishes were dear to him.

"Get it right boy, for Christ's sake get it right," Percy said silently to himself, as Tiny took on the stance of a wrestler.

If Tiny thought he was going to catch Percy unawares he was never more in error, for as he made a quick grab at him the iron bar struck him on the side of the head and was repeated before he had anything like a chance to recover. As he dropped to his knees Percy was tempted to cave in his cranium with a final blow but thought better of it, for after all, he himself had suffered no damage and by the look of Tiny, he was passed being a threat for the time being.

Dropping the metal bar he dashed desperately around the garage in search of anything movable he could stand on to draw the bolts and make his escape. Spotting a pair of trestles holding an axle up, he kicked their burden off unceremoniously and after snatching one, ran with it to the door.

It took but a few seconds to drop back the bolts, then as he stepped back off the trestle he was seized in a steel like grip that, besides nearly cracking his ribs, made it difficult for him to breathe. By the odour of Tiny's breath as he panted heavily, Percy could have well believed he was in the clutch of a grizzly bear and expected no more mercy than if he were.

Tiny was quick to move his captive away from the doors which he might have kicked against to attract attention or thrown him off balance. Percy felt like a child as with his arms pinioned at his sides he was lifted off the ground, and he cursed himself for not finishing off his enemy when he had the chance. He should have known that being no ordinary man, Tiny needed more than an ordinary whack to put him out of action, and now it seemed the mistake was to be heavily paid for.

"Let's get it over with, cock. No more fuckin' about," said Tiny as he carried Percy towards the far end of the workshop.

"Be over in a second, nice clean job," he went on as he reached his right hand down and began ripping the front of Percy's trousers open.

His action left Percy's right arm free and his hand shot to his pocket for the car keys which he automatically took from the car every time he left it. They might do to jab into Tiny's face, he thought, in his panic of clutching at straws. Then his fingers felt the aerosol can of ether he had been forced to buy that morning to start the car.

Meanwhile, the suspense of how it was intended he should be deprived of his manhood was over, for after baring

Percy's privates Tiny began offering them towards the vicious blades of the tyre seal breaker. To do this it was necessary for one arm to be locked around Percy's neck while the other hold his legs back to lower him.

Pulling the can from his pocket and taking the quickest glance possible to determine from which side the fluid would eject, he turned it behind his head and pressed the valve. The effect was almost immediate, for combined with the blows to his head coupled to the exertion of manhandling Percy, and the factor of being middle aged, the first lungful of ether set Tiny staggering.

As if for support, his grip tightened on Percy, who began to understand how the poor beast in the slaughterhouse had felt that Tiny had throttled before his eyes. The second whiff, however, made the giant go limp and relax his hold, which gave Percy the opportunity to wriggle free and roll out of reach before getting to his feet, whereupon he directed the spray fully into the tottering man's face.

Threshing the air with his arms he lunged at Percy but fell heavily, placing his head in the jaws of the seal breaker in the process. Totally unaware of his perilous position his hands, like those of a blind man, fumbled around for some form of support by which he could raise himself up.

Percy stood rooted to the spot as he watched, with fascination, Tiny's attempts to concentrate his diminished senses while his hand groped ever nearer to the operating lever. If he had not still had his head bowed as he began to raise himself the machine would have missed him, but it was as if he had made himself more comfortable for self execution. Percy could not help wincing as he heard the hiss of the compressed air closing the blades and the dull crunch as Tiny's head was crushed.

"Knackered now top and bottom aincha?" Percy said under his breath. "Still, you was lucky not ta be fully conscious."

After making sure there was no one about outside, he went through the sliding doors but dashed back some ten seconds later to collect his wheel which, on returning to the car, he hurriedly threw onto the back seat, telling Sheila that there was no one around to repair it.

Surviving such an ordeal made driving without a spare wheel no more than a petty annoyance, and if need be he would have gladly driven the remainder of the journey on four flat tyres. He was well pleased with himself to say the least over his success at finding an escape no matter how haphazardly the means were presented. Nevertheless a slight shiver went through him at the thought of how close he had come to being maimed. As much as he hoped to have got away unobserved, as long as he had all his important bits and pieces he was ready to face any charge of involvement.

In the next two days he bought a few copies of national newspapers, but only one carried a small column headed "Strange Suicide", which went on briefly to describe how an unstable man came to his end, and no mention of anyone else being remotely implicated.

SIXTEEN
Percy Island

Having grown weary of many hectic pastimes, it was only a matter of time before, like thousands of other people, Percy took up the supposedly tranquil hobby of casting a lead weight and hook, with line attached, into the sea, to wait, watch and feel with fascination, the interest that some out of sight, untamed sea creature might take in the bait.

Even though most of the time the fish got away with the worm, and he reeled in only a bare hook, it was proof that they were in the vicinity, and all he had to do was strike his rod a bit sooner to hook one.

One summer evening on a weekend when he had access to Oswald, who was then six years of age, Percy took him fishing at the harbour quayside. He picked this location to enable the little lad to drop and wind in at will, instead of the frustration of casting off the beach with his little rod.

Other youngsters not quite in their teens were expertly casting into the middle of the harbour and with shrills and whoops of excitement, pulling in eels, flatties, horse mackerel and an assortment of tiddlers that Oswald thrilled and took interest in with them. Even though Percy had impressed upon his son that he must keep a certain distance from the edge, he never took his eyes from him, for more than a few seconds at a time when he was occupied in re-baiting his hook. Nevertheless, to his great horror, after untangling a snag on his own line, he looked to where the youngster should have been, but saw only the rod on the edge.

"Oswald," he screamed, in panic, as he peered with heartbreak and terror into the murky depths below, but detecting no sign he glanced on either side along the quay in case the boy had gone to look at someone else's catch, but he had not.

Out of pure instinct Percy continued to call for his son. He felt as if his brain would burst with the helpless terror of the situation and was ready to break down and cry like the demented person he sensed he was fast becoming.

Rarely have a man's emotions been plunged to utter despair, then raised to the pinnacle of relief in so short a time, for as he decided that, through his negligence, his life could no longer continue, Oswald came running from behind a small hut where he had been to urinate.

"What do you want, Dad ?" he asked innocently, as he did up the little flies of his trousers, totally unaware of the state of near madness his father was in. As expressive as Percy's love had always been towards the child, he hugged and kissed him as never before, and as his tears soaked Oswald's face, he was the happiest of men without, at that moment, a care in the world.

As Percy gained a little insight into the sport, also like thousands of others he concluded that it was far from being what it was cracked up to be. When he weighed up the man hours and expense of the tackle and bait that went into an afternoon's fishing of fifty or so beings on the harbour arm, against what few fish, if any, were caught, the pleasure was one of anticipation only. Further, any accusations by the anti-blood sport league against the barbaric method known as angling were, he thought, not only unfounded but contrarily should have brought high commendation to the anglers for going to such great lengths to convey succulent tit bits to the wildlife of the sea.

As the results fell far short of the reward Percy considered to be a fair return for the preparation and time involved, his enthusiasm weakened. Too many times after digging an impressive amount of bait, the weather would put fishing out of the question. Or large amounts of weed would trap and break the line causing him to curse and swear in temper over losing his tackle, and far from being a hobby with tranquillising tendencies, he began to find it infuriating.

At the point of giving it up, he heard there were fish to be had in plenty at the end of the power station outfall at Southwick, so he went to investigate. Sure enough at the end of the steel and concrete causeway that jutted two hundred yards into the sea, the water bubbled as hundreds of bass leapt about like flying fish, and Percy knew he had found a veritable El Dorado.

In the interests of safety a large steel fence blocked off the end and extended seaward, with heavy pillared supports into the shape of a huge horseshoe, and it was in this enclosure that the legions of fish fed on their kind who were unfortunate enough to be drawn into the pumping machinery and disgorged in manageable portions from the outfall.

It only required to poke the rod through the ample gaps in the fence, let the line loose, and the powerful surge of the water took the bait to the creatures that jostled each other in their eagerness to be hooked. Another great advantage was the fact that live bait was unnecessary. Artificial lures such as little rubber eels were devastating. They would be let out on the flow for some hundred yards or so, then would simulate swimming as they were slowly drawn in and snatched before they could travel many feet, then it was a matter of how quickly the lure could be retrieved, and dropped back in the gush to repeat the performance.

Percy was sure that no other place in the whole country came anywhere near being as perfect for fishing as the outfall proved to be. Of course he was not alone on this fisherman's paradise, there were a number of elite and dedicated anglers who defied the electricity authority and climbed over the two sections of railings barring the way to the end.

Luckily, they did not all try to come on at the same time, but when too many did there was such a mix up of lines that the fish on the ends drowned in the flow while waiting to be reeled in. The sea did not permit unlimited time on the structure, for unless diving suits were worn it had to be vacated three hours before high tide and could not be occupied again until three hours after.

So keen was Percy to get to his quarry that he would wade out waist deep to corner the best vantage point before the others would wet no more than their ankles to come on. On these occasions many a fish slipped from his grasp as he took it off the hook, and he marvelled at the speed with which they shot away when they reached the water. In times of bad weather his dedication proved to be stronger than most, for he would struggle desperately through the wind and waves and be thankful to get to the end for something to cling to and so avoid being washed away. There he would hang on as wave after wave came battering at him through the fence. He wore no protective clothing such as waders or oilskins but just an old army camouflage jacket and a pair of wellingtons, always on the wrong feet for comfort, and which he always had to empty out after he had squelched back to his car.

When the flood tide was being fished he would liken the structure to a sinking ship as the water came flooding over in swells, and many a fish that had been put by on the side was washed back to sea by a rescuing wave. Most of Percy's companions would stay and fish for as long as he did, but when he shouted "Abandon Ship", everyone scrambled back over the prohibiting fences and went up on the beach to count their catch.

While the others took their fish home and packed it in their deep freezers or shared it with their Aunt Muriels and the neighbours, Percy had different ideas for his booty. When he was just catching two or three he gave them away to fellow tenants, but since he had been bringing off such sackfuls that he had to keep stopping momentarily to rest on his way back to the car, he had been quick to find a more lucrative outlet in the form of a Chinese take-away.

He was both surprised and delighted at the price they gladly paid for the fish which he first weighed on a machine in a chemist's doorway. After the transactions he was always treated to a meal of prawnballs and chips, followed by a generous glassful of brandy and cream soda, which he sat and enjoyed while watching the coloured television, the symbolic centrepiece of all Chinese takeaways. Afterwards he would nod off and dream of the bass splashing as they snapped at the little imitation eel. Sometimes he would chuckle as he thought of the cross-eyed ones that kept missing and had to follow it all the way in. He would be awakened by Wang Lee, the shop owner, gently shaking his shoulder.

"Time to go home now, Percy, we're closing up," he would say softly, and Percy would go home well pleased with the day's events.

Apart from the inconstancy of the weather, and the changing times of the tide, which, by their conveniences drew Percy to the outfall at differing hours of the day or night, there was the slight annoyance that everyone setting foot on it was trespassing.

Uniformed security men would stand on the path at the top of the beach and bellow through loud hailers that the police would be sent for unless the jetty was vacated.

For a time Percy complied with their wishes and left meekly with the others, but sitting on the beach pondering upon the shoal just offshore, that was impossible to cast into from the beach, was more than his flesh and blood could stand, and he clambered back on. In spite of all the requests by the officials, only the incoming tide drove him off each time. Even the most courteous personal appeals from the forthright station manager, who pointed out the dangers involved, were met with a stubborn refusal to budge. Then when his attention was drawn to the "No Fishing Allowed" sign, he sarcastically replied that he was doing it very quietly. On occasions when the police were called, and reluctantly took off their shoes and socks to wade out to him, he stood his ground, knowing that they could not pursue what could only be a civil matter.

It almost cost one of the workers his job when he was sent out on the jetty to ask Percy to leave, but a spare rod was thrust in his hands and, caught up by the infectious spirit of the location, he began to fish devotedly, because of the colossal excitement and the not-to-be snuffed at money involved, Percy went to the library and read up on the laws governing the foreshore. Magnetically he was drawn to the same seat as he had sat in when he and his friend George had been caught by the headmaster as they were looking into the symptoms of veneral disease so many years before.

Armed with what he thought was his legal right he spouted references, dates and quotes at his annoyers when next he was approached by them on the outfall. Sadly his information was only beneficial to him when the structure was below the sea, and more or less a no man's land, but when the tide went down and it was uncovered it became the property of the generating board and Percy was warned by their solicitors that if he insisted on exercising what he considered to be his right a high court injunction would be taken out against him.

Undaunted, yet respecting the warning, he wore a scarf, female fashion, upon his head when driving past the reception office on the harbour quayside.

Not that he felt he was really fooling anyone for they knew his car, otherwise how else had they got his address if it were not from his registration number.

When in the company of others on the outfall he law abidingly came off with them when the ritual hailing began, and when alone he wore a hideous mask in case the authorities felt vindictive over the nuisance he had been. One calm evening when the structure was high and dry, half a dozen youths laid their bikes on the path and ran out to the solitary figure they had seen fishing at the end.

"Caught anything?" they asked.

"No, I aint", answered Percy abruptly, as some of his catch began flapping vigorously in his bag.

"Yes you have, what's that then? Come on, show us," they demanded.

Part of the reason the officials persecuted the fishermen was because of the youngsters being attracted to the spot, and not wanting them to hang around to draw attention to him, Percy told them to "bugger off".

"Why should we? Who do yer think you are? You don't own the place," was their reply.

Until this moment, Percy had been facing seaward, paying attention to the rod he clutched through the metal bars, and in the dusk, the boys had not yet noticed the mask, but as he turned to face them, each one imagined that some ghastly creature had left the sea and taken human form. The change to pallor of their complexions highlighted the look of horror on their faces, and Percy could have sworn he saw sparks around their feet as they ran hell for leather up the beach to their bicycles.

Things settled down on the outfall, not in the way of outright congeniality, but by tolerant acceptance by the station manager that where fish were known to be, there too would be fishermen. Allowing for enough time to pass when it could not be construed as grovelling, Percy went out of his way to apologise to him for his rudeness and ignorance over the situation, and was told that he and his family would be welcome to a conducted tour of the power station any time he wished.

The occasions when they were warned off the jetty became less frequent, but when they occurred, and Percy heard anyone complaining about not being allowed to fish, he logically pointed out that if they were, it would be too jam-packed to be of any use to anyone.

Hardly had the obstacle sorted itself out to mutual satisfaction, when a far greater threat to the outfall anglers came along. A small boat with an outboard engine and a villainous looking crew of two took to casting their nets across the end of the pillars and so curtailing the distance the lines could be let out from the platform. The exercise, although only taking a minute on account of the heavy flow quickly dragging the net out to sea, did take a toll of some tackle when the lines were not drawn in soon enough.

Learning to adjust and manipulate his line to no great inconvenience, and with his acquired spirit of live and let live, Percy accepted the slight encroachment on his domain, which by his singular stand against the establishment, was now referred to by some, as Percy Island. Also by the look of the pair in the boats any confrontation would lead to a battle, and he tried to live these days along the lines of discretion being the better part of valour.

However, as encroachers rarely respect any boundaries within their range, one day, to Percy's great surprise, they swung their boat right into the outfall enclosure, sowing their net over the side and so scooping out the catch that had until then been the privilege of the anglers. As they stood off to draw in their well loaded nets, looking at them through binoculars, Percy observed that they were not even throwing back the small, illegal to keep, fish. So swiftly and unexpectedly had they pounced, that rods with lines too heavy to break were dragged out of their owners' hands and thrown unceremoniously over the side as the boatmen drew in their catch.

Flabbergasted and fuming, Percy cursed and shook a fist at them through the bars, but apart from casually putting two fingers up to him he was ignored.

"Fucking bastards, I'll have you," he shouted to them, wishing he had the Rattler there for five minutes.

"I'd put a shot in their arse," he thought. "Blow the

bastards to fucking hell." His threats were in no way idle, for had he had the tank there, he was angry enough to have carried them out.

After cleaning their nets they came in again and Percy ran to the beach where he began lifting a large piece of wood onto the structure, then dragging it to the end he pushed it beneath the gap in the fence as the boat came in for another run.

As the helmsman turned the boat in an avoiding manoeuvre, the timber struck the outboard engine which, when stripped of its blades, made a high pitched whine before becoming engulfed in smoke, and seizing up.

Now it was the boat crew's turn to be furious as, powerlessly trapped in the current, they were taken out to sea to the cheers, scoffs, and general jubilation of everyone on the outfall. How like the war it was, thought Percy, when, after overrunning the enemy position, all those who could, ran around whooping and cheering while looking for prisoners and booty.

Percy knew they had by no means seen the last of the boat or its crew, and sure enough as soon as the craft had got to the spot where the surge of water had spent itself, a sail was raised and it turned for the shore.

There were some swarthy looking fellows in company with Percy, who looked as if they could give a good account of themselves if need be, but when the two boatmen came pounding along the jetty, they, along with the meek looking ones, could not throw themselves over the side quick enough.

Only Percy's pride kept him from joining them as the fearsome pair hurried business-like, towards him. In no doubt as to their intentions, he whacked one around the head with his rod as they were scaling the anti-trespass fence, but the other man was already in momentum, and he landed on Percy before he could make it a double.

Going down heavily on his back knocked the wind out of him and he could not defend himself against the kicks to his body and face from the pair, with special enthusiasm from the man he had struck with the rod. When they left him and returned to their boat he tried to stand but his legs buckled beneath him.

Fortunately some of his fellow anglers, who had been observing the incident from further along the shore, came to his aid and lifted him bodily over the fence, then because of his stumbling they carried him up on the beach. He was given coffee and cleaned up with sea water, and in half an hour the concussion left him and even though trembling somewhat, he was able to drive home.

Catching a glimpse of his battered and swollen face in the driving mirror gave him quite a shock, for he had not seen himself in such a state since he was beaten up by the Pope brothers, which immediately brought Cathy to mind.

"Got caught up in the charge of the light brigade again, Cath," he murmured as he drove along. "Put the mockers on the light fantastic for a while as well, luv," he added sadly, referring to his dancing.

It was at such times of distress and low spirits that he could normally find solace in an evening's dancing, but apart from being unsteady on his legs, he did not wear his bumps and bruises as well as he had in his youth, and he considered he looked positively grotesque.

That night, in a hallucinative nightmare, he dreamed that he entered a dance hall full of geriatrics, some of whom smiled repulsively and beckoned to him as if he were one of them. The womens' over-made up faces and misshapen bodies gave them a fiendish appearance as they sat and waited for the decrepit, sunken-eyed males to invite them to hobble onto the floor. In between dances, some sat around connected to blood drips while others were being resuscitated with oxygen masks, as gaunt faced undertakers patrolled the hall and quickly carried off the fatalities before they were tripped over. A wheelchair waltz was announced, whereupon the vehicles were rushed in from the foyer, to be pounced upon like dodgem cars at a fun fair, and manipulated in the same manner, but with attendants weaving in and out picking up the legs and hands that were torn off in the collisions.

By the time he awoke near the middle of the following day the sweat he had bathed in during the night was dry, and he lay depressed, aching and sore, as his ordeal demanded he should, and likewise evilly disposed towards the pair responsible.

Attempting to go about his daily tasks brought too many comments concerning his battered condition and he returned to the scene of its source, as a therapy, only to find the boat, with engine restored, monopolising the enclosure again.

Obviously the boatmen were well aware how profitable and unaccountable tax-wise the fish were, and like Percy, they were prepared to go to some lengths to keep catching them.

It's no good, thought Percy, as he watched them through the excellent German binoculars he had traded bullets for, "I'll 'ave ta do their boat good 'n proper, then if they still wanna catch fish one'll 'ave ta strap the outboard to 'is arse while the other sits on 'is back an' lets the net out."

Although the craft showed a Shoreham registration on its bows it could have been moored anywhere between Brighton and Worthing, so Percy waited until the tide was too low for the boat to navigate the inlet, when it then made off in a Westerly direction. After seeing it had passed by the harbour entrance he hurried to his car and back tracked, at a greater speed than the permitted fifteen miles an hour, around the harbour perimeter to the main road.

Two miles past the Norfolk bridge at Shoreham, he pulled up and hurried to the beach where, on seeing them still coming in the same direction, he sat and watched them sail by to Lancing, where the vessel was then winched up the beach.

"Gotcha, yer bastards, now I know where ya live," he muttered menacingly.

As he had never known the boat to operate in the outfall during the hours of darkness, it was reasonable to assume it remained where he had seen it beached, and the following night when he retured with the few necessities he had gathered during the day, there it was.

It did not take long to pour the can of petrol and discarded engine oil over the boat and its nets. Then a butane gas blow-lamp was partially buried beneath the hull to enable Percy to be out of the area by the time it burned through and came in contact with the incendiary material.

Twenty minutes later, while watching through his glasses from a beach a mile away, he began to wonder if something had gone wrong with the simple arrangement.

Then he saw a small spear of light expand into a large mass of flame, and he gave a whistle of relief and satisfaction. He heard the fire engine roar by with its two tone horn blaring, when the blaze must have been past its peak, and he guessed that as there was nothing the fire could spread to, there would be no hurry to quench it.

Percy Longprong

He would rather not have had cause to do it, but most of his life had been spent in a state of blow and counter-blow, and the older he became, his retaliations became more drastic.

Percy had no illusions that his act had put paid to the boatmen or that they would be hard pressed wondering whose handiwork it was, and if smashing their engine made them furious, then what he had just carried out would no doubt turn them into homicidal maniacs. But if they want a war, he thought, I'll accommodate 'em. It was just one more proof to him of the truth in his words when he told the corporal during their little dispute at the Italian villa, that you go out and fight some foreigner once in a lifetime, but back home you are doing battle with your own nationals all the time, in one way or another.

Going to the outfall when the tide was favourable the following day, he was in too much pain to climb over the barriers and so reluctantly had to fish from the beach. Consequently when he took his small catch of three not very large bass to the takeaway, Mr. Lee thought he had taken the bulk somewhere else for more money, until he noticed Percy's battered and sad face.

"Who done that to you, my friend. A big fish eh?" he asked considerately, putting his arm on Percy's shoulder.

"Wish it 'ad 'ave been, that would 'ave been a nice week's wages all right," chuckled Percy painfully through his swollen mouth.

Mr. Lee was quite concerned and paid, much to Percy's embarrassment, far more than the fish were ever worth. Then he took him gently by the arm and sat him in his usual seat in front of the television where once again he was given a generous portion of prawns in batter, followed by the usual carton of brandy.

The following day he went to exercise his right to take Oswald out but was refused by Ena on account of his unsteady condition. He did not bother to ring the bell again when the door was slammed in his face, for as much as he loved the child, he hardly felt well enough to amuse him and had called purely out of habit.

At a loose end he decided to get a few weekend requirements from the supermarket and almost collapsed at the checkout. He declined the offer of being taken to the manager's office to await the ambulance, but instead put himself in the temporary care of an elderly couple who helped him to his car.

"Poor man looks thoroughly run down and cold, his teeth are chattering," said the woman sympathetically, to which her husband agreed and questioned Percy's capability to drive, but hastily thanking them he drove out of the car park only to pull up around the corner to remove the two bags of frozen prawns he had smuggled out in his trousers pockets. The effect of the freezing articles lying alongside his testicles were not the cause of his momentary breakdown but were only responsible for his chattering teeth.

Plainly he was not well, for apart from exhaustion and fatigue from an over exertive life, since his recent beating, brain haemorrhage had developed, which brought on feelings of inertia, and because of further damage to his spine he was experiencing spasms of paralysis. Consequently his will to earn a living was diminishing, hence the shoplifting, which he intended to live on, where food was concerned, to begin with anyway.

When next he went on the outfall, as well as a stirrup that he made up to enable him to climb the fences, he carried a three foot length of chain around his waist, and a Luger tucked in his camouflage jacket.

For the first few days he was as alert as a solder behind enemy lines, as he fished the tides in and out. Any boat that looked remotely bound in his direction he scrutinised through his binoculars as he did people walking along the beach. But in the unequalled excitement of catching fish, and quite large ones at that, the vigil was unavoidably relaxed with nothing untoward occurring. It would have been almost like old times if it were not for the occasional nagging uneasiness of wondering when, and from which direction, land or sea, his enemies would come.

In his haste to get from the car park to the causeway he sometimes forgot to pick up the Luger and chain from under his driving seat and by doing so he lulled himself into a false sense of security, for on one such day, they came.

By normal opinion and events the day was dismal and overcast, but to Percy the heavy mist that cut visibility to thirty yards, and so obscured not only his presence, but the entire outfall, was made to measure. It gave an eeriness to the gentle swells that lapped over the end as if they were from the movements of a giant creature that came into the enclosure only when it could not be observed from the shore.

Percy could not remember ever experiencing so much tranquillity. It was as if he were in a small heaven of his own as he sat on the little folding seat letting his line out into the cloak of fog that heightened the excitement of each catch by concealing their size until they were reeled in.

How secure he felt, enveloped in mist on his little island, out of sight and sound of the world's hubbub and jostling, he never wanted to even take the fish to the shop. By four o'clock the tide had gone too low to fish. The creatures were still plentiful in the shallows, but once caught they could not be pulled in against the tremendous pressure of the outflow when the level of water that kept it in check had fallen.

The mist began to lift but what remained of the day's sun was obliterated by thick cloud. As visibility lengthened and the shoreline and power station came into view, so Percy's haven took on once more its position of vulnerability. Deciding to call it a day he began to get his equipment together but as he pushed his rods through the barrier be saw the two boatmen coming along the path at the top of the beach. Fear clutched his heart as he realised his weapons were still in the car. In his state he could not have take on one of them, let alone two, and like a hunted animal he looked round for a way of escape and his glance fell upon the encrusted metal flap leading to an inspection chamber below.

Grabbing one of the supports from a fallen trespass sign he levered the hatch open and after hurriedly throwing his gear and sack of fish into the hole he jumped in after them and lay down between the huge ducts. Being only a few feet away from the outlet the sound of the emerging water was as deafening as being at the foot of a waterfall, but at least the pounding of his heart was not likely to be heard by anyone above.

On the other hand he could not hear the piece of metal he had used to jemmy the hatch being jammed across it to trap him. When the boatmen returned to the harbour they wrecked Percy's Citroen by smashing every piece of glass and denting every panel with a four pound sledge-hammer before driving away in their transit van.

"That'll give the old bastard summink else ta think

about after we let 'im out," said one of the men whose name was Peter. "Come on, we'll go up to my ol' lady's for a cuppa tea before we go back and give 'im another thumpin'."

Peter's mother lived on the West side of Southwick Green, and it did not take them long to get there. In fact it was, as the crow flies, only half a mile from where Percy was trapped. If he had seen her he may have realised that the man whose boat he burned was his son, for she was none other than the once very desirable Miss Clancy whom he had seduced on the night of his mother's wedding.

After the men had been lolling about for more than two hours Peter's companion suggested it was time to let Percy out but was told to let the old bastard sweat it out a bit longer. Peter's mother knew nothing of what their snatched conversation was about but guessing that time had some importance in the event she brought to their attention the fact that the clock on the kitchen cabinet was twenty minutes slow, which sent both men bolting out of the house.

Peter could not steer properly as he attempted to drive the transit away from the kerb. In their haste they had not noticed the nearside front tyre was flat. For a few seconds as if in defeat he lay his forehead on the steering wheel.

"Oh Christ," he whispered desperately. "Of all the bloody times," then gathering himself together he hastily got out of the van.

"Come on, we'll leg it over the locks," he shouted, as he dashed off down the road in that direction with his companion following close behind.

Back at the outfall the water was almost up to Percy's shoulders and at times when a wave came along he was completely submerged. Since he had realised he was trapped he had been shouting until he was hoarse, but against the noise of the gushing water it had been useless. He was bitterly cold and trembling, and his fingers were gashed to shreds through groping between the gaps of the hatch in an attempt to remove the bar that held it shut. Also, the exertion he had used in trying to force the trap open had caused his hernia to burst forth like another small limb growing from his abdomen, and he was in the throes of both mental and physical agony.

He had long since freed the fish from his bag and he knew how they must have felt as they wriggled out half dazed before shooting away excitedly at top speed. In a weird way he had come to love that species of fish called bass, they were energetic, brave, and mischievous, but the overpowering immeasurable interest and excitement in catching them smothered his conscience. How often he had thought, when struggling to the end of the outfall in fierce weather, that the wind and waves were doing no more than trying to beat him back from his intended victims.

Now it seemed that inside of an hour the sea would avenge all the creatures he had taken from it and he began to wonder when the apparition, that had saved him on so many previous occasions, would once more prove to be his salvation, although it occurred to him that there had been no sign of it since his mother's death, otherwise it would surely have come to his aid when he was being so viciously beaten.

The thought of drowning had always been terrible to him even before he had nearly experienced it fully at the hands of the two Germans on the shores of Crete, but to drown inch by inch and minute by minute while desperately squashing his face against the ceiling of his prison for the last thimblefuls of air, was out of the question, and after fumbling inside his jacket for his fishing knife, he wasted no time in slashing his wrists. Because the blade was none too sharp he could not bring himself to hack at his jugular unless he was still conscious when he began drowning.

Not far away the boatmen arrived panting and exhausted at the lock gates, only to find them open to let a ship through, which automatically barred the public from crossing. Unable to wait for the gates to be locked after the vessel's passing, Peter leapt from the quay, ran across amidship and jumped off the other side, much to the consternation and shouts of the harbour officials present.

With renewed vigour he covered the three hundred yards past the bonded warehouses to the beach pathway as if he were a teenager, but as breathless as he was at reaching it, he stopped breathing for a few seconds and sank hopelessly to the ground after gazing at the sea covered outfall before him.

Percy had not lost consciousness soon enough by only cutting his wrists, but he still could not cut his throat, instead he had jammed the knife in a cleft in the concrete and thrust himself upon it. Not all of the salt on his face could be credited to the sea, for a minute proportion was due to his farewell tears that far from being shed for just himself, were just one more pent up emotion for the sadness in the world.

Being impaled on the knife kept him in an upright position, and his now sightless eyes stared through the grille at the legions of fish that swam in front of him. Now that the structure was once more below the sea it was the first time his presence on it was legal, and had his fishing acquaintances been able to see him, some, who might have thought he was just holding his breath, would have been even more amazed at the lengths to which he would go to catch 'em.

As if in salute, one of the red gills attached to one of his rods had drifted out into the flow and hooked a fish that without anyone to pull it in was destined like Percy to remain there until it was fleshless. A skin diver once told him that fish had no fear of a human below the surface, for they were accepted as one of them, and if Percy could have seen the mass that swam to and fro close to him, he would have known it to be true, for they were ever so friendly.

END